One *Less* Problem
Without You

Center Point
Large Print

Also by Beth Harbison and available from
Center Point Large Print:

If I Could Turn Back Time
Driving with the Top Down
*Chose the Wrong Guy, Gave Him the
    Wrong Finger*

**This Large Print Book carries the
Seal of Approval of N.A.V.H.**

One *Less* Problem *Without* You

Beth Harbison

CENTER POINT LARGE PRINT
THORNDIKE, MAINE

This Center Point Large Print edition
is published in the year 2016 by arrangement with
St. Martin's Press.

The text of this Large Print edition is unabridged.
In other aspects, this book may vary
from the original edition.
Printed in the United States of America
on permanent paper.
Set in 16-point Times New Roman type.

ISBN: 978-1-68324-090-7

Library of Congress Cataloging-in-Publication Data

Names: Harbison, Elizabeth M., author.
Title: One less problem without you / Beth Harbison.
Description: Center Point Large Print edition. | Thorndike, Maine :
Center Point Large Print, 2016.
Identifiers: LCCN 2016022744 | ISBN 9781683240907
    (hardcover : alk. paper)
Subjects: LCSH: Large type books.
Classification: LCC PS3558.A564 O54 2016b | DDC 813/.54—dc23
LC record available at https://lccn.loc.gov/2016022744

To my AFIL, John O'Brien. I miss you so much already. I know there was so much more to learn from you. Godspeed, and I'll see you on the other side. Love from your ADIL.

Acknowledgments

First and foremost, to Tris Zeigler—thank you for being there when I was down, and for coming at all hours to be my friend. I am so grateful for your friendship.

To my friends who were there in the mud with me on a few unfortunate occasions this year, as well as at Sephora, Home Goods, and Chartreuse & Co. or in front of *Vanderpump Rules* on TV: Carolyn Clemens, Connie Jo Gernhofer, Paige Harbison, Jami Nasi, Vindhya Sarma, Steve Troha, Isaac Babik, Devynn Grubby, Jordan Lyon, Charlie Ugaz, Lucinda Denton, Paula Butler, Tracey Shannon, and Rob Connor.

So many thanks to Stacy Arnold for telling me what it's like to be a reluctant psychic. Thanks as well to psychics Adrienne Myles, Cari Roy, and Anita Arnold for more psychic help, information, and, of course, great readings.

Mike Scotti, ain't we got fun? #nowayjosecuervo #upsideofwar

Thanks to Ada Polla of Alchimie Forever, who has shared her wonderful products with me so generously. I'm a product whore and this stuff is among the best; I'm so glad to have been introduced to it! Thanks even more for inviting me to your book group meeting so we could get acquainted!

Thanks to Brian M. Hazel for his amazing friendship, as well as for the inspiration he provides in business and everyday life.

Much gratitude to the McIlmails—Tim, Jody, Zoe, Claire, Fiona, and Ferris—for being such great, often patient and always supportive, neighbors. You've made some hard times considerably easier.

Soooo many thanks to Jen Enderlin for her brilliant eye, Annelise Robey for her kind support at the best and worst of times, and to India Cooper for copyediting so thoroughly and giving such great suggestions and making it so much easier on me to go back on a tight schedule.

One *Less* Problem
Without You

Chapter One

Diana

I want to say that he knew how to work me masterfully, but that wouldn't quite be accurate.

The truth is, I made it easy for him.

He is my husband, Leif Tiesman. There's a pun in the last name somewhere, something to do with keeping me tied up, but I can't figure it out so it's anything other than sad. I'm Diana. Diana Tiesman.

People always said I looked like Diane Lane in that movie, *Under the Tuscan Sun*, and I always thought that was ironic since, in that movie, Diane Lane's character left her cheating husband and took off for an Italy that looks absolutely ideal to me—the sun glinting on her copper-penny hair, making her look fiery where *my* copper-penny hair felt more like it reflected my worth—and she starts her life anew, alone, strong.

I did not do that.

Though fantasies like that had flittered through my brain many times, my one true goal in life had always been to be the perfect wife and mother.

And like the perfect wife that I set out to be, and the bound being I became, I have been agreeable for seven years of marriage. So agreeable. I have made favorite dinners, made a point of Not Questioning Him, created a beautiful home and let him have the TV remote, and I've blown him till my cheeks ached.

Why? you must be asking. *Anyone* with *any* sense would ask that. Hell, if I were talking to my friend and *she* was the one saying all this subservient stuff, I would sure as hell be asking her why she thought he was worth so much more than she was.

But the truth is, when you're in it, that's not how you're looking at it. You can't even see the logic about your own situation, even while you might be wildly protective of a friend who isn't going through half as much as you are. When you're in it, you want the high. The win. The kiss. The body. The dizzying glee of having just had fantastic sex. Okay, maybe that's not the case for everyone, but it was certainly the case for me. Some part of me will always fight that impulse. I always resist when people liken it to an addiction—loving a person seems like it should be different from being *addicted* to them—but the reality is, that's exactly what it is.

With Leif, I always felt like if I had just a little bit more, I'd be strong enough to get away. A little more sex so I'm not longing for him, a little more time so maybe I can get stronger in my anger with him. Staying in the hot water just that little bit longer, so that the frigid cold doesn't feel so bad. Something—*anything*—to make the leaving easier.

But then he gave me that gift.

Or, rather, I took it.

It was an ordinary night. I lay in the dark on my side of the queen-sized bed, listening to my husband's deep, even breathing in the dark. As if he hadn't a care in the world.

The sonofabitch.

How could it be so easy for him to lie down and sleep, like one of those old baby dolls whose eyes closed when you tipped them backward? Meanwhile, I had to lie there in anguish, pounding heart, racing mind, skin prickling as if I were entering a nuclear fallout zone?

I knew something was wrong. I mean, I *always* knew something was wrong. But moreover, I knew exactly what it was. I wasn't born yesterday. The pain of my marriage wasn't even born yesterday. Leif had a long, cruel history of sneaking dalliances with other women, and I had a long, unfortunate history of trying to pretend it wasn't true. Or that his apology and acknowledgment meant something and it wouldn't happen again. Or that I was overreacting.

Or that it was "normal."

Man, I had a whole lot of counterproductive stances on my own husband's cheating, and I had paid the price again and again, and let him coast.

But tonight he'd come in from work after ten,

swearing he was having postwork drinks with "colleagues" (I was never sure whether it was damning or honest to list them as "colleagues" versus names so specific they were obviously meant to fool me). And at least *this* time he had not smelled like a delicate, floral perfume I would have liked so much that, under any other circumstances, I would have asked the wearer what the name of it was. That was a particularly specific humiliation.

However, he did have the telltale smear of lipstick on his cheek, and across the plane behind his ear and down his neck. Cheek could be innocent, but the roadmap from his cheek down his neck was obviously intimate. You might kiss your grandmother's cheek, but you weren't going to trail your lips across her ear and down her neck. Suddenly I had a brand-new measuring stick for suspicion.

This was suspicious. I mean, undeniably so. Even for me, who had lived in denial for so long there was a hackneyed Egypt joke in it.

Leif sighed—didn't start, didn't react to a dream, just became so additionally relaxed in his sleep next to my agitation, like a man with no secrets or guilt, that he actually *sighed*.

In a movie he probably would have sighed some girl's name. Reached for a dream head in front of his crotch.

I didn't realize I was holding my breath until the

suffocation took over and I let it out in one too-short burst, having trouble drawing back more into my lungs.

I wanted to ignore this. Damn it, I wanted to ignore this and not have a problem. I could just wake up in the morning, make his breakfast, clean the house, meet a friend for lunch, read, go to my community college jewelry-smithing class, and then come home and watch TV (with or without Leif, depending on when he got home—by day he was an ordinary-seeming businessman, but he was also attractive enough to be a talking head on TV news if there was a particularly weird criminal case) until it was time to get up and do it again in the morning.

I turned my head and looked at his beautiful profile in the half-light of the blue moon, shining in through the window and casting his skin in an ethereal (one might also say "angelic") glow.

Damn it!

He was beautiful. Not in a ridiculous way, not a soap actor you just knew was gay; he was just striking. He had liquid brown eyes that changed color with the sun, and an incredible smile that transformed his face into super-hot no matter what you might think of it in repose. His smile was broad and happy, not feminine at all, but possessing all the qualities held by the best of the 1940s movie heroes.

His voice, too—whoa. That was another thing I

had a distinct weakness for. Husky, low, soft-spoken. He was persuasive just by virtue of his tone, though God knew he had learned to cultivate it. He made himself a genius salesman without sounding like one.

He was an expert manipulator, as so many fucked-up psychologists and psychiatrists were. At least as far as I could tell, and I'd met a lot of them . . . as well as their often-unfortunate spouses. At any rate, he had my number anytime he needed it. We'd have disagreements that started with me on fire and ended with me *apologizing*. Often I couldn't even remember later what the argument had been about, although the feeling of anger tended to linger, a rudderless boat without an anchor or a shore.

I glanced at the familiar ceiling of our bedroom. A few glow-in-the-dark adhesive stars still strained to beam against the dark ceiling but all but failed with the passage of time and, I guess, the absence of faith. They were just something fanciful I'd put up to delight him with when we'd first moved in; the "light" from them had annoyed him, and I took them down. Still, every once in awhile I'd still see one in the dark that I'd missed, and it would remind me of what now felt like my foolish optimism.

The light ding of a phone pierced the darkness.

I stiffened. It wasn't my phone. I didn't have that ding set up; he was Android, I was iPhone.

But I knew his text sound as well as I knew his voice.

And it didn't normally come from his phone at this hour, deep in the dark.

An emergency, I thought at first, a habitual thought I would later be embarrassed about.

But while I was still in emergency mode, I glanced over at his phone, just long enough to see that "Eastern Shore Plumbing and Air" was writing "I want you now" to him.

I want you now.

The phone had gone black again, protected by its password shroud of privacy. There was no way to see what else had been said between Leif and Eastern Shore Plumbing and Air.

I leaned back against my pillow, my heart pounding so hard I thought it was probably shifting the fabric of the old Mickey Mouse T-shirt I slept in.

What now?

And, seriously, what now? I couldn't question this and get an honest answer. Obviously he had entered some girl in his phone under a false and seemingly uninteresting contact name. Clever. If only because he could count on me never questioning it. Even if I could, or *would,* have searched his phone, that contact would never have raised my interest.

What an idiot I was.

I put a hand on my chest and tried to calm my

breathing in the dark. Meanwhile Leif was sleeping as peacefully as a puppy, his breath slow and even. In fact, those slow, even breaths increased my anxiety by the moment. Every relaxed sound he made ramped up my heartbeat and the heat coursing through my veins.

But I don't know anything, I told myself. *Maybe it was a wrong number.*

That wasn't impossible. I'd gotten nonsense texts in my life. Well, once. And it had been my friend trying to text a work colleague. But still, I hadn't understood it, as it had clearly gone to the wrong person; it didn't make sense within the context. Who was to say that wasn't what was happening now?

Slightly reassured, I turned on my side, facing away from Leif, and tried to close my eyes and go to sleep, vowing to think about it in the morning but to allow myself the grace to just go ahead and sleep tonight. Nothing good ever came from a lot of exhausted late-night emotion. Ever. Did it make a difference if I sweated this now or later?

My heart pounded about twenty-five times in the darkness.

Screw this.

Yes, it made a difference. I'd been here before with him. A hundred times. I knew what was going on, and this business of trying to fool myself into believing the unbelievable was ridiculous. How many times was I going to do that to myself? Or allow *him* to do it to me?

And at what cost?

This was damn close to gaslighting.

That's when I got the idea. Yes, it was risky; I could get caught, and a huge fight would ensue. And there was no doubt who was stronger in an argument: Leif was relentless, seemingly capable of believing his own lies to the death. I could never win. I could only give up. And I had—many, many times.

Not this time.

It was hard to say what made the difference. A different alignment of stars? That single straw that, added to the rest, could crack bone? Or maybe it was just a long-overdue desire to know and deal with the whole truth and its effect on me.

Whatever it was, it propelled me stealthily out of bed and around to Leif's bedside table, where I took his phone in hand, cold and hard as a stolen gun. He shifted, and I froze, ready to drop it back on the table and make a mad and dangerous dash to the bathroom, as if I hadn't been next to him at all.

But his breathing resumed, and I carefully made my way back to my side of the queen-sized bed. There were squeaky floorboards, but I'd never memorized which, so every time I stepped on one I froze and listened for the telltale evenness of his breath.

It seemed like forever, but when I finally got back to my side of the bed, I hesitated and decided to get in without an abundance of care. Had I gotten up in the middle of the night to pee, I wouldn't have come back like a thief, and maybe on some subconscious level my stealth would register with him as "something amiss," not just me simply returning to the bed.

I took the chance and got back in, rolling over on my side to face him. As predicted, he didn't stir. I moved my foot to his and twined my lower leg between his, as I had done so many times before, and he reached out and put a hand on me.

Perfect.

Holding my breath, I hit the ON button, and the screen flared to life so brightly it was as if someone had shouted. I took the blanket and covered the screen, exposing only the START button, then reached for his hand, put the button under his index finger, and held my breath.

The phone dinged to life.

Leif did not.

Thank God, thank God, thank God.

I rolled over, keeping the screen down, and stayed still, occasionally tapping the touch pad to keep it alive, until I was sure he wasn't waking up and catching me red-handed.

Then I got up again and took it into the bath-room, closing the door quietly behind me.

Now I was committed. If I was caught, I was

screwed, so there was no reason for me not to see as much as the good Lord was willing to show me.

I sat down on the edge of the tub and went to messaging. Eastern Shore Plumbing and Air was at the top of the list, and when I opened it up, I could have cried. There were so many texts. So very many. I scrolled through, and they rolled on and on.

I'd like to meet you, he said. *I'll be going to visit my mom in Connecticut in a couple of months, maybe I could stop by your place in Jersey along the way.*

My stomach rolled. Gross. This was someone he'd "met" online, and he was willing, and ready, to turn a family visit into an adulterous tryst? That easily? What if I had said I wanted to join him on that trip? What if I'd insisted I wanted to see my mother-in-law? Would he have discouraged me, or snuck onto his phone when I wasn't looking and told the Plumber they'd have to hook up another time?

Your dad lives in Michigan? the Plumber asked. *Did I tell you* my *dad is from Michigan too? It's like this is meant to be!*

I paused over that. *It's like this is meant to be!* Such a bold statement to make to a man who was married. Though the poor girl probably didn't know he was married. There certainly weren't any references—loving or otherwise—to his devoted wife.

Instead there was *I loved hearing from you last night, but next time dial *67 if you remember. This is a work phone and I don't want my boss getting any concerns about how I'm using my professional tools . . . Speaking of which, I'd like to put my tool right in that tight little snatch of yours. You made me so hot, I was dying!*

I didn't remember Leif being hot and bothered at any recent point. Was he lying, or did he take care of it in the shower and then manage to join me for dinner and compliment my pan-seared lemon shrimp and the good job I'd done on painting the foyer, as if he didn't have another interest in the world beyond day-to-day domesticity?

I continued to scroll through the messages and didn't find anything remarkable beyond the fact that now and then he called the girl "Red" and she referred to him as "Buck," which . . . was that some sort of joke they'd agreed upon, or was that a name he'd actually given himself?

I tapped the screen and went to the e-mail app. There appeared to be two names: his own, at Gmail, which was the one she used if she ever had to forward something or give it out; and another one, *Buckthesistem* at a weird domain I'd never heard of.

Sistem? Was that some sort of gender-specific play on the word "system"?

The phone trembled in my hand as I clicked his in-box. I was in it now; there was no turning back.

Whatever I wanted to know was at the touch of my fingertips. And I *needed* to know it, no matter what. That I was clear on. I'd been living in nervous apprehension for too long, never quite trusting anything he said, whether it was that he loved me or that we were running low on toilet paper. I'd heard lies that mattered and that didn't, and that sent me into a tailspin of doubt.

I *certainly* never believed him when he said he was working late.

For perhaps ten minutes I scrolled through his e-mail, and apart from a few seemingly innocuous messages to his friends, there was nothing. I actually began to feel a little bit better. Not *okay,* by any means—the texts with "Red" remained inexcusable—but something inside of me just hoped to God I *hadn't* been duped time and again.

That hope died fast when suddenly I got to a date, about two months prior, with a collection of Craigslist answers. He'd been on a business trip to Las Vegas. A long one that included weekends, which struck me as odd at the time. But still, he *did* have business out of town a lot, did a lot of consulting on legal cases and whatnot, and I never wanted to be the kind of wife that did inordinate investigating of something presented as truth.

In other words, I never wanted to be the kind of wife I was being at this moment.

But I was in for a penny, so I might as well go

in for the whole pound. Even while I clicked, during that fraction of a second between clicking and opening, I hoped he'd been trying to sell or buy some car part or something. But it wasn't the case.

Come play with me? 100 gifts an hour, you come to me. 200 gifts an hour I go to you. The link was too old for me to see anything beyond that which was in the e-mail, but there was plenty in there. Leif described his physique, in painful (and possibly inaccurate; to my memory we never *measured*) detail, and asked where she—assuming it was a *she*—could be found. What room?

There had to be missing e-mails—though I couldn't tell why he would have deleted some but not all, or why they weren't all in the history of the one I was looking at. Still, even though there were enough gaps for Old Me to have slipped through the cracks, this me was seriously disgusted.

I mean, what were "gifts"? That could only mean payment, right? My husband, who declared every small new thing I timidly suggested we try in bed for freshness to be "weird," was willing to go to Vegas—where, by the way, clean, tested prostitution was *legal*—and *pay* some Craigslist person for anonymous sex?

I cut-and-pasted her ad headline into the current Las Vegas search bar and came up with a new ad with the same wording. This time there were pictures. A woman, her face obscured by long dark hair but revealing enough to show she wasn't . . . conventionally attractive, was posing with her foot up on a dirty avocado-colored bathtub, bending over, with a soap scum–covered shower stall behind her.

This? This he was willing to *pay* for?

It's hard to describe just what this did to my heart. And I don't even mean my metaphorical "broken heart" (which surely existed and was damned to get worse) but just literally my heart. It clenched, felt so tight I could barely breathe. I thought I was going to throw up.

There was no forgetting this. There was no ignoring it.

There were more Craigslist correspondences there, but I couldn't even bear to look at them. None would say, "Just kidding, can't believe you fell for that, Di!," so all they could possibly do was exponentially increase the horror and betrayal I was feeling now.

I had to stop. For my own good, I had to stop.

But before I did, I clicked each one to forward it to myself—then noticed the faint arrow indicating that the e-mail had been forwarded.

Shit!

I fiddled around, trying to find a way to undo the indicator, and finally ended up just deleting the e-mails from his list completely, and then emptying the trash.

He'd probably never miss them. Surely he hadn't kept them for any purposeful reason. He'd probably just forgotten to delete them—raising the disturbing question of how many other e-mails there had been that he *had* deleted.

It was too much to comprehend.

In fact, really, all of it was too much to take. And it all just reminded me that I'd been taking too much for too long.

After returning his phone to the nightstand, I went down to the kitchen, no longer giving a damn if I disturbed his precious sleep or not. I needed to relax. To him that would have meant that I should take one of the sedatives prescribed for me and just shut up, but after months of ever-increasing numbness on the pills, I'd realized that I was becoming Rip Van Winkle, which felt awfully close to becoming Judy Garland. I didn't want that.

That's when I started making herbal teas. I'd gotten a book on them from the Internet, an introduction to growing, drying, and infusing herbs. It was pretty elementary, but I found that my own chamomile tea was far better, and stronger, than the stuff I bought from the grocery store aisle under the General Foods International Coffees.

So I'd gotten pretty good at making my own infusions, if I do say so myself. Kava, vervain, and chamomile to relax. I know most people like to put a hint of lavender in, too, but that was too perfumy for me, so I kept it mild.

Was it as quick as the pills? No. But that was good, because if it worked as quickly as the pills did, it probably would have been just as problematic. I didn't have room for more problems in my life.

So I heated the water on the stove and put the dried leaves into the silk tea bag. I added extra kava, as that was the most relaxing of the ingredients; then, in a moment that might have been ill advised, I got out the Corsair vanilla bean vodka.

I was inventing an elixir, I told myself. Vodka Kavas. The perfect nightcap.

As soon as the water started to boil, I poured it over the tea leaves, then let it steep for three minutes, taking a shot of vodka straight as I waited. Why not? It had been a bad night. No one could tell me I wasn't entitled to a quick shot of help.

As soon as the tea was ready, I removed the bag, dropped a few pieces of rock sugar in, and added a generous dollop of the vodka.

It was fantastic.

Or maybe it was just *needed*. Hard to say at that particular point. It was probably both, to be honest. At any rate, it warmed my soul going down, and eased my mind once it hit.

Maybe it eased my mind a little too much,

because soon I started to get a little wobbly in my anger. And by "wobbly" I mean "irrational," and by "irrational" I mean I decided it would perhaps not be a *terrible* idea to make a tea to poison my husband.

Chapter Two

Prinny

The truth was, she hated being called Prinny.

"Lillian" was so much more dignified. And that's what she wanted, to be dignified, rather than Daddy's Little Princess, aka Prinny. Even her "halo of golden curls," as her parents had referred to her hair, made her look like a child's imagining of a fairy-tale princess. Sounds like a silly thing to complain about until you realize no one takes you seriously. Prinny. It wasn't a name that *could* be taken seriously. And yet Lillian might as well not have been her name, since no one had ever called her that.

Even her classmates had ended up calling her Prinny, so the label her father had, with good and loving intentions, put on her as a child had now stuck with her almost thirty years into life. It had long since stopped conjuring a fairy tale and had more recently, she felt, made her sound like a little old spinster from *Gone with the Wind*.

Not that she didn't appreciate the fact that her father had cared so much; she did. He was all she'd had. Until she'd lost him. Now she had only an adversarial stepbrother and a kind but meek sister-in-law with whom she was barely in touch.

Prinny's mother had died when she was only six years old, so she didn't really remember her very well—in fact, sometimes she wondered if her "memories" were memories at all or if they were just her own psychic intuition of what her mother had been like—but the one thing that everyone always said about Ingrid Tiesman was that she was the picture of dignity and sophistication.

It was hard for someone who had been basically called a baby all her life to live up to that.

Yet Prinny had loved her father hugely, so she never wanted to ask him not to use the affectionate term for her that was so special that even his tone softened when he said it in a way she never heard it change at any other time.

"Where's my Prinny?" he'd ask when he came in at the end of a long day at work. Given the speed with which the maid would also bring him a Scotch on the rocks, in her earlier days, Prinny had never been quite sure whether *his Prinny* was her or the drink. But soon enough she realized, after he'd downed the first and asked for "another rocks," which would appear as promptly as if it had already been ready and waiting to go, that she was the Prinny and the drink was . . . well, the drink was his binkie.

In the end it was his poison. But that's an old story. Who hasn't heard it or told it or both? She lost her mother when she was six, she lost her father at twenty-six, and somehow, in the twenty years between, she'd never quite learned how to be a grown-up.

People thought she didn't know that, but she did. There was always a vague panic humming like a bad subwoofer under the weight of Led Zeppelin, telling her that the time was coming when it was all going to blow up in her face. She didn't have it in her to handle the weight of a real, adult life.

Her mother had died at the age of twenty-six. Prinny had passed that landmark with the full expectation that something magical would happen and she would suddenly understand all the little things she needed to about getting by, day to day, on her own and handling things like insurance, business, all the things her dad had always handled for her.

Instead, her father's liver finally cried uncle and he died, leaving her alone in the world, with an estate executor who was in charge of pulling all the financial strings in her life, and an older stepbrother, Leif, who, in the three years since, had been hell-bent on taking over her portion of their shared inheritance so she would stop "squandering" it.

All of life was a game of *Leif Says* now. Fortunately, Alex McConnell—the executor of her father's estate—didn't seem daunted by Leif, even as the battle waged on and on, because Prinny sure was.

Prinny was also pretty daunted by Alex McConnell, though she could never admit it to a soul. He was married; the picture on his desk of him and his beautiful wife posed in a typical beachy vacation spot proved that Prinny could never stand a chance with a guy like him. There were types, and he was a gorgeous, smart, successful, *married* type. And though Prinny had never met her, she knew the wife was the sort of gorgeous, pouty woman who always got her way, and whom a man would chase around the globe forever, just for the favor of her smile.

Prinny would never be that woman.

But she was in love with that man, and she had to settle for her time with him being business related. In fact, she had to settle for her *life* being business-centric. She needed to succeed on her own; she needed to be self-sufficient. She wanted to understand her finances, her investments, and everything she'd need to keep her going, even if she was alone forever (as she feared she might be).

She needed absolute financial independence.

That was the only thing that would give her complete control; the only lifestyle that didn't care if she was a little insecure and a little round in the hip and a little flakey, and very shy with men.

She would have said *especially men like Alex,* but there was one who was even worse for her nerves, though he offered none of the fun that her interactions with Alex did: Leif. Somewhere deep inside she was terrified of Leif, even though one of the only things she remembered well was her mother reassuring her that Leif was more scared of her than she could ever be of him.

Didn't matter. Leif was powerful, and he was doing everything he could to sabotage her inheritance and, it seemed, her very life.

That's why she'd opened Cosmos. She needed to have a legitimate business, legitimate expenses, a storefront, all those things, so that Leif couldn't accuse her of being incompetent. Anyway, that's what Alex had advised her.

He hadn't exactly advised her to open a meta-physical shop, however. In fact, when she'd told him that was what she intended to do, she sensed some backpedaling on his part, and the fact that at least several times a week drunks stumbled in, thinking it was a bar, didn't help her case much.

But still . . . it was what she was born to do, she knew it.

When she was around eleven years old, her

favorite nanny, Marie (whom she liked to think of as Mary, as in Poppins, despite her Jamaican sun-dark skin, with a note of mahogany Prinny always puzzled over), had taken her up to the broad-beamed walk-in attic of the house and showed her something that would change her life.

As soon as she opened the door, Marie had put a finger to her lips, *shhhh,* even though they were the only two home. "You do not tell anyone a word that I show you this," she said, her accent—which Prinny could still not identify to this day, especially since she had only her childhood memory to rely on—thick and mysterious.

Prinny had nodded eagerly, doing the sign of *cross my heart and hope to die,* though she always crossed her fingers during the second part of that, since, apparently, it was incredibly easy to die unexpectedly. Even her mom had done it!

Don't think that way, the Voice said in her mind. *Life is magical, wonderful, and meant to be lived fully.*

Marie closed the door behind them and took Prinny's hand, leading her into the thick, hot, dusty air, to a trunk that was only slightly illuminated by the high vent at the peak of the roof. It was August in D.C., which was about as hot as hell or anyplace like it could get. Prinny had trouble breathing, but she knew she had to be silent; she couldn't let out the cough that was trying so desperately to escape.

"I found this by accident," Marie said, then added, as if she'd been questioned, "I was up here looking for a fan for your room, and I found it accidentally, but I think you should know."

Even at that young age, something trembled through Prinny. What had she found? What could it possibly be? Was it a body? Was it *about* to be—her own? She'd been reading Nancy Drew books like a fiend at that point, and it was all too easy for her to believe that people weren't who they said they were. Ever.

She hung back, ready to turn and run, but Marie felt the resistance and turned to face her. "Oh, child," she said, that indeterminate accent somehow thickening and softening all at the same time, "this has to do with your mama, so you *know* it's a *good* thing."

In her mind, Prinny saw colors. Lots of colors, pictures, cards, and . . . rocks?

Prinny looked into Marie's eyes, trying to scrutinize, with all the wisdom and experience an eleven-year-old could possibly muster, the truth of her intentions. Her eyes were so kind, Prinny thought she couldn't possibly be lying.

And Marie had never, ever been mean to Prinny, never raised her voice, much less a hand, and she'd been with her longer than any of the others, more than a year now. She'd even made sure to put pictures of Prinny's mother here and there, even though Prinny's dad kept taking them down, because she insisted it was important that Prinny feel her mother's presence in the house.

Prinny never told anyone that she did. Constantly. Sometimes she even *saw* her mother. But even at that age, she knew she couldn't say that without scaring people.

So Prinny went with Marie into the thick stale air, and watched as she opened the trunk. "This, child, is what we call a treasure chest." She sat down on the floor and patted the dusty wood next to her.

"What is it?"

"Your mama's things."

"You mean like clothes and shoes?" Prinny tried to work out how there could be more when the people had come and taken away rack after rack of clothes that smelled of her mother's familiar Jean Patou Joy perfume, "for charity," as her dad and Leif had said.

Yet for a moment, Prinny's heart leaped at the idea of smelling that delicious, comforting scent one more time, of perhaps wrapping herself in one of her mother's garments, untouched since Mama herself had carefully put it away. She wanted to try on the strappy, high-heeled shoes and see if they fit yet.

In fact, she was diving fully into a fantasy of clopping around the attic in her mother's shoes, looking for a mirror (there had to be one up here; wasn't there a mirror, cracked or otherwise, in every spooky attic?) when Marie handed her a box.

Prinny took it uncertainly. It was a small box. Not a shoe box. Too small, even, for a filmy scarf to fit in it. "What's this?"

Your legacy. Your history. Your gift.

"Cards," Marie said reverently. "Cards that tell the future!"

Suddenly the box felt like it was trembling, and Prinny dropped it, though it was probably her hand that had trembled. It was now. "Did they tell Mama she was going to die?" She knew they had. She just *knew* it.

Marie appeared to consider. "Maybe. I don't know what your mama learned from them."

Prinny suddenly felt scared. "Why are you showing me this?"

"Oh, child." Marie moved toward her and put a meaty arm around Prinny's narrow, bony shoulder, pulling her into her ample bosom. "Because these are the tools of *magic*. This is a *gift* your mama has left for you, and finally we have found it."

"Magic?" Witches sprang to mind. Of course. "Magic" was not a bad word in Prinny's mind. Not at all. Magic was something she wanted to believe in. No, she *needed* to believe in it. It was her only way to connect to her mother and to the happy life she felt had already eluded her.

"Come look." Marie started taking things gently out of the box. "Look at this bag of pretty stones she collected." She handed it over to Prinny.

It was a mesh bag, about the size of a paper lunch bag, at least half full of pretty stones, some cut, some smooth, some sparkling in the dim light, and others dull, receding like little rock shadows at the ocean's edge. "What are they for?"

"All different things," Marie said, helping Prinny open the bag, then taking them out one by one. "This one is rose quartz. That's a magic rock to help you find love."

"But Mama had Daddy!"

Marie smiled. "Maybe this is why." She curled her fist tight around the rock and held it to her chest for a moment. "It's very powerful. Also for self-love. You know it's important to love yourself, don't you, child? If you don't, how's anyone else gon' to?"

Prinny didn't understand that concept, but she didn't care. She liked the idea that she had found some magic talisman that had given her mother and father to each other, and when she touched it, it buzzed against the tender skin of her palm. She would save the stone, she determined right then and there, so that someday she would be able to find her own husband.

Though it did occur to her later, and she hated herself for it, that maybe it hadn't been so lucky after all. Had she been willing to give up her life so young, just to find love at twenty-one? Even at eleven that had seemed like a pretty bad deal.

"This one"—Marie took out what looked like a great big diamond—"is a plain ol' crystal quartz. Very *very* magical."

"It looks like a diamond!"

"Indeed it does. It is good for everything. Very good luck for everything."

"But she died!"

"It was her time." Marie gave Prinny another hug, and it spread over the child like a soothing balm. "She chose that long before she ever came to this earth. She came here so she could create *you,* and *you,* child, are destined for greatness."

Those words never left Prinny's mind.

You are destined for greatness.

They had supported her through some pretty hard times, but they had also taunted her when the going got tough and she felt she should have been more successful, in more ways, than she was.

She'd always thought that by thirty she'd be married, have kids, be living the life that had been taken from both her mother *and* herself. She'd thought she'd finally be starting to heal all the things that broke when she was six and her mother "disappeared."

Too late for that possibility. She was months away from thirty now.

And even though she still clung to Marie's words—*you're destined for greatness*—as time marched on she believed them less and less.

Nevertheless, that day in the attic had changed

her life forever. At first she'd just sneak up there whenever her father—or whatever subsequent nanny was on duty—wasn't looking and go through the trunk.

She never dumped the whole thing out or tore through it, taking it all in and trying to understand it. Instead she lifted out all the books and made them into a pile, so she could tell what she was looking at as she went along, then took things out piece by piece, letting each one be the treasure of the day.

The bag of stones was first. There were so many of them, and she sat in the attic—now with a flashlight—and looked through a metaphysical book she found in the library to identify each one and its magical properties. It was a cross between being a geologist and a witch doctor.

The amber and blue lazulite was to reduce worries. She could use that.

The purple amethyst was for peace and happiness. There had been a small one in the bag, but a large bookend of it as well, deep in the dark of the trunk, sparkling like treasure in Captain Hook's lair.

Moonstone was just a beautiful name, and a beautiful moon-gray stone, and according to the book it was for protection from negativity. But there was a warning not to be near it during the full moon, as the energy could get too frenetic. Prinny didn't know what that meant, but it didn't sound good, and since she didn't know the phases of the moon, she set it aside so she would never accidentally interact with it at "the wrong time." Later, of course, she learned the phases of the moon and their power and got quite adept at harnessing the power of the moon and the moonstone, if only in small ways.

There were a bunch more, but the one that interested her the most was the selenite. It looked like an ordinary crystal, or, to be more specific, like the bauble on the end of a cheap necklace from Claire's after it aged for a while, but the book said it called in the angels.

Prinny was sure that her mother was an angel now, and she'd do anything to bring her back, so she kept the selenite on her at all times, a long, slim cirrus cloud, right up until it crumbled to chips and dust in the front pocket of her jeans.

That was when the idea to have a metaphysical shop first occurred to her: when she was just a teen. Not that she would have called it a metaphysical shop, because she didn't know what that meant at the time, or how it would work. All she knew was that this magical stone that she hoped to God would bring her mother to visit had broken to bits and she needed another one.

Which isn't to say that the crystals and stones were the only things of interest to her in the trunk. There were cards, not just the tarot cards that Marie had first pointed out, but beautiful cards decorated with fairies and flowers and positive messages, like happy fortune cookies. There were candles, too, that still smelled nice but were melted into lumps, and whose purpose Prinny would never know.

For a long time, through three more nannies, Prinny kept the chest a secret. No one else ever went up to the attic, and she didn't want anyone growing alarmed at the contents and deciding to remove it "for her own good."

That was exactly the kind of thing grown-ups did.

But she did eventually take the books down to her room, one by one, and read them at night, trying to understand the workings of the occult. Except she didn't like to think of it as "the occult" because that sounded so devilish, and everything she'd found in the box—as well as everything she remembered about her mother—was just so fun and kitschy and even frivolous. Cards with fairies on them, bright-colored candles, sparkling gems and crystals . . .

When she was sixteen, five years deep into her ever-strengthening interest in fortune-telling, she broached the subject with her father.

"What was Mama like?" she asked him one night as they sat, just the two of them, eating his favorite meatloaf and mashed potatoes—prepared by the new cook he'd given his mother's old recipe to—for a late dinner.

He looked taken aback. "What do you mean, what was she like? You remember her!"

"Not so well, Dad." She shrugged. "She's been gone for nearly two-thirds of my life." The words hurt, not so much because she remembered and missed her mother, because she really didn't remember her very well, but because she hadn't had a mother long enough to mourn her properly. All she had was the few remnants her mother had left behind, and her own imagination, which was putting together a picture that might or might not be accurate.

"Not that long," he said, frowning. "Surely not so long. It's only been"—he thought about it—"nine years now."

"I'm sixteen."

A pained look crossed his face. It was as if he'd never considered the impact on her before. Then his expression softened, and he said, "You look very much like her, you know."

Prinny felt her cheeks grow warm. To be told she looked like the truly beautiful, sophisticated blond woman in the pictures was like being told she looked like Grace Kelly—someone had said that about her mother once. Prinny had had to Google the name, but when she did, the images took her breath away. To be compared to a woman who was said to look like her was a nice compliment, to be sure, but the kind of thing that was embarrassing to acknowledge graciously because then it sounded like she agreed.

But coming from her father, it was a different thing. Maybe he really meant it. "Did you know her when she was my age?"

"Very nearly. I met her when she was twenty. Imagine. Just a little older than you are now."

The fact that she'd died less than a decade later hung in the air, a sad little bit of dust floating between them, unacknowledged but fully known.

"What sort of things did she like?" Prinny went on carefully. "I found a book on tarot cards upstairs on one of the shelves a few years ago, and I guess it was hers, because that sure doesn't sound like you." She smiled, but something inside told her that this could be a touchy subject and she'd better tread very carefully.

He laughed, genuinely. "Oh, she loved that stuff! Loved it! When we first met, she told me a psychic had told her I was coming for her. She said she was never afraid of being alone for too long because a psychic told her I was on the way to save her." His smile dimmed, presumably at the thought that he ultimately couldn't, and didn't, save her.

"Was she psychic?"

He gave that wry smile that to this day she remembered as being quintessential *him*. "Every single time I tried to surprise her with a present or a trip she was."

Prinny had to laugh. "But was she *really?*"

He shrugged. "Who knows? I never really bought into that stuff myself."

Prinny was incredulous. "Even though someone *told her* you were coming?"

He stabbed at his meatloaf. "It's not like they gave her my name, baby. They just told her a man was going to come into her life. She was nineteen and gorgeous, so who couldn't have predicted that? If it hadn't been me, it could have been anyone. It could have been Jean-Claude Van Damme. He could have been your father."

She screwed her face up, both at the obscure choice of celebrity and at the idea of that one in particular being her father under *any* circumstances. "That seems like a stretch."

"All I'm saying is, it didn't take a psychic to tell a beautiful girl like that that a man was going to love her."

Prinny smiled. There was so much love in him still for the mother she'd never know except in the pieces he gave her, that she couldn't help hoping such a good man was on his way to her, too.

She wanted to know who the psychic was who had told her mother that, but she knew her dad wouldn't know the answer. And even if he did, chances seemed slim that she could find the same person and that they'd remember Ingrid Tiesman. Or, rather, Ingrid Barclay, as she'd been at the time.

"When they said you were coming along, did they tell her Leif was coming with you?" Leif had been ten years old when Prinny's parents had gotten married.

"Now, *that*"—he took a forkful of mashed potatoes—"is a damn good question."

"If they did, that would prove they were right, wouldn't it?"

"That they were lucky guessers. Or maybe that they were good enough at talking vague that she made it fit."

"If she believed, there had to be something to it! I mean, if that was her *thing*—"

"Princess, it was just one of her things. Your mom had a whole lot of different interests. That's just one of the quirkier. She told me that she liked playing those *psychic games*—that's what she called them—when she was a lonely teenager. Those things brought her comfort, so I say why not? That doesn't mean they were magic."

Prinny had had the same experience with them herself, though she was shy about admitting it, particularly since it would probably make her father feel like her loneliness was somehow his failing. "Did she keep on seeing that same psychic?"

"Nah. Not that I know of. I never even heard the name. But now and then she'd see one of those neon signs, like in Georgetown, and she had to stop, no matter what time of night it was, and get a quick palm read or whatever they did."

"You didn't go in with her?"

He gave a dismissive shake of the head. "Not my thing. Gave me a chance to sit in the car and get the scores on the radio."

"You were never even *tempted* to find out your future?"

He shook his head, but kindly. "You don't get a lot out of it if you don't believe."

"So you really don't believe." The idea that he didn't gave her the uncomfortable feeling that he didn't believe in *her*.

He shook his head. "She loved reading those cards, though. She'd shuffle them up like a professional blackjack dealer, then ask me to pick one. Damned if she couldn't make it all sound true, too. But that's how those things work. Don't be fooled by them. It's like horoscopes—they're just vague enough so that you can read whatever you want into them."

Actually, Prinny disagreed. She'd been teaching herself to do readings, and all the ones she'd done on her own life were spot-on. Her father would say that was a perfect example of reading into them to make things fit, but she knew there was more to it. She suspected her mother had had the Gift and that she'd passed it down to Prinny.

The only thing was, she didn't know how to *use* it. Or maybe, more specifically, she didn't know how to harness it. Because the thoughts came to her wildly. She could ask a question and get an answer right away, but the problem was that all of the questions were hers and she didn't always remember the answers so it was tough to say how fast or accurate her prognostications were.

She *had* talked to plenty of psychics, though. Mostly phone psychics, though she stuck to the ones that had a money-back guarantee if you weren't absolutely *amazed*. And most of the psychics she'd talked to, without any prodding from her, had told her she was going to open a business to light the way for other people.

Other people like Prinny and Ingrid.

So when her father died and Leif started making noise about her not being responsible enough to handle her portion of the inheritance— implication, she was not responsible enough to handle *life*—she knew she had to come up with a viable business.

And what better than one her own mother would have loved? What better than a business that would help and comfort people, the way it had helped and comforted Prinny and her mother in their lost years?

She could see it before she even bought it: the baskets of beautiful shining, glimmering, glittering stones and crystals; an array of oracle cards (now there were so many more than in her mother's day: mermaids, unicorns, saints, and angels); colorful book spines lining the shelves with titles like *Most Magikal Herbalism* and *A Wink from God*. It was clearly Meant To Be, as far as Prinny was concerned.

And as far as Prinny was concerned, she knew when things were Meant To Be.

And, seriously, *where* better than in Georgetown, a place filled with funky little shops and at least one neon PSYCHIC light that had been up as long as Prinny could remember, and might well be the very one her father had spoken of stopping at in the middle of the night on her beautiful, eccentric mother's whim?

To say nothing of all the other browse-about places that made foot traffic so likely. Three seasons out of four the weather was nice enough to stroll along the streets and shop, and people also loved Georgetown in the snow.

It was perfect.

And so Cosmos was born.

It *had* to be.

Chapter Three
Twenty-eight Years Earlier

"Did you see that?" Jessica, aka "the New Maid," nudged Lena, the cook, who was the closest thing she had to a friend in the Tiesman household, and pointed into the dining room, where the family was getting up from dinner.

"What?" Lena was distracted, trying to clean the plates, but the baby's wailing turned her attention to the dining room. "What happened?"

"That little shit just pinched her."

"What, the baby?"

Jessica was instantly incensed. "Yes, that's why she's crying. He thought no one was looking, and I watched him do it! Jesus, she's not having food allergies or any other reaction. She's being abused by that kid!" She shook her head and tried to resist the urge to go in and beat the crap out of him in front of his parents. "Son of a bitch."

"She's not a bitch, she's lovely."

As if on cue, Ingrid Tiesman went to little Prinny and swooped her into her arms. The child settled quickly, but Jessica could see the angry red spot as if it were throbbing.

Then, almost worse, she saw the little smile on Leif's face.

It was disgusting.

"Aren't you supposed to be clearing the dishes?" Lena asked. "And not gawking and judging?"

"I don't wanna go anywhere near the kid."

"It's your *job*. And *I* can't finish *my* job until you bring them in. So get on it."

"In a *minute*." She watched the scene before her.

Ingrid took Prinny toward the stairs, stopping, for a moment, to let her husband give the baby a kiss. She had quieted by then; the pleasant little thing was even smiling, despite the fact that tears still rested on her cheeks. She always rallied, that one. Such a good, easy baby. Such a contrast to her brother.

"Do you want me to take her up to bed?" the boy asked, approaching his stepmother and sister. Jessica couldn't tell if the gleam she saw in his eyes was real or just something she imagined because she expected it.

And the poor baby reached for him! Actually *reached for him!* Her tormentor, yet her little eyes lit up when she saw him, like he was a movie star or something. It was horrible.

"I've got to stop this." Jessica started for the dining room, but Lena stopped her.

"That is *not* your job."

"Fuck my job." Jessica bustled into the room. "Leif, did you drop something?"

"No." He was reaching for Prinny, but it didn't look like Ingrid was going to give her up. Thank goodness. Ingrid was no dink; she knew her stepson was a monster. No one could miss it, for Pete's sake! He was mean as a snake, through and through.

"I thought I saw something glinting under your seat," Jessica went on, searching frantically for anything that might explain it. There was nothing, but at least she'd interrupted whatever his intentions were toward his poor little sister.

It wasn't only what he'd just done; that was icing on the proverbial cake. A cake he would happily have put snakes, snails, and puppy dog tails—along with a good measure of snot—into. In fact, he *had* put toothpaste in the middle of select Oreos in a package; that had been a delightful discovery. And the time he'd stolen the neighbor's cat and kept it in a plastic grocery bag for two days before being discovered? Even though that could have ended much worse, Jessica was pretty sure the cat left with a haunted look it hadn't had before.

She'd heard tell of other things he did in the neighborhood—cruelty to small animals, mostly— though she'd never been able to catch him. *She* believed the stories of other children, but it wasn't enough to convince the parents to get him to a psychiatrist.

People saw what they wanted to see, but even more than that, people managed to *not see* what they really *didn't* want to see. And while it seemed like Mrs. Tiesman might have some awareness that things weren't right with the kid, she was very kind and supported her husband in his determined efforts to make this family strong and happy.

Jessica was one hundred percent sure that was never going to happen.

"So I thought you might have dropped something you needed," Jessica went on, finishing lamely.

He turned and glared at her. "I'm going to put

my *sister* to *bed*." He looked back at the baby. "Come on, Prinny Princess," he said in a voice dripping with sarcasm.

Jessica looked at Mrs. Tiesman with a tight smile.

Ingrid Tiesman seemed to get it. "It's all right, Leif. I need to change her anyway. You know how you feel about that."

Everyone who had seen—and especially those who'd had to *clean*—the soiled diapers he'd taken out of the Diaper Genie and smashed to the wall when they first brought Prinny home knew how he felt about that.

Ingrid ruffled his hair and swept out of the room, Prinny safely in her arms.

She didn't see—as Jessica had—the look of sheer, unadulterated hatred he had shot at them as they left.

"Listen to me," Jessica hissed in his ear. "I saw what you did, you little shit. You pinched Prinny and made her cry. You've been doing that all along, all over her body, making your poor parents mad with worry over what is wrong with her."

"They're not *my parents*." He gave her a cold look, then opened his mouth and began to wail a fake cry, but she instinctively slapped her hand over his mouth.

"Do it and you will be sorry." Her anger was such that it took him aback. She could see the fear flicker momentarily through his eyes. "I *swear* it." She took her hand off his mouth slowly, ready to clap it back if he made one peep.

A moment passed in which he leveled that flinty gaze on her.

A gaze, she knew, that would probably someday make doomed girls swoon. Doomed girls loved assholes, and this kid was going to be the king of them.

"You *bitch*," he said, then literally spat in her face.

She slapped him, hard, a reflex she couldn't stop.

And with that one move, she knew her job was over. He was sure to tell, and even if he didn't, she'd have to because she was *not* going to keep secrets in conjunction with this little heathen. There was just no way.

So she went up to her room to pack her things. He was probably reporting on her right now, showing his red skin and crying his icy blue eyes out. She was going to be kicked out quickly and soundly.

But she wanted to warn Ingrid Tiesman what she was dealing with. She wanted to tell her about Leif pinching Prinny, and hurting animals, and even the part about messing with the food. She *assumed* it was only toothpaste in the Oreos, but it wasn't like she'd eaten a bunch to be sure. That could have masked any number of other things, and there was not one thing she'd put past Leif Tiesman.

Eleven years old and she wouldn't put it past him to actually try to kill someone.

But what authority did she have to say anything? She was a maid. Not a childcare expert, not the nanny; she wasn't supposed to have anything to do with the children at all. She was just the busybody who had something to say about something that was none of her business.

Honestly, now that Jessica was thinking about this, even if she wasn't fired, she'd be afraid to stay in the house one more night. She'd unleashed something in the boy, and he knew that *she* knew it was out there. She wasn't safe anywhere near him.

She took out the spiral notebook she used as a diary and began to write her letter of resignation.

Chapter Four

Chelsea

Don't move a muscle. If ever she were to be held up at gunpoint and heard these words uttered behind her while the cold, hard mouth of a gun wedged into the nape of her neck, she would at least earn a gold star—or her life—for following directions.

If she were ever on a reality show and the challenge was to cover her own body in honey and bees and stand stock-still no matter how many times she was stung, she would win. She hated those gross-out shows, but she was certain she would have the mental concentration and detachment to win that challenge.

If she ever had a kid, and he tried to goad her by pretending he was going to shove a finger up her nose, then she'd gain points from onlooking moms who admired her patience and stillness in the face of annoyance as she did not move a muscle, even if the sticky, Jolly Rancher–covered digit made its way past her nostril.

So now, if she ever got famous—no, *when, when* she got famous—she'd be able to tell interviewers about that laugh-riot era in her twenties when she'd picked up extra cash (essential cash, really, nothing "extra" about it) by working, among other less-than-glamorous things, as a living statue at Union Station.

The job was fine. Easy, compared to many. Certainly compared to manual labor. If you said to a plumber or a trashman that you thought your job was hard, and then admitted that your one requirement was to stand still and let people pose with you as if you were Snow White in Disneyland (a job she'd practically kill for at this point), you'd sound like a spoiled idiot.

As if you didn't already.

One of the biggest problems, and one she never remembered to adjust for, was when she had set herself facing one way, doing a pose facing away from the clock, then realizing that her shift must soon be up. Because inevitably, she'd be facing anywhere but within peripheral view of the clock, and statues trying to look at the wristwatches of passersby were creepy, not cool.

"Mom! Mom! Look, I think that statue just moved!"

Dammit. She'd scrolled her eyes to the left to try to possibly see at least the little hand on the clock.

"No, I don't think so," said the mom, in that *Blues Clues* way that means you are absolutely right and urges you to investigate further. "A *statue,* Hank?"

Hank? *Hank* for a six-year-old? That's the name of a weirdly tall and whip-thin farmer guy who *just wants to drink his beer and have some goldang quiet.*

This poor little man. Hank.

"I saw it! I did! It's *magical!*"

"Oh, I don't know. Magic? Or a trick?" The mother laughed uncomfortably. She was probably starting to think it was time to have the Talk about Santa Claus, so a moving statue was one thing, but a *magical* one was quite another.

She should come to the store. *That* magic would probably *really* freak her out.

"Can we take it home?" Hank was too old to ask something like that. Was he accustomed to seeing large objects in public places and thinking he could just grab them?

"Not today. But why don't I take your picture with the statue?" And something about the way the mother suggested it made Chelsea know—she just *knew*—that tonight, when she *really* needed to get out on time, Mom was going to take her damn time trying to figure out the camera settings on her phone, then try to get the perfect shot. It was like waiting in line for the one working bathroom stall in a bar behind someone with a wooden leg, a catheter, and no real hurry to get out of your way.

Hank slowed down in his approach to her, suddenly wary. He brought his hands together and looked up at her, his half-smile frozen.

She let her eyes go unfocused, so they'd be less likely to catch on movement, and waited until his mom was gazing down at her phone to get the camera open.

Then she looked down at Hank and winked.

He gave a tiny squeal.

She had him! He was charmed. She could *totally* be Snow White (or Elsa or Cinderella or Tinker Bell) in a Disney park. She'd charmed a child, the toughest audience there was.

"Mom!" Hank tugged on his mother's arm. "He did it again!"

He?

Chelsea sighed as undetectably as she could. Forget the charm. She'd probably just scared him. Her mammoth, white-painted self had scared a child. She hated getting this Grecian woman costume. She'd always suspected she looked less like an Olympia and more like cartoon Aladdin after he became a sultan, and Hank's reaction just proved it.

This would *not* be a hot portfolio picture.

"That's fun, huh?" The mother circum-navigated the area, then crouched down like a tourist pretending to be a real photographer.

Both of them were waiting for her to move again. The trick was to wait until just after they decided she wasn't *going* to.

It took a frustratingly long time, particularly since she had to leave. She had to get to the shop. She had appointments lined up, and they paid better than this gig, though they weren't likely to get her on Broadway anytime soon.

Prinny wouldn't say anything bitchy if she was late—that wasn't her style—but she'd let out a breath that sounded like that yoga breathing technique, Ujjayi Pranayama. Except way less relaxed, and way more irritated.

Just as Hank started to walk back to his mom, smile almost entirely faded, Chelsea shifted her arms to a Superman stance and spun herself to face the clock. Four fifty-five. She had an hour to get undressed, redressed, and on the road to the shop.

"Mom!"

"I've got it!" The camera started clicking its little digital click sound as Hank maneuvered himself in front of Chelsea.

She'd wait for them to finish and head off—didn't they have somewhere to be? This was a train station, for God's sake, not a sunny park on a Saturday. It took all of about fifteen minutes to see everything there, and that included a jaunt into The Body Shop for emergency hand sanitizer (something Chelsea purchased frequently in this place).

It took them a few more minutes of examining the marble floors—Hank surreptitiously looking back at Chelsea every few seconds to see if she'd moved again—but they finally left.

Chelsea turned like a soldier when they were out of sight, facing the direction that led to the back offices and locker rooms. Yes, locker rooms. Not dressing rooms.

She lowered herself down onto one leg and extended her other forward off her pedestal. (*Ha,* the number of times ex-boyfriends had encouraged her to do just this, jump off her pedestal and be real.)

Then she let the other down, unfocused her eyes, relaxed her face so she looked as bland as the girls who kept getting the roles she wanted, and made the march back to her locker, as still and unanimated as one could imagine a walking statue would be.

Once she was beyond the threshold of the door, and into the hot room that smelled like chalk, makeup remover, and hot bodies, her muscles melted, and she skulked to the bench to sit down.

She peeled the costume off and shoved it into one of the five-gallon Ziplocs provided for the statues' wardrobe, then jumped into a steaming hot shower. Well, actually, it was a *shoilet,* a small closet space that held a toilet and had a shower-head in the ceiling, just like you'd find in the "luxury cabins" on a cross-country train. The space was so small she was sure that if she put on three more pounds she'd have trouble fitting in it. But she didn't have time to worry about that now, or ever. She had to work with what she had and pray that someday these would be funny stories of climbing up the ladder to fame and success, rather than the actor's equivalent of a former frat boy's Tales of Glory.

Slapping on her exfoliation gloves, she poured on the thick orange goo used to remove latex paint and sticky things from skin. It had solvents and little beads that helped get the stuff off, no way was it good for your skin. It wasn't exactly Bliss Spa peppermint scrub. Still, it did the trick faster than if she were to painstakingly take the stuff off with makeup remover wipes or endless latherings of soap.

It was a full ten minutes until she was finally back to her peachy, if rubbed red and blotchy, skin tone. She had just dropped her towel when the door slammed open and a shirtless, slick-skinned guy burst in.

"Hey," he said, perking up with a smile when he saw her. As she scrambled to cover herself, he didn't cover his eyes or make an awkward apology. Instead he laughed and entered the locker room with even more confidence.

A sound that might have been an attempt at "um" came from her mouth, and she tightened the terrycloth around her chest.

"I pride myself on being on time," he said, walking past her and whipping his backpack off. "And then on my first day, I'm running this late. You know I actually got off the Metro and ran the last two miles?"

That explained the slick skin. She would have guessed baby oil and unnecessarily bare pecs, but a shirtless run made sense, too, with a guy that looked like this.

He bent over, his hands on his thighs, breathing deeply. Chelsea could tell from the tight torso that he was definitely no stranger to working out.

"Whoo!" He stood up. "I'm Jeff."

Jeff held out one hand and swept off his backward-turned hat with the other one.

Pulling the towel closer with her forearm, she shook his hand. "Chelsea. I'm not usually so naked. Or silent. I just wasn't expecting anyone to come in. Especially not—"

She stopped—what on earth had she been about to say?

Unimaginable as it might seem, there was a whole *world* of living statues. Just as every restaurant and coffee shop has its own little society and its own dramas, relationships, and feuds, so, too, did Statue Land, and it was firmly divided into two camps.

In one were the teenagers to twenty-somethings who consistently put in their two weeks, then stopped bothering to come in or even call, instead climbing aboard a BoltBus to Manhattan or elsewhere to pursue real dreams.

The other camp was made up of the older people who never went anywhere. These were called, terrifyingly, the Dying Statues.

As the weeks and months passed, Chelsea was coming dangerously close to changing camps. In sad fact, she probably already had in the eyes of the others. Suddenly she was the college graduate wearing Hollister and realizing that not only had everyone else stopped wearing Hollister, but she *especially* looked ridiculous for still wearing it at her age. Like it might as well have been Gymboree.

All of the young statues, girls and gay men for the most part, got dressed in front of each other, no problem, dropping clothes to the ground and chatting naked as they got ready, like a squad of *America's Next Top Model* prospects.

Jeff didn't give off a gay vibe.

Slightly too self-conscious for this communal bathing style, Chelsea took pleasure in working the early shift, which usually left the locker room open and empty for her alone.

"I wasn't expecting someone I didn't recognize," she filled in for herself. Perfectly reasonable option.

"Well, now that won't happen, even if I do burst in on you again, right?"

"Right." Chelsea averted her gaze, realizing she was staring at him as he pulled things out of his bag and put them on the bench.

"How long have you worked here?" Jeff asked, raking his hand through his short brown hair. It stuck up for a moment, amusingly, then dropped back down into place.

"About four months." Closer to six, but she didn't really want to admit that.

"Cool. You'll have to tell me the tricks of the trade!"

"Stay still. Be a statue. That's about the size of it here." She smiled. "Much more challenging than people think, of course."

He laughed. "Good advice." He turned around, his flat stomach facing Chelsea. He had that abs-framed-by-obliques thing going on. "Hey, I'm just moving into the area. I don't know a soul. Do you want to maybe grab a drink or something after a shift this week? Or coffee, if that's more your thing. Just someplace right here. You can give me the scoop." One side of his mouth went up in a smile.

She was completely taken aback. Chelsea knew one thing for sure about herself, and that was that she didn't strike most people as entirely approachable. When she wasn't smiling, she had a chronic case of Resting Bitch Face. When she was smiling, she looked like a Dumb Girl.

Was this guy actually *attracted* to one of those looks? Or, more likely, was he a particularly masculine gay guy looking for another bestie? She was also fine with that. Frankly, she was kind of intrigued by the idea either way.

Then she thought about the week ahead of her. All early mornings and late nights. She had the store. She had the statue gig. She had auditions, and any free time she had she really needed to be spending memorizing lines and practicing. She had no time. No time, *literally*.

"This week is really busy for me . . ." She drifted off, knowing he was going to think it was a bullshit excuse. She was going to come off as unfriendly at best and bitchy at worst.

"I'm not coming on to you or anything." He gave a laugh. "Really, I just want to meet some people."

Hm. Was that insulting?

Had he just insulted her?

Was she *disappointed?*

Better to just play it cool, no matter what his deal was. "Really, it's *just* a terrible week for me." She gave an awkward smile, then emphasized it with an unintentionally insincere-looking shrug.

His expression shifted. "Gotcha. I'm sorry, didn't mean to get off on a weird foot. I'll see you around." He smiled, exposing straight white teeth. Model's teeth.

"I'm gonna rinse off in the shower," he said, his voice clearly dismissive now. "If you're not here when I get back, it was nice meeting you."

"You, too." Chelsea nodded and watched him go to the showers, taking in the divots at the bottom of his spine, right above the low-slung shorts.

She was gawking at him not because he was the most breathtaking human she'd ever seen, but because it was the first time in ages that she'd felt this—those pre-crush butterflies that make you stammer and replay the scene where you made an ass of yourself later as you fall asleep.

What the *hell* was the matter with her? She might not have even a spare hour in her schedule right now, but she could have been *nicer* about it. She wanted to kick herself.

When she heard the shoilet turn on and the curtain rings scrape across the metal rod, she dropped her towel—without a witness this time—and got dressed in a hurry.

It would be very uncool if she were to still be there when he came back out.

The bells jingled on the shop door when she arrived. She was ten minutes late, but Prinny was a nice boss. She knew Chelsea was running around like a chicken with her head cut off, or, to be exact, an actress with a seemingly endless stream of outrageous bills to pay.

Prinny Tiesman was organizing the impulse buys at the front and turned when she heard the jingle.

Chelsea was fascinated by her boss, because she was one person whose motivations and goals weren't always clear. She'd be hard to play on film. Prinny came from an *extremely* wealthy Loudon County family, whose wealth had been divided between her and her brother upon their father's death, yet she didn't seem to spend money on anything other than necessities.

Meanwhile, her brother was reportedly horrified that she got half. The business manager in charge of Prinny's inheritance was always insisting the store needed a solid plan and profit margin in order for Prinny to protect her assets, but Prinny seemed a lot more concerned with pleasing the finance guy than with saving herself from this mysterious fairy-tale "wicked stepbrother."

Chelsea had never met the wicked stepbrother, but she kind of wanted to. What would an evil, youngish, rich, and powerful man like that look like? Not that she'd be *interested* in an evil man, not romantically, but from a theatrical standpoint both options—bulbous-nosed wart-covered monster *and* handsome devil—seemed clichéd. It would be more of a surprise if he were utterly ordinary. Maybe even wore terrible suits from Walmart. If Walmart sold suits.

Anyway, Chelsea had no idea which category he'd fall into because, despite her job, she was *not* psychic.

Though she *could* read cards, and she could definitely read people. Prinny had very fixed ideas about Spiritual Integrity, so the business was running with as much integrity as possible. Even though Chelsea was not psychic, per se, she was extremely good at reading voices, gestures, and choices and had managed to convince Prinny that she was outside the normal range of perception and, if not clairvoyant, then certainly intuitive—helpful in any business really, Chelsea would imagine.

"Hey, Prinny," she said, shutting the door behind her and starting to unwind her scarf.

Her boss knitted her brow. "What's wrong?"

"Wrong?"

"Something's up." She pointed her finger and then stirred the air with it.

Most people would ask this question because of a dark mood cloud rising above the person who's upset. Sometimes people want to be asked what's wrong. Chelsea was not this sort of person. She was far more likely to pull out her best mood, so as not to have to answer any uncomfortable questions. And for her, any questions about herself were pretty much uncomfortable.

But in this case, Chelsea wasn't hiding anything. Not on purpose, anyway. Prinny was Prinny, however, and she was the real deal when it came to this sort of thing. Either psychic stuff was genuine or she was an exceptional people reader, even better than Chelsea.

"Something's going on," Prinny said.

"I feel fine, really. I think?"

Prinny planted her hands on her hips. "No, it's nothing bad. Just something new. Maybe something to do with a guy?"

Again, a generally basic question from anyone but Prinny. Chelsea often was faced with these sorts of inquiries from her, and more often than not she had to dig through her mind to find whatever it was Prinny was picking up on.

In this case, Chelsea wondered how far into her mind she was delving.

"I mean . . . someone just asked me out. Well, not *out* out."

"Ooh, what did you say?" Psychic defenses down, girl-talk game face on.

"I told him I was busy."

"You are," Prinny said. "But too busy?"

Chelsea shrugged. "That would depend on the circumstances. I was too busy under these circumstances."

"Hmm. Not cute?"

"No, he was cute. Really cute, actually. I honestly don't have the time."

"For heaven's sake, Chelsea, you can always take a night or a few hours off. I haven't seen you go on one date this whole time you've worked here."

"I know."

"Not your scene?"

"I really just don't have time, that's all."

Prinny nodded at her, both of them knowing she could have made the time if she wanted to.

"You should go out with this guy. Find the time. It's time to get over the breakup. I have a good feeling about it."

"Honestly, he didn't even ask me out. He's just new in town and asked me if I'd grab a drink with him. He's looking for friends, that's all."

"Well, if that's the case, that's even worse! Someone makes an effort with a stranger, just hoping to make a friend, and you rejected that? Shame on you." She smiled, letting Chelsea know that she meant it but was teasing her.

"I'll let him know next time I have a few hours."

"Good."

A tiny flint in Chelsea's chest caught alight as she wondered, cautiously, if Prinny really was picking up on something. This surprised her. She'd feared that hope was gone.

"What's his name?" she asked.

"Jeff."

Prinny nodded. "Hm."

"What?"

Prinny laughed. "Nothing! I'm trying to pick up on it, but you keep interrupting. Anyway, I'm not getting a gay vibe. That's good for a good-looking eligible guy in this day and age."

"I'll say." Chelsea shook her head. "It's a jungle out there."

Prinny nodded. "Just make real sure you're the predator and not the prey."

Chapter Five

Diana

It was scary how obvious the idea of killing my husband seemed once I thought of it.

I could get away with it, I was almost sure. There were so many tinctures that could go wrong—or *right* if that was what I was doing—and create a "natural death" that no one would ever suspect I might have made it happen. There's an art to everything. Curing disease, boosting immunity, quelling depression, calming anxiety.

Even killing.

Maybe even *especially* killing.

I sat in my dimmed kitchen, drinking my own tea with the hopes of calming down, but my thoughts raced so hard that I felt they were knocking into the sides of my brain, banging a headache in that would never go away. Pain that would never go away.

"Hey." The lights clicked on, and I winced like a nocturnal animal, squinting in the direction of the doorway, where Leif stood in his briefs, tanned body looking every bit as muscular and delicious as it had when I'd met him ten years ago.

He *still* made me catch my breath. Even all this time later. My first thought was *I should be ashamed of myself for being so weak.* But that wasn't fair. If he were faithful and his wife still loved and admired him like that, it would have been great. The ideal situation.

I shifted in my chair, as nervous as I would be with a stranger, unsure what to say that wouldn't just come out as *I read your texts and you're a cheating sonofabitch and I hate you I hate you I hate you!*

"Did I wake you up?" I asked, hoping if I had, it had been just now in the kitchen and not when I was prowling around the bedroom like a cat, invading his privacy.

"You weren't in bed." He gave that pirate smile I'd always loved. "How am I supposed to sleep without you in the bed with me?"

You seem to have managed to do a lot of things in bed without me. Sleeping is probably one of the lesser ones. "I was having some anxiety, so I

71

decided to make a tea." I pointed at the cup, as if I had to prove it or something.

"Do you need one of your pills?"

A little splinter of irk pierced my consciousness. "That's not actually the answer to everything."

"It's what they're *for*."

"I don't like the way they make me feel."

"You prefer this?" He gestured at the cup, which was rapidly starting to seem like a child in the middle of our conversation.

"Yes, I do."

He sighed and shook his head, indulgent but a little bit annoyed, clearly. "Should I get my mom on the phone?"

"What? *Why?* So she can talk me into taking a pill?" It wasn't such an absurd suggestion, actually. She was the one who had prescribed them to begin with. Presumably she *did* think they were a good idea. "This is stupid."

"Okay, okay." He held his hands up, the universal sign of sarcastic surrender.

"It's more convenient for you when I'm a zombie, isn't it?" I asked suddenly.

He frowned. "What?"

"Put me to sleep so I stay out of your way and don't ask any inconvenient questions?"

"What are you talking about?" But something in his expression shifted and made me think I'd struck a nerve and he knew *exactly* what I was talking about.

My heart was pounding. I wanted to back off this, quick, but I'd started it, and in my gut I knew I had to finish it. "Don't pretend you've never cheated on me, Leif."

He wasn't one to blush or go pale, but the set of his mouth tightened. "That was a long time ago. You know I'm sorry. I'm sorry for it every single day. You know it was a onetime thing."

I knew with absolute certainty it was *far* from a onetime thing, and the Plumber tonight was just more of the same old same old. Or maybe she wasn't even the same. Maybe this one was different.

That would be the worst. If one of them was actually *different*. Different enough to replace me.

Suddenly I wondered if I was the one dispensable part. Icing. The thing that made a muffin into a cupcake but was sickeningly sweet by itself.

That's what I'd been with him. Sickeningly sweet. So forgiving, so understanding. I'd gone so far out of my way to forgive him and assuage his guilt that it was amazing I hadn't gone under in the Pacific Ocean.

"I don't believe you," I said, low and steely. My tone wasn't on purpose; it was just all I could work up.

"What are you implying?"

He knew. Of course he knew. He *had* to know because he'd been with her!

Still, I didn't want to tip my hand. I couldn't allow him time to work up a defense.

"Just that you spend a lot of time *at work,* Leif. A lot more hours than most people do, and sometimes you come home smelling more like perfume than printer's ink."

His brow lowered, and the blue of his eyes seemed to cloud like cheap ice. Don't your pupils dilate when you *love* someone? He was looking at me as if he *hated* me.

"Do you have any idea, any idea at all, how many responsibilities I have at work?"

My spirit cowered, but I tried to keep my body straight. "How could I? You never talk to me about it. You never have me to any office events, not even the holiday party. What kind of company president doesn't have his wife at the holiday party?"

"The *professional* kind."

"Yeah? Or is it because your girlfriends work there and you don't want us intermingling?"

He waved the suggestion away as if it were a gnat. "You're being completely ridiculous. When did you get to be such a jealous harpy?"

The question incensed me even while some part of me feared it was true. What I needed was the strength and dignity to walk away and not hammer at an issue that was clearly intolerable. "You know what?" I said with a strength I didn't feel. "I'm done." I stood up and rinsed my cup out, trying to ignore the tingles that went down my spine where I felt his eyes on me.

I also tried to ignore the feeling of him coming up behind me, his warmth pouring out toward me, going right through the cotton nightshirt I was wearing.

But I couldn't ignore it. I'd never been able to. And even though my mind was telling me to get the hell away from him, my body refused to move.

He put his arms around my waist and pulled me close against the heat of his torso. "Baby," he murmured against my ear, his voice low and sweet. He could have been threatening to strangle me and I wouldn't have been able to stop myself from sinking into the bliss of his embrace.

But he wasn't threatening to strangle me. It was worse than that. He was threatening to seduce me.

"Don't," I said, but my voice was feeble. He might not even have heard me.

"I love you." He trailed his lips along behind my ear and down my neck. I shivered and knew he felt it.

Triumph for him.

"This isn't love."

He chuckled softly. "Whatever it is, it's hot. You know it and I know it."

Oh, I *did* know it. It was always hot. Hot enough to compel me to stay in this toxic relationship. It wasn't that I needed him to change. Obviously that was never going to happen, but even if it could, there was too much water under the bridge. There were too many things I could never forget.

"No," I said, but reached my hand behind me, as I had a million times, and held it on his hip.

"Yes." He turned me around and moved me still closer. It was as if I were melding right into his body.

"This is over." I felt his hardness against me, and my core sprang to life. The button had been pushed. I wasn't just walking to my doom, I was *running* to it.

As I had so many times before.

"You're my wife. It will never be over."

"Why do you even want me? You have so many *extracurricular activities*. Why hold on to the old ball and chain when there are so many things, so many *people,* you prefer to me?"

"Because you are my wife. I married you. I made a vow, and I don't break my vows."

I noticed he didn't deny it that time, and something in me died even while I knew it was the truth and any other objection would have been bullshit. "You've broken plenty of your vows," I said tartly. "You can't cherry-pick which ones to honor and which ones to completely ignore."

"You are the one I chose." He ran his hands down my bare arms, and my skin rose in goose bumps beneath his touch.

"Once."

He lowered his mouth onto mine and drew me into his familiar kiss. It never got old. What *was* it about him? I'd had the most frustrating moments of my life with him, the most heart-broken moments of my life over him, but somehow I couldn't bring myself to resist him.

So I kissed him back, tightening my arms around him and running my hands up his back.

He slipped his hands under my nightshirt, his skin so warm against mine that I thought I might melt. He pulled the shirt off over my head, leaving me naked in front of him, and trailed his fingers down my back and across my hips before pulling me closer against his hardness.

"I don't want to do this," I murmured against his mouth, even while I allowed his tongue in and played at it with my own.

"Yes, you do."

"No . . ."

He walked his fingers down my abdomen and reached between my legs, instantly finding the proof he wanted.

My body's betrayal.

He smiled against my mouth. "Yes, you do."

"You hurt me."

"No, I didn't."

How could he even say that? "Yes, you did!" I said with more strength. How could he dismiss so much pain so completely?

"You know me, you know the deal. You stay because you want it, too."

"No, I stayed because I believed in you, like an idiot. I didn't know how big a liar you were!"

"Shhhh." He kissed me silent again.

And I let him.

Damn it, I *let* him.

"Turn around," he said.

"No."

"Yes." He spanned his hands on my ribs and turned me, forcefully, to face the counter. Now his touch stopped feeling good and left an ache behind.

"No!" I said, and I tried to wriggle away, but he held me in place easily.

"You know you want it." He touched my wetness again. "And I know you want it." He used his hand to guide himself into me and began to move.

At first my body betrayed me yet again. I had spent a long time loving this man and his touch. But very quickly his movements grew harder, slamming my pelvis against the cabinets we'd just paid way too much to have replaced. I'd hated them when he picked them out, hated them when they were installed, and now I hated them more than ever. Who would have thought those brass plumbing-pipe drawer pulls would end up being so painful to me this way?

"Stop!" I was begging. My voice trembled. Everything in me was alert to danger.

He put a hand over my mouth and used his other hand to spank me. Hard. It wasn't the first time he'd slapped my butt in bed, it wasn't even the first time it hurt, but a resolve grew in me that it would be the last.

"Leave me alone!" I cried, and tried to get away again. I had to be drying up fast. Nothing about this was a turn-on. It was pain. Pure pain. Nothing more to it.

"Shut up!" He banged into me so hard, the slapping noises echoed in the kitchen.

Tears burned in my eyes and spilled out, plopping onto the cement counters Leif had insisted were the latest and greatest thing, even though I'd found them as industrial and depressing as a Walmart floor.

Finally he turned me back around, looked down, and saw me bleeding where the hardware had cut me.

He drew back, reviled.

Leif hated blood. Total phobia. It was amazing; as strong and bullying as he could be, the minute he saw blood he'd go pale and shaky. Not *visibly* shaky, but definitely shaky.

"What's the matter?" I asked, anger sharpening my tone to a point. "Don't like your handi-work?"

"That's not my fault."

"It is."

"You were just as into it as I was."

And, in a way, he was right. God, I hated that most of all, but in a very real way he was right. He'd pushed all the right buttons, and my body had responded exactly as it always had, exactly as he wanted it to. Exactly as he *expected* it to.

That damnable moment of pleasure ultimately just prolonged my pain.

Most of it was emotional. I could get over the physical. I'd done it before. The most painful thing was that he'd just lured me in, against my will, again, and he'd done it *so easily*. Piece of cake.

I was sleeping with the enemy, not just because I was afraid of him but more because I was afraid of my own weakness. As long as I was anywhere near him, I was never going to be able to let go.

In that sense *I* was my own enemy.

He turned and went back to bed.

And I? I followed. Just as I always had. But this time I didn't snuggle up against him, wrapping my arm around him and spooning up against him. (Did it mean something that I was always the one doing the holding and he was always the one being held?) This time I turned away from him and sniffled quietly in the dark as my pillow grew more and more damp from my tears.

I couldn't live like this anymore. This wasn't even living. It was killing me. It was time to let go. I didn't know if I had a chance at life at all, but I knew that as long as I was with Leif I would not be long for this world.

The problem was, I had nowhere in the world to go. My parents were gone; my sister, Meghan, was estranged (in part because she'd never liked Leif, though the truth was she wasn't much more likable than he himself was).

So the bare fact was that I was really all alone in the world without him.

In fact, maybe that was another reason I'd stayed so long. Once upon a time—when I was young, stupid, and madly in love with him—I had dreamed of the family we'd have together. I'd *planned* on it. After we got married, he changed his tune about wanting children, however.

Now I was twenty-nine and looking at a long, lonely life if things didn't change.

I spent a long, sleepless night thinking about it. I stayed on my side, facing away from him, even while my arm and shoulder cramped and grew sore. I could not face him.

I didn't know that I could ever face him again.

But I couldn't kill him, either. I wanted to say the idea had been tempting, but the truth was that it had only felt like a "solution" because it was theoretically possible, not because I'd actually *do* it. It was my cyanide pill, and, like all who carry a cyanide pill, I knew that eventually this situation was going to kill *me*.

I was going to be the only casualty.

He would skate by, as he always had, looking out for number one and apparently having a great time doing it. The only price he ever paid was the occasional few minutes of mollification and seduction he had to spend on me.

I couldn't harm him.

I couldn't even faze him.

All I could even *try* to do was to save my own life.

In the morning, as he got up and got ready to leave, I pretended to be asleep so he didn't talk to me. So I didn't have to look at him.

Partly, God help me, so I didn't weaken toward him.

It seemed like it took forever, but finally he left the room and I heard the front door slam behind him. I often thought he did that on purpose, slammed the door in a last-ditch effort to wake me up or make me uncomfortable. Just one more way to niggle at me.

This time, though, it just signaled relief. He was gone.

Thank God.

I got up and began to pack. I didn't know where I was going or what I would do. The shared bank account that I had access to had only a few thousand dollars left in it, but I would take everything I could. It wasn't like I was going to be able to use my credit cards. Or even my car. I was going to have to leave that behind as well.

I was going to have to leave everything I had and everything I knew behind.

And once he saw what I'd done, I knew, he'd never forgive me. This was a game-ending move, but I had no choice.

With my suitcase packed and my phone charged, until I could get a cheap TracPhone, I stopped in the kitchen one last time and poured myself a shot of vodka and sipped it slowly while I looked at all the choices he'd made that created *his* home instead of *ours*.

All he had ever cared about was himself. Why had I thought I could change that?

That's when it occurred to me that there was one person in the world who *would* understand this. One person who might—just *might*—be a friend to me at this time.

I opened my phone contacts and dialed my best—and absolute only—hope for salvation.

Chapter Six

Twenty-five Years Earlier

The party was beautiful. Glitz. Glamour. Glitter. Fancy. Champagne and hors d'oeuvres went by on silver platters. All the servers and the bartender were in black tie.

Unbelievable. And this was her *future*. She'd gotten the job! Not only did she get to live for free in this big, gorgeous house, but she'd be *paid* to do it!

Boy, for a girl from the wrong side of the tracks in Silver Spring, this was *living*.

And it was living exactly the life she was meant to have.

She was born to be a mother. As a child, she had put her dolls to bed every night and played elaborate pretend games with them that involved feeding them, playing with them, and teaching them. In college, her friends had even jokingly called her Mom. She was always the caretaker, whether she was the five-year-old tucking in a plastic baby doll or the twenty-one-year-old emptying a water bottle down the gullet of a drunk friend.

Though suburban life—husband, 2.5 kids—was probably where she was headed (she didn't understand the disdain for it), she was sure going to enjoy the time she spent nannying for the Tiesmans.

Always a dreamer, Elisa felt like she was living out her fairy tale. Or at least a semi–fairy tale: the glorious house, no money worries (not that she'd be rich, but she was frugal anyway, and this position would include room and board), she wouldn't be hungry or cold . . .

The father, Charles Tiesman, was incredibly

nice. Warm and kind. His friends even called him Charlie—wealthy and powerful as he was, he was Charlie! Imagine that!

His wallet, she had noticed when he pulled out a twenty-dollar bill to cover her cab ride, had a picture of his daughter front and center. Her name was Lillian, but he called her Prinny—short for Princess, he'd explained with a proud little laugh. Elisa had resisted giggling when she heard it. She had a feeling the nickname would stick well into Prinny's adolescent years—long enough that she'd probably feel too guilty ever telling him it embarrassed her.

Prinny was the kind of kid who walked around happily—and loudly—at all times. She was four, but had a spark in her eyes that made her look practically reincarnated from some hundred-year-old yogi from Tibet. Honestly, she looked like she truly understood everything in the world around her.

She had a belly laugh that was absolutely contagious, and bright eyes that beamed like lights, almost always happy and definitely always kind.

Charles's wife (she was Charles's second wife, after what Elisa had gleaned from the other workers was an acrimonious divorce from his first) was very thin and fragile-looking, but Elisa suspected that to be an illusion. When she *did* smile, which seemed reserved for genuinely happy moments, it was a big smile that reached her eyes. It was most often directed at her children, Prinny and, of course, the other— Leif. That would be the woman's, Ingrid's, stepson. She was so warm to him, but he was so cold back.

Leif was quiet and unsettling to Elisa. She couldn't figure out why exactly; he was too old to need a *nanny* per se, so her job was primarily to take care of the toddler, Prinny. But Leif was still there; he was around a good percentage of the time, and Elisa had never felt the same kind of discomfort with any other child. Something about that pale complexion and his utterly colorless eyes mixed with his almost constant, yet somehow *hostile,* silence was deeply unsettling.

If Prinny seemed oddly tuned in to her surroundings, Leif seemed strangely detached from his. Yin and yang. And frankly maybe a little too much on both their parts.

The cook, Lena, whom she had grown to quite like over the past few weeks, had warned her not to get too close to the situation at all. Not from any angle. Apparently other nannies had tried and failed and ended up hurt and fired as a result.

Hurt.

That was definitely not the plan. Elisa just wanted steady work in this beautiful place until she couldn't stand the bliss anymore. So far she expected that to be never.

This was her first party at the Tiesmans'. She'd gotten the feeling it was going to be a pretty big deal, but had no idea how—and she knew the word made her sound like a rube—*fancy* it was going to be. She'd been to *weddings* far, *far* less extravagant.

Elisa arranged the slices of white cheddar cheese and Ritz crackers in a neat circle on the blue plate. She'd learned upon getting the job that this was one snack both children could agree on. Both of them were hungry, and neither of them was allowed out into the party, where tables were filled with caviar, salmon, oysters, filet mignon, lobster, salads, and a bunch of other fussy non-kid food.

To be honest, rather than building up a plate that would look like it was for herself (*nanny steals caviar, gets the sack*), she just went with what was in the fridge for the children.

Plus, this way she got to gawk at the party from the swinging doors without being in the midst of it.

She put everything away and took the plate back down the hall to where she had left Prinny quietly watching *101 Dalmatians*.

Walking up to the door, she could hear that Leif was in there with her, and whatever they were doing, they weren't doing it quietly.

She quickened her step and pushed open the door.

Leif—fourteen years old and too tall and too old to have any disagreements with his toddler sister, much less physical ones—was standing above Prinny, who was on the ground clutching her face, her chest catching in silent sobs.

"Leif!" Elisa exclaimed, rushing over. "What is going—"

He smacked the plate and the sippy-cup of grape juice Prinny had requested from Elisa's hands before she had a chance to stop him.

She took him by the shoulders to calm him, but the effort lasted only a few seconds. As soon as she had a grip on him, his angry gaze shifted to behind her. He looked suddenly horror-struck.

Elisa turned and saw Mrs. Tiesman.

"What on earth is going on in here?"

Leif wriggled away from Elisa and backed up against the wall to point at his nanny.

"Prinny and I were playing—just kidding around! And then she smacked her and tried to wrestle me onto the ground!"

The impossibility of Leif saying this, making up such a lie on the spot, struck Elisa silent.

"Leif, *again?*" Charles Tiesman showed up at the door, and it was obvious from his urgent expression that the ruckus had been audible far beyond the room.

Prinny took in a sharp breath, her sobs now becoming audible. Elisa saw that a hot red had spread across one entire side of her face. Her heart twisted, and she longed to go to her and soothe her.

Her father did instead, before shaking his head in confusion at Leif.

"No," he said. "Why would you—"

"Me?" Leif's jaw dropped, and his arm shot out like a railroad gate, one boney index finger pointed at Elisa. "It wasn't me. I didn't do anything. It was her!"

"I beg your pardon." Elisa straightened her spine. "Tell your parents the truth."

His eyes shifted uncertainly. "I guess she thought *I* was trying to hurt Prinny, but I wasn't! I don't know why she had to get so"—he sniffed as though crying, but Elisa noted that he had no tears welling, and his pupils were like pin dots—"so *violent.*"

Elisa found her voice. "That is *not* what happened!" She was unable to keep the note of childish frustration out of her voice. As if she were one of the kids, too, and had to defend herself to the parent. "I just walked in and found him standing over the poor little thing, and she was sobbing her sweet heart out. Heaven knows what he was doing, or *planning* to do."

"Ask Prinny!" said Leif, a look of disbelief on his face, and a posture that said *go right ahead.* But when he looked at Prinny, something in his expression shifted.

He looked scared of her.

"Prinny, were you and I just playing? Having *fun?*"

Elisa and the Tiesmans all looked to Prinny.

Her tear-filled eyes looked to Leif, and then to Elisa. She looked confused and afraid.

After a long moment, she nodded and looked down.

"Told you." Leif crossed his arms, noticeably not looking at Prinny again. "Plus, she spilled that stuff everywhere." He indicated purple stains on the white wool carpet. "Is Prinny even allowed to have juice this late? I'm worried the sugar will interfere with her sleep."

The next ten minutes were a blur for Elisa, who was unceremoniously stripped of her job and turned out onto the street with her purse in her arms. The boxes of pastels and colored pencils she'd brought were still in the house, along with a cardigan she'd left the day before, but none of those things had sprung to her mind while the unbelievable happened.

She walked to the bus stop, wondering why, *why* that fourteen-year-old boy had done whatever he had done to his sister to begin with, never mind what he'd done to Elisa. In the end, he had lied to protect himself; she supposed she understood that. Kids didn't understand the ripple effects of their lies. Neither did some adults, but he had time to figure it out.

But why was a big kid like him making a little

girl like Prinny cry? It looked like it had been physical, its own heinous problem, but if it hadn't, if it had been emotional torture, could anyone say that was *better?*

She wished she could have told the parents the truth before she left. Wished she could have warned them, as what she saw coming down the tracks was far worse for more people than losing this one job was for Elisa.

For a moment, she'd even thought she'd seen sympathy and openness in Mrs. Tiesman's eyes. Certainly sympathy—the woman was always kind, but she was protective of her husband and the children to a fault. Inarguably *to a fault.* She seemed to just want a happy family, even though the truth was that the kid was troubled.

So even though Leif wasn't biologically hers, anyone could see that she tried like hell to love him, and forcibly pull him closer in to her as a mother, and her daughter as his sister.

It's just that anyone could *also* see that he was never going to let it happen. Not one cell in his body had any interest in having a close and loving family around him.

And, presumably, that family he did have didn't want to know the truth about him, or they would have seen it long before Elisa was haplessly trying to convey it to them while getting the bum's rush out of the house and her job.

Which left her with her own problems to worry

about. Like figuring out how she was going to pay her rent next month when she had only three weeks of work with the Tiesmans behind her and unemployment took forever to process.

Oh, yeah, and how she was going to eat?

She really, *really* didn't want to go back to exotic dancing. She'd sworn she never would. It was demeaning; it went against everything that she believed in. She'd sworn it was only a temporary way to fund college, but the money had been so good she'd let it go on a few months after college while she looked for the perfect position.

So to speak.

That was what she thought she'd found in the Tiesman household.

Not so.

Now, thanks to her previous career, she had about one month's worth of expenses saved up. But that wasn't going to get her very far if she didn't find more work tomorrow.

Or more like yesterday.

The entire thing was so maddening. How dare that punk risk her livelihood and career, just to save his own spoiled, mean-spirited ass?

Someday he'd pay for this, and, if he kept going on the path he was on, probably a whole lot more.

Karma was a bitch.

Chapter Seven

Prinny

"Should I do it in an Irish accent?"

"Irish?" Prinny reeled in her patience. "Why? Why an Irish accent? Why?"

Chelsea straightened her spine and, clearly, her resolve. Her acting chops were chomping. "Because, Prinny," she said, enunciating every syllable, "the Irish were among the first to get into this, you know, Celtic Druid woo-woo stuff. People look for that here, just like they're always looking for Enya music in our record selection. So." She shrugged, as if she'd left Prinny in checkmate. "It just makes sense."

"So maybe you should just record the message in Gaelic?" Prinny asked, feigning innocence. "Let everyone assume that if they don't understand, it's *their* shortcoming, not ours?"

Chelsea's eyes lit up, and she raised an index finger. "You think you're kidding, and I did *not* miss your sarcasm there, but you may be right! You said you wanted to set us apart from the rest. Why not do something radical? Just let me see if anyone else is doing it." She took out her phone and started tapping on the screen.

Prinny sighed. It was the end of the day, and

she didn't have the energy to be exasperated. "Stop. Look, let's just do it in the neutral newscaster sort of voice we agreed on. It's a phone system, not a Meryl Streep movie. Do it like we talked about."

"We *just* talked about cultivating business. How are you going to do that by being generic?"

"It's a way to statistically track the percentages of calls for each given topic," she said. "We can tell what people want by which number they hit, and when we know what people want from us, we can grow the business in the right direction."

"They will only opt for what we offer them, and as we already discussed, we're not offering that much."

"So we offer a few things that maybe we're not doing so much of, to see if there's a market for them."

"Is this one of Alex's ideas?"

Prinny was embarrassed to admit that, yes, it was. It was a way to validate the business aspect of the store and ward off the never-ending threats of her stepbrother, Leif, who wanted to take control of every asset their father had left them.

But Prinny was hard-pressed to admit all of that. So instead she simply said, "It's one of those dotted-i, crossed-t things, yes."

Chelsea cast a suddenly compassionate look at her, then started the recording. "Press one," she said, in a perfect neutral female accent, "to fall out of love." She looked to Prinny with an eyebrow raised.

Prinny nodded. "I think that's good."

Chelsea sighed. "I know what he wants. I don't think it's going to do much to bring in business, but I get what you're saying. All right. So is there anything else?"

"I think you need to say the option first. To give them an idea of what they're here for. You know?"

"No."

"To fall out of love, press one."

"What difference could that *possibly* make?"

A normal employee would never be this difficult. An actress? Virtually every interaction went like this. But the store needed her there to play the role of a safe, reliable psychic: one that would read the cards accurately—as Prinny had taught her—then let the clients come up with their own answers and never advise anything objectionable.

One didn't need to be *psychic,* per se, to read cards. The cards told the story whether the person could intuit anything further or not. So the reason she'd hired Chelsea was to read well and deliver advice convincingly and in a comforting manner. With fate being as flexible as it was, it was important to let people make their choices clearly.

Chelsea kept her eyes on Prinny, waiting for an answer.

"A lot of people would just hang up after

hearing 'press one' because every day we get that with our banks or our utility companies or whatever other drudgery we have to deal with, you know? So 'press one' sounds like you're being rerouted, whereas starting with 'to fall out of love' immediately grabs the attention of both people who want to fall out of love *and* people who want other such options." Honestly, she couldn't even believe she had to say this kind of thing with a straight face, but she did. This was her work, and this was an employee she was in charge of, doing a job she had created, so there was no out.

"Got it." Chelsea gave a nod. "But I still think you need a more exotic accent."

Prinny felt her shoulders sink. "No."

Chelsea reached up and twirled a finger in her blond, beach-waved hair. "But people are calling for fortune-telling, gypsies, magic. They want something *romantic!* I use an accent just about every time I do a reading, and they love it."

"You *do?*" Readings were private. Fake as Prinny knew them to be, the party line was to give good, sound advice that anyone on any daytime talk show would give. Chelsea had been hired as the store gypsy because she could give those supposed readings with a straight face, but Prinny had had no idea she was trying out a variety of accents on clients. "What happens if people Yelp that they liked or hated the Irish psychic and someone else says the psychic is French? Or

Spanish? Or Polish? Or whatever else you decide to be that day?" Lost revenues circling the drain whirled in her mind.

"I keep track," Chelsea said, waving the nothing away. "What, you don't think I have notes on everyone who comes to see me? Once I establish their issue—love, money, health, or family—all I have to do is nudge them and they spill it all and I record it and write down all the names and situations to reference when they come back." She gave a purposeful dramatic pause. "And they always come back. *Always*. So I guess I don't suck too bad at this."

Prinny pinched the bridge of her nose to try to stave off what she had come to think of as the Chelsea Headache at times like this. "Fine. Fine." Chelsea wanted to use her acting chops, so fine. "But how about something just vaguely exotic. Not wholly foreign, not something that people with hearing problems might have trouble understanding, for example, but just the vaguest . . ." She searched for something Chelsea could hook on to. "Gabor sort of accent?"

Chelsea frowned for a moment, then looked up to the left, then to the right—all of which was clearly unstaged, which made it that much creepier—then said, "Okay, I've got it."

"You do."

"I do."

"Can I hear it?"

"Let's just go."

Prinny shrugged and nodded.

Chelsea closed her eyes, took a long breath in through her nose—as if she were about to belt out an aria at the Met—and said, "To fall out of love, press one." Her eyes remained closed for a moment, and she touched her thumbs and index fingers together as if she were meditating, then opened her eyes and looked at Prinny. "Okay?"

The truth was, it was pretty good. A vague, unidentifiable accent, exotic enough to be intriguing, but not so much that it was confusing. Maybe Chelsea had been right; maybe what they needed was some gypsy in the phone messages, even though all of Prinny's business education had supported the idea that neutral was best.

This was no ordinary business.

"Okay, go on." Prinny gave a cautious nod.

"For financial abundance and prosperity, press two," Chelsea said, and did not look to Prinny for an opinion.

Prinny did not object.

"If you have family difficulties, press three."

At this point, it was not the accent but the content that was driving Prinny crazy. It was wrong to let people think they could just call up and get solutions to all their complicated life problems. Even a real psychic could only clarify: show them where they'd been, where they were now, and—sometimes—where they were headed if they didn't change course. But the thing was, most people knew where they'd been and, even if they didn't admit it, knew where they were now. And the future was liquid; it could always change. Predicting it with certainty was like jumping into someone's car on the highway and deciding which exit they would take. If you didn't influence them, they would take the exit they'd been heading for the whole time, and there was no way that even the best psychic in the world could predict that. Anyone was capable of swerving off course at any moment.

That was one of the *good* things about life.

Most people didn't see it that way, though.

So Prinny had to support the business and what they were presenting and people were receiving. And that was prognostication in all forms: purchasing tarot cards and oracle cards, buying books on witchcraft with which to *force* their future intentions, and, most of all, coming in for a reading with Chelsea—Miss Ada, to the masses (so she could be replaced, if necessary), unless she'd been giving other names in other accents— in order to find out that their dreams would come true.

No one ever wanted to know that their lifeline was short, or that they should up the life insurance on their husband, or that the niggling little suspicion in their belly now and then was legit, or that, yeah, their kid was experimenting with pot and dunking the Amazon-purchased drug test into the toilet water to dissolve the results.

No one wanted to know that stuff.

So Prinny stood back and let Chelsea do her thing.

"For revenge, press four," Chelsea said, with a slight but unmistakable edge to her voice.

She looked to Prinny with a question in her eyes.

Prinny gave her thumbs-up.

Good.

Chelsea continued. "For intense stress relief and/or weight loss, press five."

Prinny shrugged inwardly. That might be the best bet for the power of suggestion they could provide. Believe you have willpower and are not craving junk food, and so it shall be.

Hopefully.

"To get a promotion or otherwise improve your professional life, including getting rid of a bad boss, press six."

Okay, yes, that was wordy, but it covered a lot of ground that wasn't interesting enough to stand on its own in three parts. Prinny herself had consolidated that collection, because the romantically forlorn did *not* want to listen to a long laundry list of boring business problems; they would hang up long before the last digit was proposed. So this worked, awkward as it was. It would speak to the people who were calling with job problems.

"For love spells, press seven."

That was it. That was bank right there. And they had to leave it at seven because *so* many people who were calling wanted someone to fall in love with them, and they'd waded through all the other options to get there. And anyone who was already into the hoodoo of calling for help like that would be totally sensitive to which number they had to press to achieve it.

Prinny held up her hand. "Chelsea, can we somehow hit harder on that one?"

"What do you mean?"

"Elaborate on it." Then, seeing Chelsea's slightly confused expression, she said, "Make it more clear. More . . . sexy." She knew that would ignite Chelsea's imagination.

And it did. Her eyes grew bright. "You mean, like, 'For love spells to enchant and win that person you have been loving from afar, press seven . . .'" She raised an eyebrow.

Prinny thought about it. It was basically everything she'd been thinking they should say. Except . . . "And to live happily ever after."

Prinny didn't believe in that. Seriously, how many people end up with that?

Chelsea squealed and laughed and clapped her hands. "Oh my God, Prinny Tiesman, you are *brilliant*—to live *happily ever after,* that is exactly what everyone who calls for a love spell wants. Believe me. I've talked to hundreds.

Maybe thousands. They want dramatic results."

Yes. Of course. Love was the most compelling thing of all. That was one reason they were waiting for those callers to wait until seven. They'd be back; to fall out of love, to get revenge, for whatever they remembered from the earlier part of the menu that they might need or want later.

So far, so good.

"Go on," Prinny said.

Chelsea shot her a look, then cleared her throat and moved into the microphone. "For good luck in all areas, press lucky number eight." She looked at Prinny. "Isn't seven supposed to be lucky?"

"Everyone has a different lucky number."

"You sure?"

Prinny nodded, and so Chelsea fanned herself with her hands, then raised her chin and went on.

"For protection and hex reversal, press nine."

Prinny cringed at that one because it was such a damaging lie. Plenty of people used it, of course; they acted all tough on the outside, then revealed that they thought they were cursed, their crops were dying, their wives were straying, their *codpieces* weren't operating according to the original manual.

Each of these cases needed to be treated individually. *Very* individually. Anyone who thought they were cursed tended to be at least somewhat open to the reversal. All that was required was their belief that the hex was gone and—poof!—the hex was gone.

So Cosmos was off to a damn good start in determining where their biggest customer market was. That was Prinny's idea behind the specific radio differentiation; she knew that much could be snuck in and out, yet not all the sneaking would be tolerated.

Finally Chelsea—who was gathering her things to leave, even as she spoke into the microphone—said, "If you need further help, please press zero. If anyone is here to assist you, they will pick up. Otherwise, please leave your name, problem, and the number of livestock your family possesses at this time."

"Very funny," Prinny said. "Just leave it at press zero, okay?"

She nodded.

Chelsea started replaying the recordings, doctoring the levels, and loading them onto the voice mail system.

"That was good," Prinny said to her.

"Good of ye to say so," she said, tipping an imaginary hat to her. And Prinny just *knew* it was a green top hat. Probably with a sarcastic shamrock poking out of it.

"Don't bring the Irish back here."

"How about the blonde from India?" It had to be said, her accent was pretty spot-on. *Simpsons* worthy.

Chelsea did this all the time. Tried her accents out, too often with actual customers at the cash register, to see if she could fool them into thinking they were authentic. But when she tried the Indian accent on an actual Indian customer, or the Mandarin Chinese accent (she was very specific) on an Asian customer, it grew very awkward.

To Prinny's eternal frustration, all the actual workings of this already-insane metaphysical shop were her responsibility.

She needed to consult with Alex.

Not that he had to give her permission for anything she wanted to do. They both knew that. It was just a game they played, where she'd present some harebrained idea and he'd question her on it, which was lucky because he'd stopped her from wasting a lot of money on more than one occasion. She needed to be able to retire someday; she *needed* to not lose her nest egg on an idea that *seemed* great in one mood but was actually nuts to the rational public.

Alex saved her from those decisions.

Alex was a perfect man with a perfect job and a perfect family, in what was undoubtedly a perfect Northern Virginia house. He was married to a perfectly coiffed blond socialite named Britni Spencer-McConnell.

Isn't that cute? Alex and Britni.

It would be just great if Prinny wasn't in love with Alex.

Chapter Eight

Chelsea

It felt like the moment Chelsea's eyes drifted shut, her alarm blasted like Reveille. It was actually "Chop Suey!" by System of a Down.

She shot up out of bed like a cartoon character in an ejector seat, then shut off the alarm and lay in bed for a few moments, doing breathing exercises to calm her pounding heart. Next, she refreshed her browser on the casting Web site she used, as had become her routine before bedtime, in the morning, and at other random points throughout the day.

"Audition Results to Come . . . ," it still said. No matter how many times she refreshed the page, the results were still *to come*.

Letting out an audible groan, she threw the blanket and sheet off and made her *Walking Dead* way to the bathroom, putting on her morning playlist. She connected her phone to Bluetooth, so that she had no choice but to be immersed in loud, rousing sound. "Off to the Races" by Lana Del Rey blasted through the room.

Hair up.

Wash face.

Brush teeth.

She decided to leave her hair up in a top bun because she just didn't have a shower in her. One look at the tub and she couldn't think of anything she wanted less than to be soaking wet, especially with water that might or might not get cold today. Even if it would wake her up more, it just didn't feel like it was worth the gamble.

So she set about her makeup routine and hoped for the best.

Make Up for Ever foundation, Too Faced Better Than Sex mascara, perfect MAC liner cat eye, and Lime Crime's Red Velvet lipstick. That was her standard look. It wasn't a cheap drugstore routine, but it was simple and so, in its way, economical.

She didn't do the clown contouring that had been so popular a couple of years ago. Well, no one *called* it clown contouring, but that's how just about everyone who tried it looked. Including Chelsea herself; as much stage makeup as she'd done in her life, she found subtle but distinct makeup much more effective.

It was the same with brows; people didn't seem to be able to do their brows without ending up looking overdone. (Or if they did, they did it so well that she didn't notice.) Thankfully, Chelsea didn't have that worry, as she was blessed with good brows. Well, blessed might be an exaggeration—more like she had a mother who didn't inform her that she needed to pluck them when she was young. The downside of that was that she spent a good portion of high school looking about half an inch shy of Frida Kahlo. The upside was that now, she was in a much better position than a lot of girls to rock the Cara Delevingne look.

Next, she had to get the clothes right. She had a standard audition outfit. One that she always felt good in. Stretchy scarlet tank that was tight enough to show off her body—*Look how easily you could dress me, I'm practically a paper doll!* and also *I have just enough breast to push up, and just enough to strap down!*

Tight, deeply dyed jeans—*Look, I have a thigh gap and trendy high-waisted pants, plus I can successfully pull them off!*

A black blazer, sleeves rolled halfway up the forearm.

It was just enough ballerina, just enough business, and just enough every-girl to have as a standby. You never wanted to go in looking like a character, even if you thought you had a pretty good idea about the one you were auditioning for. You could be spot-on and get the role, or you could be way off and have made a bad move.

Then she began her healthy breakfast routine. The one that was a huge pain but, she told herself, would be worth it when she got discovered (or found someone to discover her) and had healthy, glowing skin, shining hair, and the svelte body that was soooo important for acting.

One Ziploc of preselected, precut veggies into

the juicer. Beets, carrots, apple, broccoli, cauliflower, ginger, and celery. Pound the glass like a pledge at a frat party chugging Natty Lite. Recover while scrubbing each of the five pieces of the juicer. She had it down to a five-minute science.

Then a Cali Shot, a shot of apple cider vinegar mixed into eight ounces of water with the juice of half a lemon. That and a protein powder+appetite curber+maca powder+chai tea+vanilla almond milk to take along in a blender bottle and she'd be set until lunch . . . which she packed herself so as to avoid the temptation of Chipotle when she was starving in a couple of hours. Because this breakfast was healthy but it wasn't quite as filling as the carb-heavy brunch of pancakes, eggs Benedict, omelet, and strawberries and cream she would always, *always* prefer.

Everything else she needed was by the door. She slid into her boots—and started her commute.

Every time she sat on the Metro she felt like she might just be the person happiest to be there. Her routine was so jam-packed, and her schedule, too, that she was simply happy not to have to drive. She got to lean back and be carried to work through a dark network of tunnels under D.C. That was a relief.

The night before had been rough. She'd been out far later than she had planned to be with her friend Andrew, an eccentric playwright who was having "an utter breakdown." They had been friends in high school, and though they hadn't always been best friends—he could be exhausting (witness current exhaustion)—they had always remained in touch. Since he'd moved to the city, they were each other's lifesaver in the water that was D.C. He had rubbed shoulders with a lot of people that she would give anything to be in a room with, and he loved having her on his arm for his own image. Apart from just really liking each other, they were the perfect professional pair.

Struggling playwright and struggling actress. How dramatic the pair of them were.

Andrew was the kind of person you'd find yourself up all night with—going through a couple of bottles of wine and mental breakthroughs—before you knew it. So when he'd called the night before at eleven thirty complaining about the utter breakdown, in his usual overdramatic way, she had not felt quite like going over, even though he was only one Metro stop away. Tired as she was, though, she was left with no option. It wasn't exactly because he needed her—if she went over every time that happened, she would live there—but he was writing a script for a local director who had moved from Manhattan in an effort to boost the theater scene in D.C., and thus perhaps *she* needed *him*.

Of course, she agreed to go over.

She put on a swingy white tank top, black harem

pants, and her red lipstick. On went the wool hat that went perfectly with the *Oh, I was just off to bed when the fashion police showed up knocking at my door!* look.

It was an outfit she would wear anywhere. Coffee shop. Beach boardwalk. City sidewalks. But when she looked at herself in the mirror, something stopped her.

It was too bare. This wasn't a date. At this rate she didn't know if she'd ever date again.

She pulled on a black hoodie and left without glancing at her reflection again.

She walked down to the Metro in her costume of anonymity, knowing at least that she would have the excuse of the late hour to lean on if he criticized her "thuggish look."

But he didn't, because she hung the hoodie on her purse before he opened the door.

Her fashion choices had the desired effect. Andrew, diminutive and performing from second one, rested the Marlboro Red in his lips (Chelsea just knew he enjoyed the dichotomy of his diminutive appearance and his "cowboy cigarette") and exclaimed, "Jesus, Mary, and Joseph, girl, you always look like you stepped off the pages of French *Vogue*." His observant gaze glanced downward before he turned back around. "Ew, except that hooded sweatshirt. Throw that away."

His living room was one of those minimalist

types that didn't have a piece of furniture that wasn't selected on purpose and at great cost. Andrew was the type not to have a sofa at all, for example, until he found the Perfect Sofa. Which is why on past nights, she had perched on cushions that were slightly too small and thin to be floor cushions instead of on the firm gorgeous sectional she now reclined on.

They had a bottle of Chardonnay, something probably hard to get that she probably didn't appreciate half as much as any of his other friends did, and she breathed in secondhand drama and secondhand smoke until three in the morning.

"If I could get past this stupid"—he made a spiraling motion in front of his forehead—"*block* that I have. It's the perfect time. People are paying attention to my writing. They're *listening* right now. And of course, it's the driest time of my life."

"Almost." She smiled and gave a warning gesture at the glass of wine sloshing in his hand, although somehow he never spilled it, no matter how much he gesticulated.

He rolled his eyes, a smile playing at his lips, and took the last swig of it. "I've got to find something. I've got to find something to write."

This was *not* her wheelhouse. She wasn't sure what to say, even though this wasn't the first—or last—time they'd have this conversation. "Well, what do you want to do this time? Comedy?"

He shook his head. "That was a disaster last

time. I mean, I involved an actual *rubber chicken*. And the rest of it wasn't ironic enough to support that. Why didn't you stop me?"

She raised her eyebrows and jutted her chin forward to ask if he was kidding her.

"Okay, fine," he said. "I wasn't listening."

She nodded. "Tragedy? Dramedy? Stage horror?"

He bit his tongue and then leaned forward, tilting his head thoughtfully. "Hm."

"Which one?" she pressed.

"Dramedy."

"There you go, that's a start, right?"

"Tragic hero."

"Or—"

"Or *heroine!*" He slapped his forehead. "God, I haven't done a female lead in ages."

She looked around the room, not sure if trying to act like she didn't think of herself as an option was the right choice. But he wasn't paying attention anyway.

"Dramedy. Heroine. Something scandalous. Something big. Scary. Taking the classic 'let's make light of this in a slightly terrifying way' thing, but taking it darker."

Chelsea watched him.

One thing she would give him was that he was an actual mad scientist when he really started working or had a stroke of inspiration. His eyes simultaneously unfocused and intensified, as if he were focusing on something in another dimension that no one else in the room could see, something he knew he had to capture while it showed itself to him or it would vanish.

"Spunky girl. Sweet. Smart but trusting." At this point, he was making senseless gestures in the air, like a wizard conjuring his vision. "Dark filthy corner of hell on earth, one which she never even saw coming. She can't lose that mojo, though."

Chelsea could tell he was about to digress into disjointed details, and she would need to be silent. But she also knew she needed to stay and be part of it in his mind. She removed the wineglass from his hand, which didn't shake him from his reverie. It reminded her of posing as the statue.

When she returned, the glasses were refilled with a Syrah blend she'd found on the counter.

"Did you do a red wine rinse?" he asked, accepting the glass, still zoned out.

"Yes?"

He took a sip and then gave her a teasing glare. "Another night . . ."

She leaned back and let him keep thinking. It wasn't until his silence had lasted nearly twenty minutes, and she envisioned the hangover she would have in the morning if she continued to sip her way through the discomfort, that she decided she needed to be smart and leave.

"I've got to go now," she said, making a point of yawning and stretching broadly as she stood up. "We're both up too late."

"Probably true. Let me call a car for you."

"Oh, no, no, I'll take the Metro."

He looked aghast. "Darling, you are way too Gigi Hadid for that." He went to his leather man purse on the desk and took out a fifty. "Uber, cab, I don't care, but no Metro at this hour. Besides it's closed by now."

Knowing she'd make a profit, she reluctantly accepted. It was what he'd intended; neither of them acknowledged it, even while they both knew it was true.

And that's how, a mere six hours later, she came to be exhausted but on the train, relieved to have even twenty minutes to lean back on the window and rest.

She drifted fast into something resembling sleep but awoke with a start when the train rattled to a halt at her stop. Despite her exhaustion, she managed to stand, then floated like a ghost to her audition.

The waiting room was filled with girls that looked so similar to Chelsea that it might have been a casting call to fill her role in the story of her own life. Instead, it was just a small part in a political drama taking place in the city, *Veto*. *Veto* was centered on Connor McNamara, an intense, completely misogynistic—but sexy!— "right hand of the president" type. *He knew everyone's secrets, but hid his own.*

In season one of the show, he described his

perfect woman as "a tall, waifish thing with an ass I can grip with one hand and lips I'm afraid to puncture with my teeth." So far, every woman—except for one—his character had been with had been some version of this. Evidently, since these were callbacks, which meant everyone in the room had already passed some level of acceptance, this season's character would have big eyes and no tits.

That explained what she was doing here. At least her titlessness could come in handy for something.

"Chelsea Cole?"

Chelsea's gaze shot up. She'd been staring at the girl across from her and thinking that there was about a hundred percent possibility that she spoke in baby talk most of the time.

"Yes, that's me. Sorry." She grabbed her clutch and the script, its pages curled backward from her countless rereadings.

Feeling like she was being led into a doctor's office, Chelsea followed the girl who'd called her down a hallway and into a big room with fluorescent lights. Unlike in a doctor's office, however, there was a panel of people waiting to judge her, even on her most subtle inflections.

A camera was set up, pointing at a spot in the middle of the room where she was presumably about to stand and then sink or swim.

An audition begins the second you enter the

room, Chelsea knew, and so she always became whoever she needed to be before crossing the threshold. This time, though, it wasn't easy. Back in college, the most she'd have to fight through to give a good audition was a mild hangover that lasted till early afternoon. Sometimes, she had performed even better then. Something had been working, because she had gotten a lead in everything she auditioned for. She'd been Liza Doolittle in a dinner theater production of *My Fair Lady*; Anna in a production of *The King and I*; Lady Macbeth; Hedda Gabler; even Mary Shelley in an indie play called *Chillon* about the writing of *Frankenstein*. It was almost impossible for Chelsea Cole not to get a good role. She had been a shoe-in every time. Everyone had secretly hated her for it, and she didn't mind that one bit—because back then, she *knew* she would be the one who really made it. She knew it the way everyone says *you'll know.*

You'll know when you find the right college.

You'll know when you find the right guy.

You'll know . . . *you'll know.*

You'll know.

But she had been wrong. And now she never believed she *knew* anything.

Today she was hangover-free, and yet her mind and body were in a complete state of unfocus. She was tired. *So* tired from being up half the night with Andrew.

When she'd started studying for the initial audition, she'd done everything right. She'd watched the show so she knew exactly what the other characters were like. She had read and reread the character description in the audition blurb. She had decided that her version of Hadley Anderson would be a combination of coy Audrey Hepburn and the side-piece bimbo in *Gone Girl*, infused with a bit of the sly cleverness that lay deep in the eyes of every character ever played by Kate Hudson.

She looked at her reflection in the mirror and practiced the dumb-girl pout, the clever narrowing of her doe eyes, and added the posture of someone trying to act tougher than she was. It was the perfectly mixed cocktail, and she hadn't been surprised at all when she got a callback.

But right now, her lips weren't pouting, her posture was timid, and her eyes probably looked more Bambi-watching-the-gunman than anything else. To make things worse, by the last time she read through the lines out in the waiting room, she had started to feel like she didn't even have half of them memorized.

"I'm Chelsea Cole, and I'm here to audition for the role of Hadley Anderson." She straightened her back and gave a small smile.

She was nervous. Where had these nerves come from that suddenly plagued her before she ever put herself on display?

"Hello, Chelsea. If you want to place your things right over there on that chair and return to your mark, we can begin."

"Perfect," she said quietly and then took the direction.

When she returned to the spot, a woman with dark hair and glasses cleared her throat. "All right, now, there's been a bit of a change in the script. And, well, really in the character. So if you could . . ." She licked her thumb and forefinger and separated one pack of stapled papers from a stack. "Just go ahead and read these. It's a different scene, taking place later in the episode. The character is close enough that it shouldn't seem unrecognizable."

Chelsea stepped forward, thinking briefly and unexpectedly of the shop and wondering exactly what Prinny's plans were. She cleared her head. She was about to do a cold read. This was no time to think about work.

The pages seemed stark and too bright, the letters too close together. Her lines were high-lighted in blue—the most difficult to read. Why couldn't they have chosen classic yellow?

She smiled.

"Begin whenever you're ready. Tim will read Connor's lines."

She gave a nod and then zoned in on the page.

"Connor, please, I can't keep doing this—*you* can't keep doing this. If we get caught—"

"We won't get caught!" Tim read the lines with a booming, intimidating voice that made Chelsea feel even more underprepared and even more underwhelming. She tried to funnel the timidity washing over her into something useful.

"So what am I supposed to *do?*" She had no context for the scene. No idea what it was they couldn't keep doing. She could guess, but she didn't know. Was she supposed to be angry? Sad? She should have glanced over the lines before launching in. "Christ, Con, it's like you think I'm some kind of—some kind of—"

"What, Hadley? Some kind of a hooker? Some kind of a *prostitute?*"

Shit, thought Chelsea. Even she wanted to hit the guy. "Don't you dare say that to me. This is *different.* You know it is."

"How is it different? I pay you. We fuck. You do everything I want. How is it anything more complicated than that? Huh? You want to tell me?"

"I do everything you want because I lo—" Chelsea was surprised to feel tears starting to sting her eyes. "Because I want to." Her voice cracked, and she felt the attention in the room focus on her. "It may have started out that way, but you know *damn* well it's not like that."

"You're going to tell me what it's like? You know who I fucking am, Hadley. You know I—"

"You're goddamn *right* I know who you are, Connor. I know you have a *hell* of a lot more to lose than I do."

"You better hope that's true, because you're about to lose everything. But before that . . ." Tim hesitated, as the script instructed. "I need you to get on the bed."

Chelsea stared at Tim, who was reading the lines with a blank face behind the table. She felt briefly unaware of the camera or any of her nerves. This was what she loved. That high that meant she had broken into being someone else. It was like finally reaching a meditative state.

"I guess you can't have everything you want after all. Not even if you pay for it."

It was the last line of the stapled pages. It indicated that she should walk out, but she was practiced enough to know that they didn't expect her to stalk off away from her mark.

"All right," said the woman. Her flat tone shook Chelsea from her meditation and reminded her to be nervous again.

"We just have a couple more scenes for you to read through, and then you're set to go."

Heart pounding and skin hot, Chelsea read through them in a haze. She read nothing as well as the first scene. She left feeling unconfident and idiotic. She hated when she couldn't rid her mind of other thoughts enough to focus on the task at hand. The worst part was that the stress over her bad audition would be what distracted her from whatever else she needed to do later.

She was walking out of the building when her phone buzzed. A text from Andrew:

> Thank GAIA for you queen, thanks to our convo, I believe I've finally got my lead character. She's spirited, tough, eternally authentic. Like you used to be before you got bodysnatched. Haha. Xoxo

Her stomach twisted like a wet rag being wrung out. It was far from the first time he'd jokingly told her how much she'd changed lately. The worst part was that she knew how true it was. Anyone who knew her could tell.

The hell of it was, she didn't even have a good reason to pin it on.

She needed to get back into life. She couldn't let a breakup break her.

Chapter Nine

Twenty-one Years Earlier

It happened exactly how Kathy always thought it would.

It's not as if she'd ever really sat around dreaming about these moments, but she doubted if any girl could say with complete honesty that she hadn't even envisioned it.

For nearly all four years of high school, she had kept to herself. Well, to herself and her best friend, Judy. And really? It wasn't that bad. She had never been dying to be part of the cool kids' clique. She never longed for the everyday scrutiny that popularity invited. If anything, she wished simply that she *looked* a bit more like those girls. She wished she looked like one of them—with their shiny hair, clear skin, even smiles, and perfect, tiny bodies—but *wasn't* one of them. She was smart. She knew that would make her infinitely cooler. At least someday.

Yet she couldn't help dreaming of the shallow qualifications for popularity. She envisioned herself tanned and narrow, her brown hair actually holding a curl long enough to look beachy and casual instead of lank and in possible need of washing. She had pale green eyes— the one thing strangers always complimented her on. Unfortunately, like the dreaded "she has a great personality," it was a compliment that seemed to carry an invisible "but" with it. *But she has great eyes!*

When those girls, the Others, pulled on their jeans, they buttoned them easily and didn't have to shimmy into them and tug on belt loops to get them into a comfortable place. They could wear tank tops without spilling out of them. They could wear loose sundresses and look like they just climbed off the pages of *Teen Vogue*, instead of looking like they were trying to cover up "problem areas."

Kathy was eighteen. "Problem areas" wasn't even a term she should know yet. That was an expression usually reserved for postpregnancy mothers shopping in the full-figure sections of department stores. Not for eighteen-year-old girls living out the last few weeks of senior year.

What must it feel like for them? she wondered as she sat outside on the bench with her backpack on her lap, at the perfect viewing distance from the popular kids.

It was hard not to watch them when they were all together. She'd worry about looking like a longing creep, except they never bothered looking outside their own little realm. They were all used to inviting and performing for an audience. Feeling gazes on them was such par for the course that they didn't seem to notice it anymore.

The crowd of beautiful people was gathered outside the cafeteria by the picnic tables. Guys sat with their knees apart enough to make a space for their girlfriends to stand and coo over them (not much distance needed). One twosome— voted in superlatives last month as Cutest Couple—stood together, him leaning against one of the tables, his hand resting comfortably on her butt. The fabric on the sundress she wore was

123

thin, and showed the exact shape of her beneath.

Two of the girls sat leaning back on propped arms, letting the sun sink into their skin. Both had their bellies showing under midriff tops. No— "belly" implied something that wasn't there; even "stomach" sounded too round for what they had between hip and chest. They were absolutely flat boards. Kathy wondered how they had space for their organs in there. Or maybe even their organs were petite and cute.

Kathy wasn't bitter about any of this. She had the things that mattered more. A good family. A cozy bedroom. A Labrador retriever that was on her heels the second she got home. And she had her best friend, and they were headed off to the same school in the coming autumn. She didn't feel the anger or resentment that often went along with unpopularity. But that didn't mean she wasn't fascinated by them. Especially . . .

He emerged from the cafeteria, practically in slow motion with a fan blowing and a soundtrack playing for him.

Leif Tiesman. Kathy felt sure that no one could possibly blame her for being hopelessly in love with *him*. Come *on!* He was the stuff of fairy tales. The stuff of time-travel romances, back to the days of chivalry and manly men. The stuff of steamy music videos.

And he didn't have a girlfriend. He didn't date the head cheerleader, as the usual script called for. In fact, he'd never had a girlfriend. He "hung out" with people for different periods of time but never seemed to settle into anything.

One of the things that made him even hotter? Out of all the girls he'd hooked up with, a handful of them weren't the school's Most Wanted, just normal girls. In fact, one of them had glasses and braces. She was really pretty beyond those things—Kathy would never have judged her whatsoever—but it was just a little surprising that Leif had looked beyond the usual "hot guy roadblocks" and seen her for who she was. It was more than surprising, really. It was awesome.

Judy came out of the back doors and walked over to Kathy.

"I am *beyond* overwhelmed," she said.

"Why?" Kathy scooted over to make more room for her.

"All this studying for finals and I can't get any focus in class! All anyone can talk about is prom, and it's like all of my teachers are ready for the school year to be over, too. It's like, hello? I'm still learning here?"

"Oh, you're going to be fine."

"Maybe! Who knows at this point? It's like, sorry, college, I guess I'll just drown when I get to you. I still haven't mastered the algorithm for Tesla's—"

"It's Kate, right?"

The two girls looked up to see Leif standing in

front of their bench, sun behind him. Kathy could practically smell the sun on his bronzed shoulders.

It *wasn't* Kate. It was Kathy. Always. No one called her Kate. But come on, like she was going to correct him.

She nodded. "Yeah. Kate, Kathy, whatever." She felt Judy's gaze bore into her.

She ignored it.

"Leif," he said, in a way that clearly said he knew she'd already known that. She couldn't blame him for that arrogance; it would have been false modesty to act like he didn't understand his position in the school.

"Hey. So. What's up?" She resisted moving her hair from one shoulder to the other. She was uncomfortably warm, especially now that he was talking to her, but it would just look like a weird, bad copy of a Wannabe Hot Girl Hair Flick if she did it.

His dark eyes glanced to Judy briefly. "Could Kate and I get a moment?"

Judy's own eyes, plain brown, were narrowed at him in confusion. It was the same look she gave her math homework right before she said something like *There's no way there's an answer to this. It's impossible*—then tackled it anyway. She didn't actually say anything, though; she just shrugged and, giving her friend a glance that seemed unnecessarily judgmental, went over to a bench on the other side of the doors.

"So what's going on?" Kathy—suddenly *Kate*—asked Leif when he took Judy's spot, then reached an arm along the back of the bench, which kinda-sorta resembled his actually putting his arm around her.

"I know we don't really know each other," he said, "but we kind of do. You can't be in the halls with someone for four years without feeling kind of like you know them."

She didn't point out that they had also been in middle school together. "Right, totally."

"So I kind of feel like I know you." His smile made the skin around his eyes crinkle. "Do you feel like you know me?"

How she longed to be clever. To respond the way she would if she actually *did* know him. If she did, her answer would be *I think you have to have a conversation at least once before really saying you know somebody*. In retrospect, she'd wish she had said that. What had stopped her? That was what the hard-to-get girl character would say.

Instead, she said, "Yeah, definitely."

"Cool. So do you think you'd want to maybe . . . hang out sometime?"

He glanced behind her, and she felt vaguely aware that his friends were back there. But she dismissed that concern quickly, pushing it under the sea of her excitement.

It might not have been at the top of her list to

be one of the cool kids, but when the hottest guy in school—and the hottest guy you'd ever seen in real life—asks you out, you're automatically one of them.

"Um, sure," she said, sitting up a little straighter and pulling the backpack in toward her not-entirely-flat stomach.

"Cool." He nodded. "You want to go to the movies or something? The new Batman movie is out."

Again, she gave the answer that opposed her natural inclination. "Yeah, I've been dying to see it!"

Not true. Not true at all. But *Leif.*

When she got home, the first thing she did was head for the kitchen, calling out for her mom. She knew she'd be there; she always was at this time of day.

Sure enough, there she was, standing at the stove. Holding a wooden spoon and a handful of spinach, she turned around, looking a little alarmed at her daughter's excited tone. "Kathy? Everything okay?"

She dropped her backpack. "Uh, yeah. Guess who asked me out."

Her mother's lips drew up in an anticipatory smile. "Who?"

"Leif Tiesman."

Kathy wasn't offended by the shock on her mother's face. It *was* weird and unexpected.

"Did he *really?* To do what?"

"Movies."

"Wow!"

"I know. It's really out of the blue, but I mean, he's dated all kinds of random girls. Remember I told you about Rosie with the braces?"

"Well, it's not a surprise he should ask you out, sweetie, you're beautiful—but you don't really know each other."

Kathy sat down on the stool. She was always amused and flattered when her mother—a wisp of a woman—told her she was beautiful.

"I know, but who cares?"

"Not me!" Her mother laughed and went back to the stove. She set the wooden spoon in its rest and started ripping up the spinach to drop into the pot. "Want some veggie soup in a bit?"

"Sure."

"What time is he picking you up?"

"Oh, I'm just meeting him there."

Pause. "Hmm." Another pause. "Not sure I like that. Not very gentlemanly."

Kathy rolled her eyes, sort of pleased to find herself in a cliché teenage scenario like this. "It's fine, I'd rather meet him there anyway. Like you said, I don't know him that well. Maybe he drives like a maniac, you don't know!"

This was actually something she thought to be true. He'd been the center of gossip once when he was suspected of being the driver who crashed into a garage door across the street from a party. His car looked fine, but he also had piles of money, so no one was ever quite sure if he simply repaired it before anyone saw.

After tearing through the closet with her mom's help, Kathy finally settled on a pair of black stretchy jeans, a navy V-neck, and a gray leather jacket from Nordstrom. Its zipper angles were very flattering. On the whole, when Kathy looked in the mirror, she felt good. She was no Abercrombie model, but she understood her body and knew how to make it look as good as it could. Maybe in freshman year she would have beaten herself up for how she looked, angry that the muscles she had developed had never replaced the fat around them.

She was strong. She could run a 5k with good time. She was young, powerful, and capable. She was also healthy. Her skin glowed and her hair shone from her healthy diet. She had pearly white teeth, devoid of cavities. Her skin was buttery smooth. Everyone has a weak spot. Hers was her weight, and she had grown to accept that when nothing changed it. Some people are just bigger. Kathy was one of them.

Her mom helped her pick out exactly the right makeup to wear: neutral tones on her eyes, pitch-black waterproof mascara, and only the slightest tinge of bronzer. They mutually agreed to skip lip gloss, repeating the conversation they'd had many times about how it was gross-looking even under the best of circumstances.

Half an hour later, walking from her car to the theater, she saw Leif talking to a group of three girls. When he saw her, he gave her a nod and then gestured in her direction as he said something to them. For one mad second, she feared that he'd invited a bunch of girls out. She didn't have time to think through why he would do such a thing, because by the time she got to him, they had walked away. She heard them whispering as they went. Who knew about what? It could have been mean comments about her, or it could have just as easily been adoring ones about him. Either way, she didn't really care. Either way, she was the one out on a date with him.

"Do you want some popcorn or soda or something?" he asked her as they passed the concession stand.

"Oh, thanks, no, I'm good. I don't really eat that stuff." For a moment she regretted saying it—that's the sort of thing that sounds insulting and judgmental to those who do. Her regret was quickly wiped away when she saw the look of surprise—and was that admiration?—flash over his face.

Huh.

He didn't say much during the previews, which she supposed she couldn't blame him for. Not everyone thought that any visual entertainment was improved by running commentary.

But that wasn't all. The previews, the movie—it was all watched in silence. No leaning over to make comments. No nudging of elbows or *should we hold hands?* tension. Just two people who didn't know each other, watching a movie one of them didn't want to see.

When they left, he asked if she wanted to see "something cool."

"Sounds pretty ominous," she said. "It's not, like, your pet snake or anything, right?"

He gave a little smirk she didn't understand until later. "No. It's definitely not my pet snake."

He took her hand then (his was surprisingly cold, maybe even a little clammy) and walked her down the side of the movie theater to the back. They passed a Dumpster that smelled like sticky soda, fake butter, and the worst of other garbage.

They kept walking, out onto a grassy hill that overlooked a big man-made pond. Not a pretty one, just a big gross hole filled with water, condoms, and empty Natty Lite cans.

He sat down on the grass, and she wasn't sure she wanted to. It wasn't exactly a nice little patch of grass. But so far, this was the only interesting part of their date. The only thing that hadn't felt like babysitting a ten-year-old boy she didn't know. Or—she realized suddenly—*like* that much.

"What did you want to show me?" she asked him.

"Show you?" He looked bewildered.

"You asked if I wanted to see something cool."

"No, I didn't."

What? This was crazy. "You did, you asked if I wanted to see something cool and I asked if it was your pet snake and you said no."

He shrugged. "I don't have a pet snake."

What did that even mean? Was he acknowledging he'd said it or calling her a liar by virtue of the fact that he didn't have a pet snake? This was too weird.

She was very glad she had her own mode of transportation to get back home.

She needed to make a polite excuse—*any* excuse—that would get her home to her couch, where her mom would give her a lemonade with mint, so she could tell her every single detail of how much Leif Tiesman turned out to suck.

As she opened her mouth to say she was tired, he grabbed her face—gently, but still definable as a grab—and kissed her.

She let it happen. Old mental habits compelled her. *Leif Tiesman Leif Tiesman*—the drumbeat of his name in her head insisted that this was what she wanted.

But it wasn't. It wasn't what she ever would have imagined. His tongue was forceful and too wet. His breath smelled like he hadn't brushed his teeth since he and his friends had taquitos for lunch at 7-Eleven.

No, she decided suddenly, just *no*. It didn't matter what she'd ever thought before, or what a whole host of other idiot girls at school wanted, *she* didn't want *this*.

So she tried to pull away, but he pressed harder. It wouldn't be until she went to college the next year that she fully understood what she had narrowly avoided that night. At the time, it just felt like a guy who wouldn't get the hint. But that wasn't all.

She pushed him, her triceps working overtime, just like she'd trained them to do, and he toppled off of her, onto the grass.

She ran.

Weirdly, her main thought was that she couldn't wait to take a shower.

That thought disappeared when she heard his footsteps behind her, giving chase. She increased her pace, and he did, too. He was really *following* her? Picking up even more speed, she wondered wildly exactly what he planned to do if he caught her. He was an athlete, but so was she, whether he knew it or not. All she needed to do, she realized, was shake him off. She didn't want to run to her car, parked in the dark lot—it had gotten emptier in the time they sat on the hill.

No, all she needed to do was get into the public eye. He was a self-obsessed jerk. He wouldn't want to look stupid or weird in front of people. He wouldn't want that because he *was* stupid. It wouldn't even occur to him that a guy physically chasing a girl down was cause for real concern. He just wouldn't want to run into someone he knew.

Particularly the three blondes.

Just as she'd thought he would, he stopped as soon as she was visible in the light from the virtually empty theater. Out of breath, he gave a shake of his head and ran a hand through his hair before coughing a couple of times and sidling off to his silver Mustang convertible. He started the car, and his speakers blasted—Eminem—then he drove off.

She'd thought of taking a day off the next day. She could go to the movies with her mom and see a movie she *wanted* to see—didn't Kate Hudson have a new rom com out? But Kathy was determined to keep her chin held high the next day and go in.

It didn't matter, though. She knew the second she walked into the school that something was off. The looks clued her in. The whispers got her thinking. And Judy's report had her fuming.

Judy said she'd heard people talking about it outside before classes started. The field hockey team—domain of the Hot Girls—had already begun their summer practices, which took place at six in the morning. Apparently all the girls were out at the picnic tables—also the domain of Hot Girls—and talking. About Kathy.

About Leif and Kathy and Leif's Bucket List.

She couldn't contain her anger when she heard the extent of Judy's story, which was really Leif's lies. Somehow, she had to concentrate for three periods before lunch. This didn't happen, but she burned through about fifty mental drafts in her head of what she'd say when she found him.

It didn't happen like in the movies. Not everyone watched. There was no background music to come to a stop. No one clapped or watched her walk away with new admiration.

But she did what she needed to.

She walked up to Leif, thinking how ridiculous and feminine he looked in his tank top, and stopped right in front of him. His smile faded. Clearly he thought she had no reason to be mad.

"Did you tell everyone I gave you a blowjob?" she asked, wishing her voice were stronger.

"I told like one person." He shrugged, as if it wasn't his fault and therefore it couldn't matter. "News travels fast."

"I didn't give you a blowjob, Leif."

He cocked his head at her, but his eyes showed that he was very aware of anyone and everyone who might be close enough to hear. "Well, it didn't feel much like one, no. I didn't say you gave me a *good* one."

His friends laughed. One dolt even put a fist to his mouth and said, "Ohhh shit!"

Disgust built in her throat like vomit. "You

know damn well that I didn't give you one *period*."

"Ew, quit talking to me about your period. I already told you that was off-limits." More laughs.

"Oh my God, are you kidding me right now? What are you, twelve?"

His friends went silent.

"You're lying about me doing anything with you, unless you count when you kissed me. Felt like a pack of rabid wolves, by the way," she said, directing it at the girls. "Smelled like it, too."

"You'd think you'd be a little more grateful," he said, still *somehow* thinking he was coming off as cool.

"If I understand this correctly, you asked me out thinking you would get me to go down on you, so that you could complete some bucket list?"

"Yup. I can't remember what it was for, though." He looked to his friend, who took a sip of root beer and then filled it in for him.

"For getting a BJ from the ugliest chick in school."

Everyone behind Leif laughed.

Heat rose in her cheeks, and she loathed her face for betraying her yet again. Not by being less attractive than any of the faces she was surrounded by, not this time. By raising a blush and making it seem like she gave a damn about his opinion.

"You're a terrible kisser. That was enough to tell me how *great* things would be if I went further. No thanks. As you well know, I didn't do anything with you except get the hell away from you last night."

"Okay, Miss Piggy. Whatever you say."

This time she was undaunted by his insults. They were just too dumb to take seriously. "And you can call me fat all day long if you want. I don't care. But you're boring as a brick, and you always will be because you're too stupid to do anything about it."

"Wow, you really are on your period," he responded, somehow still eliciting a laugh from his buddies. The girls, at least, had stopped laughing. Even a moron could tell this wasn't funny.

"As for your bucket list? Whatever the *fuck* that's all about? You're a loser. I am the fattest chick in the school, and you couldn't get it." She turned to the girls. "Watch out for him. He's pushy and doesn't listen to the word 'no.' He'll even run after you, try and chase you down, until his out-of-shape lungs do him in."

And then she walked away.

Nothing changed for the long last few weeks of school. She hadn't really expected it to. She knew her words meant nothing to him, or to any of his cronies. Her truth didn't matter, yet she couldn't let his lies go unchallenged, which made for a nightmarish push-and-pull that was futile and did nothing more than drain her of her energy and confidence.

He'd never understand that, of course. Never understand what he'd done to another human being who was just struggling along to get it right herself. And he wouldn't care even if he *did* understand it.

He was just that crappy a human being.

She hoped to God that someday he got what he deserved.

And maybe she'd even get to be the one to deliver it to him

Chapter Ten

Prinny

Alex McConnell (more specifically, *Alejandro* McConnell, which people didn't expect when they saw his light brown hair and bright blue eyes) was the lawyer in charge of Prinny's father's estate (more specifically her share of it, thanks to Leif's complaints), and even though all of the decisions were ultimately hers, he advised her on everything she came up with that required spending money. And all too often he declared it an idiotic idea and advised against it.

Actually, all too often he was right. Prinny was

no fool, though; she knew when he was right, and she used his nix as the last word, so she seldom made a huge mistake.

But today's idea? She felt a little like she was grasping at straws. The business wasn't doing nearly as well as she needed it to, but she wasn't sure of the best way to change that.

"Mr. McConnell will see you now."

The receptionist's soft voice seemed almost harsh compared to the plush comfort of the overstuffed leather sofa in Alex's waiting room. The lights were low—lamps, not overhead fluorescents—and the music was the kind of unidentifiable instrumental stuff you'd enjoy during a massage, yet quiet enough not to inter-fere with reading. Just a whisper, to keep the room from feeling stark. That was probably important in a lawyer's office, making sure the room didn't feel harsh.

She stood up, took a breath, smiled at Amy (the receptionist, who always wore the Wild at Heart scent from Victoria's Secret), and pushed the heavy oak door to his office open.

"Don't tell me," he said with a welcoming smile that showed his straight white teeth and crinkled his eyes. "You want to sell black cats, and we have a problem with the Humane Society."

"No, no." She sat down in the chair opposite him, as she'd done at least once a week this past year, in order to try to present her new business

140

ideas in the most . . . *business-y* way possible. Though she didn't always have a good, or *believable,* idea to throw at him, this was the only way she ever got to see him. And, damn it, she wanted to see him.

She shook her head. "Try again."

"Magic wands, made in England, hindered by their status as live plants?"

"We already went through that. And they *would* have sold really well." Unbelievable. Live plants she could understand regulating. Sticks? It was absurd.

He laughed, a good genuine laugh. "We did! Would you believe I forgot that?" He shook his head. "What have you come up with this time, Miss Tiesman?"

Prinny raised an eyebrow. "What makes you think I'm not here just to chat?"

"That would be an honor, of course. And a first."

So he genuinely had no idea how she felt about him, how she missed him if too many days stretched on and she hadn't seen him. Good Lord, hadn't he seen right through that bullshit idea to do a *Witches of Washington* documentary? She'd barely been able to find any good stories of historical magic in the most political town in the world.

In fact, as she'd written the halfhearted proposal, she'd felt certain her contention that there should be public funding for Washington

Witch Research would have been a clue to him that she was joking.

Unfortunately, that was probably who he thought she was. The crazy witchy girl, head full of cotton and bad ideas.

"Okay, listen," she said. "I know I'm not going to bowl you over with my business savvy on this one, but I need you to trust me. I'm about to take the business in a new direction that's going to bring in far, far more revenue. So I need to budget in a new salary and an expansion, even if you think I'm being stupid."

His face grew serious. "Prinny, I would never think you were being *stupid,* and if I've ever given you the idea that I sincerely thought anything of the sort, I'm truly sorry."

She was so touched by the earnestness of his expression and tone that her throat grew tight. So she tried to imagine Leif saying the same thing, and of course, she couldn't. Even if Alex allowed her to expand, Leif would fight it every step of the way.

And even though she was able to see that her business was going to take off, and she could see the exact amount she needed in order to budget for it, she couldn't explain *how* she knew it. And to people who didn't understand, which was *most* people, she sounded a little kooky.

She knew that. She wasn't stupid.

"Thank you," she said to Alex, and her eyes

rested briefly on the picture on his desk. Where were they, he and his wife? Belize? She always thought it was Belize, and therefore she always had a mental block against the place.

"So let's get down to business here. How much do you want, and what are you doing with it?"

"Why do you always look so nervous when you ask that?"

He laughed. "Ever since you asked for manufacturing and licensing money to make Beatles tarot cards, I am a little skeptical of your cutting-edge ideas."

"Hey, that was *not* a bad idea!" She'd been joking, of course, but there were Beatles playing cards, so why *not* Beatles tarot cards?

"Not bad, no," he agreed. "What's *today's* idea?"

"Workshops."

"What kind?"

"*All* kinds. Tarot reading, wand whittling . . . baking herbal edibles."

He raised his eyebrows and laughed out loud.

"Seriously! Like a center for education. Except fun little activities."

"Wine and crystal ball reading?" His face stayed hard, but his eyes had a glint of teasing in them.

"You're kidding, but that's not a terrible idea."

Alex—and nobody else—could make mildly derisive jokes about her business and it didn't bother her. He was respectful of it ninety-nine percent of the time. Besides, when he joked with her it felt like the Real Him, and she would never argue with seeing that side of him.

"Okay." He shrugged. "You've already got the space, so what's the problem?"

"Well, *that's* the problem. We don't really have the space. *But* the video rental place next door is going out of business." As she said it, she knew that, workshops or not, she needed to physically expand the store. *This* was the path she needed to take.

"Video rental place?" he echoed.

She nodded. "Weird it was still in business for so long, right? But if they could make a go of it as long as they did in this day and age, that proves almost anything can work in our part of town. Things go from irrelevant to trendy in a heartbeat. We just have to pick something that'll work."

He wasn't so convinced. "What about where Chelsea does the psychic readings? Why not just use that room?"

"Way too small. We're talking about working up interest, getting groups in, maybe every weekend, and selling the accompanying materials for whatever the workshop is for."

"What about the apartment upstairs?"

"Absolutely tiny. And very apartment-y. You know, kitchenette, full bath, all of it a mess. If I used that space, it would totally feel like I was trying to make a silk purse out of a sow's ear."

She paused. That was stupid. "That's the wrong metaphor, but you know what I mean. It would seem very homemade, not professional. I'm already up against it—as you know—so the last thing I need to do is invite criticism for the business."

He considered this. "You'll have to find out the rent on the space next door."

"It's half of what I'm paying for the main space now."

He considered, jotted something down on the pad in front of him, then frowned.

"Yes?" she asked.

"Yes." Very Captain Von Trapp, that voice. She'd had to admit to herself that she found it sexy. "Seems like a decent idea to me, not that you care what *I* think." He chuckled.

She forced a smile, hoping he didn't know how feverently she *did* care what he said.

"But I need documentation to present when this inevitably comes under scrutiny," he went on. "A paper trail so no one can call BS on this."

Her eyes drifted to his wedding ring.

He is dreading the coming end of his work-day. He does not want to go home.

The unbidden intuition gave her a shameful rush of hope.

"Prinny?"

"I'm sorry, yes, documentation."

The picture caught her attention again, but when

she glanced at it, Alex's wife was in a different position, one arm wrapped around a different man, a blond Bradley Cooper type, her hand on his crotch. Prinny stared for a moment, but there was no mistaking it. The picture had completely changed, like something from *Alice in Wonderland*.

She blinked hard and looked again. The other man was gone, and Alex and his wife were standing just as they always had in the photo, tanned and smiling.

But the word "cheater" was now echoing in her mind.

This was too bizarre.

"So," she said, putting a hand to her chest, then taking it down just as quickly. "That's it? I just jot some numbers in a proposal? The same old same old?"

"There is never anything *same old* about you." He actually flushed slightly and looked down for a moment. "Not in this biz, anyway."

"I know. It's like I'm spoon-feeding Leif hope."

Alex laughed heartily. "You know he's watching for you to make any misstep so he can take this back to court again."

"I know." Brotherly love. What a great thing. "But he can't just arbitrarily get into my books. He has to have a court order for that, doesn't he?"

"Yes, but he's argued over less than this before."

She looked at the picture. Same as usual.

Whatever had happened wasn't happening again. "Okay, granted, he has. To hell with him. So how soon can I get my hands on the money?"

"Inside twenty-four hours."

"Oh. That's not too bad."

He looked at her kindly. "It is *your* money, Prinny."

"Why do I have so much trouble remembering that?" She raised an eyebrow.

He laughed. "It's part of your charm. Now get to work."

She mock saluted him. "You know me. Always ready to do a thorough proposal for documentation to keep my Scrooge of a brother off my tail." She shook her head. "I wish he'd just stay out of my life."

Alex nodded but didn't comment.

He couldn't, of course. He had to remain professional, and Prinny contending that she'd be better off if Leif would disappear wasn't the sort of thing he could endorse.

"Thanks for your time," she said to him as she gathered her things. "I'll get the paperwork to you in a few hours."

"I'll look forward to it." He chuckled and held out his hand.

She took it, embarrassed at the heat she felt rise in her cheeks. She could only hope he didn't notice—but how could he miss it?

Prinny thought of the feeling she'd gotten when

he looked at his ring. Why didn't Alex want to go home? Would she find out?

Her hand still felt warm and tingly as she walked out of the building into the evening air In fact, she could have sworn it was actually *buzzing* until she realized her phone was on vibrate and was in her purse, ringing.

She stopped and took it out.

It was her sister-in-law. That was weird. She *never* heard from Diana. In fact, she rarely ever even *thought* of her unless they ended up at the same event—usually a funeral or something equally gloomy, where Diana was accompanying Leif, and Prinny had to mingle with them.

Prinny answered.

"Prinny, it's Diana."

The voice barely sounded familiar. Of course, each of them knew who was on the other end of the line in this day and age. If she'd been talking to a friend, or if she hadn't heard the distinct tremor of nerves in her sister-in-law's tone, she might have laughed and pointed that out.

"How are you?" It was all Prinny could think of to say.

"I'm good. I'm all right."

Prinny nodded, pointlessly since it was a phone call, but what else to say? They didn't have an easy rapport, so Prinny couldn't simply say, *All right, cut the chitchat, what's going on with you?*

So instead, she just waited another few seconds

to see if Diana would get around to it herself.

"I had to call you because you're the only one who could possibly understand," Diana said finally.

"Understand what?"

"It's about Leif."

Prinny froze. "Is he . . . is he all right?"

Diana's hesitation gave Prinny just long enough to become aware of a surprisingly strong reaction to the possibility of something being wrong with her brother, but not long enough to sort out what that reaction was.

"Yes, I'm sorry, he's fine. Leif is fine." She let out a swear word under her breath. "I'm sorry, maybe I shouldn't have called."

"Diana, what is it?"

"Well, it's just . . ." Suddenly Diana sounded like a whining teenager, venting about a boy. She seemed to notice this, as her words faded away from her.

Prinny knew her well enough to encourage her not to be too afraid to say whatever was on her mind. To say whatever it was that had made her reach out to a sister-in-law she rarely spoke to.

"Whatever it is, you can tell me. Are *you* okay?"

"Everyone thinks Leif is so great, so charming, so generous, so smart, so *perfect*—"

"Right." Prinny pushed the phone harder against her ear, as if leaning closer to listen. Was she about to hear that Diana, the Good Wife, had doubts? Doubts that he had surely earned?

"And he's not entirely . . . I love him, you know I do. I wouldn't have married him."

Prinny didn't want her to backpedal. Didn't want her to weaken whatever unexpected resolve she had gained.

"I've *never* understood why everyone thinks he's all of those things you listed. The perfection, kindness, et cetera."

"Because you know he's *not* any of those things." Diana took an audible deep breath. "You know he's a stingy little man who would do anything to further his own goals."

Prinny stopped on the sidewalk. Was this *really* Diana? Or was this some sort of setup? Was Leif trying to get Prinny to say something on tape that could somehow incriminate her? Not that agreeing he was a jackass was actionable, but still . . . this wasn't the meek Diana she remembered.

"Diana, I'm sorry, but I don't understand. Is there something going on?"

"I need to get away from him. I need a safe place to get away from him so he can't find me. I don't mean forever, but just until I can come up with a solid plan. He would never suspect you of helping me, so he wouldn't even look in your direction. Please. I'm desperate." Her voice broke, and she cried quietly.

"I'm sorry, I don't mean to be dense but—well,

look, if you need somewhere to go, that's fine, it's not that. But he didn't . . . did he *hurt* you? Are you afraid he's going to hurt you?"

"No!" Diana said, then gave a sharp bark of laughter. "Not physically. To the contrary. I'm afraid if I don't get away now, I'm going to kill him."

Chapter Eleven

Diana

"So *this* is your shop," I said to Prinny, marveling at the bursts of color everywhere. Packs of elaborately painted tarot cards, sharply etched runes, books of every size and color, and what seemed like a million gem-colored stones lined the walls, sat on shelves, and glistened in buckets.

"This is it." Prinny spread her arms, then let them drop to her sides. "Has Leif complained about it a lot?"

"Leif complains about everything a lot," I answered, knowing she was probably expecting a smile or indication that I was kidding, but I wasn't. Not at all.

"He was a pretty dour teenager, as I recall," Prinny agreed. "I was terrified of him."

I looked at her sharply, my body registering alarm at a myriad of things this could potentially mean. "Yeah? Why? Did he hurt you or something?"

She looked surprised. "No! That is . . ." Her face went soft with thought for a moment. "Not really. No more than anyone else going through sibling rivalry."

I wanted to say that there shouldn't have been sibling rivalry between two siblings that were ten years apart, particularly not when the older one was a boy. Well, a boy who, in this case—I happened to know—was mean. And vindictive.

Especially when it came to his sister.

But what good would it have been for me to point that out to her? Surely it was nothing she didn't already know and she wanted to be reminded of.

"He and I had some of that, too," I murmured.

The bell rang over the door, and I hoped Prinny didn't notice me startle at the noise.

I looked, fully expecting it to be Leif, but of course it wasn't. That would have been more surprising than it not being him.

It was, instead, a small woman, wrapped in a shawl that looked too warm for the balmy evening, with a kerchief that covered her head like a babushka.

"Excuse me a moment." Prinny held up a finger and went to the woman. "Can I help you?"

The woman looked down. "I'm looking for a new tarot deck," she said in a hushed voice. "It's

Tarot in the Shape of a Heart, created by Jami Myles. Do you have it?"

Prinny smiled, and I could swear she was trying not to laugh. "As it happens, we are the only distributor of Jami Myles's products, so you have *definitely* come to the right place!"

"Imagine that."

"You must be psychic." Prinny was able to say those words, so often uttered in sarcasm, with an absolutely straight face.

Even more surprising, the woman nodded. "I believe I am, but I could never let on to anyone who knows me."

"You should come in for a reading, and we can do some psychic testing."

"Oh, I couldn't do that." The woman kept her eyes averted. What the heck was her deal? Did she have dangerous laser eyes that she had to prevent from hitting any soft tissue or paper that they might burn? She was acting so strange.

I watched as Prinny led her through the card section, handing her a deck or two before leading her to the books. All the while, she was talking in this soothing voice that even made *me* want to ask her what my future was. Except for the fact that I was terrified to hear an accurate truth, I might have done it.

They went through the store, and the woman collected so many things that Prinny went to get her a basket.

I have to say, everything she got seemed like great fun. Of course, this from the person who had Gipsy Witch Fortune Telling Cards and a Ouija board. To say nothing of the Magic 8 Ball, which I poo-poohed as an absurd gimmick even though I wouldn't have called a boy I had a crush on without consulting that gimmick first.

Prinny completed the sale, all cash like a drug deal, watched the woman leave with a small wave, then looked at me and laughed. "Like we don't know exactly who she is!"

I went blank. "Do we?"

"Don't you?"

"Do you?"

Prinny laughed, a pretty musical laugh. "Does the name Barbara Lingburgh ring a bell?"

I quickly scanned my brain for where I'd heard the name before. "The senator?" I realized at last, though I couldn't tell you what state she was from.

"The very same."

"*She* comes in here?" I realized how bad that sounded and quickly tried to correct myself. "Not that there's *anything* wrong with coming in here at all—it's just that everyone knows Nancy Reagan was mocked horribly over her astrologers, so it seems pretty chancy coming in here." I stopped and felt a little breathless, like I'd tried too hard and accomplished too little, but fortunately Prinny didn't seem to register either of those sentiments.

"Right?" she asked with a smile. "The press would not be kind to her, or to us. On the other hand, as long as they spelled the name right . . . you know the saying."

"I do."

"She's nice, though. I really like her, even though she comes in here like once a month and seems to genuinely think we have no idea."

"Do you get other customers like that?"

"Oh, yeah." Prinny gestured toward the chairs in the book area, and I followed her in there and sat with her. "You'd be amazed how many embarrassed people come in here."

"Embarrassed?"

"Big-time. This is shameful for a lot of people. Religion plays a part for some, but mostly I think people are afraid of being mocked. It's like saying you're married to an alien or something."

I smiled. "And somewhere out there, there is a shop completely devoted to the care and feeding of aliens, and they're saying the same thing about witches."

"Touché."

"I was kidding."

"Let's hope!"

I had to laugh. Prinny went on to tell me about rock stars who'd been in (they weren't usually ashamed), actors from local shows who claimed they were just doing research, and one local weathergirl with big dreams, big hair, and a pretty big budget for love potions and candles.

Honestly, it sounded like a lot of fun.

And something about the place really soothed me. I know it sounds crazy, but I felt like I was at home, even while I'd never quite felt so out of my element.

It was partly the smell. I'd never smelled incense that didn't smell like the old "hippie" variety, but Prinny was burning something called Antique Rose that made me feel like I was inside a Renoir painting, swirling in the color and warmth and safety of the brushstrokes.

"So why are you leaving Leif?" Prinny asked, looking me directly in the eye as soon as a lone customer had left.

I gave a short, dry laugh. "Do you really have to ask why?"

My attempted deflection didn't work. "Yes, unless it makes you uncomfortable or steps on your toes."

"Not at all," I lied. It was arguably her business; I just couldn't stand to admit what a fool I'd been. For so long. If I even tried to tell the whole truth, I thought I would probably shrink down to nothing, I'd feel so small. So instead I went for the overview, the kind of thing anyone can understand. "We just had some differences we couldn't get over. The kind of thing you ignore at first and then realize it's driving you crazy."

"I've had that feeling before," Prinny said.

"Where someone is so hot for the first month and by the third month you cannot understand why he hasn't cut his stupid nose hair or whatever."

"Exactly."

"Except . . ." Prinny hesitated, then sighed. "You don't seem to be that kind of person. I can well believe Leif is aggravating, but I can't quite see you buckling under it. Is there something else?" She looked at me so kindly I almost caved in.

"Not really."

"Then how come you came here? Why was I the only person who could understand?" She didn't quite smile, but her expression was so soft it gave the feeling that she did.

"Because . . ." I tried to gather my thoughts, but it wasn't so easy. "Do you want some tea?" I asked suddenly.

"What?"

"Tea. Remember how I make teas and tinctures?" I said. "It's become my main hobby now. Probably comes from my old days as a bartender, though I learned a lot about herbs in my job at the acupuncturist."

"Bartender!" Prinny cried. "Tea sounds good, but I've got a full bar's worth of liquor in the back room from our holiday party six months ago. Would you rather have a good stiff drink?"

"If you can heat up some water, I can make the best of both worlds," I said, feeling a surge of optimism. *This* was something I was good at. I wasn't good at talking, I wasn't good at being a wife, I wasn't good at being strong, I wasn't good at being an estranged wife, but, damn it, I was good at concocting.

And I needed a concoction.

I don't travel much, but I never left the house for long without at least some emergency herbal supplements. My problem with anxiety had been tremendous back in the day, and then my problem with tranquilizers had been even bigger once Leif's mother, a psychiatrist, began prescribing them in amounts that my Internet research told me were too great.

Sometimes I wondered if they were in cahoots—my husband and my mother-in-law—to either kill me or turn me into a nice, agreeable Sleeping Beauty.

That's what he'd married me to be, you know. He told me so himself. He'd wanted a wife who would be pretty (but not too pretty), mild tempered, agreeable, and impressive if he ever had to convince a jury of his innocence. He actually said that to me! And while he said it with a laugh, somewhere deep inside I knew he wasn't really joking.

I looked pretty good for him on paper, no matter what his ambitions were, and he had political ambitions *and* criminal tendencies. While I realize this didn't make him all that different from other people with political ambitions—especially in this town—Leif was smart enough to set himself up early so he could say he had a long-standing good marriage to this good woman with a middle-class background and good sturdy childbirthing hips.

He must have been really disappointed when it wasn't easy for me to get pregnant. I had been disappointed, that's for sure. But as the years have gone on, I find I'm more and more grateful that I didn't bring someone else into this mess. What would I be doing right now, for example, if I had a child? Would this be safe?

Would home?

Would anything for a Tiesman child be safe? Looking at Prinny, I didn't think so. Because she was the sweetest thing, honestly. There wasn't a bad bone in her body, it was easy to tell that. Why, then, did my husband hate her so much? It seemed to go beyond him resenting her inheritance, though he certainly did that. But no, it was more than that. It was like he hated her for *existing*.

For breathing.

I'd never really understood it, but now, talking with her gentle self and being as grateful as I was for her help under these weird circumstances, I understood even less about what had led Leif to this.

We sat back down, holding cups of my Lavender Lemon Balm Tisane with some vodka unceremoniously dumped in. "So tell me," Prinny said, then paused to blow the steam off the top of her drink. "Is Leif not supposed to know you're here?"

"I'd *really* prefer he didn't."

"Is that, in fact, why I was the only person you could turn to?" Prinny asked, then spared me the trouble of answering. "Sorry, I just thought we should get this out of the way. I get it, I just don't want you to feel like you need to maintain some sort of story, and I especially don't want to have to pretend I believe it."

"So you . . ." I waved my hand around vaguely. "This is real? You're really psychic?"

"Yes," she said evenly. "But it didn't require clairvoyance to figure out why you're here. I know my brother, and I know the signs of someone who has been abused in some way. You don't have to tell me anything you don't want to. I just want your promise that you won't tell *him* anything about my business. My business business or my personal business. We both know he'd like to destroy me, and I have to believe that you're not here to help him reach that goal."

I was horrified at the very thought that she might believe I was here to harm her when she was being so kind as to take me in. "Absolutely not. I swear it."

"Good." She looked at her tea. "No poison in here?"

"Oh, yes—vodka."

She laughed. "Excellent." Then she took a sip,

paused, and took another. "This is amazing," she said, looking truly surprised.

"Good, right?"

"It's *really* good. Was it easy?"

"Oh, sure." It was tea. With vodka in it. What was so hard about that?

But Prinny looked like a baby who was tasting her first ice cream. It was like I was a genius mixologist rather than just a neurotic woman who needed the occasional shot of herbal relaxation.

"And it's a mixture of teas?"

"Not even, it's just a few things thrown into boiling water and steeped. Honestly, you could do it with just about any herbs and spices you can think of, as long as they aren't toxic."

"I feel like you're a genius," she said with a laugh and took another sip.

"Then you just keep right on thinking that, sister," I said, enjoying that someone else was finally taking me seriously. "You keep right on thinking that."

Chapter Twelve

Chelsea

When Chelsea got to the store that morning, Prinny wasn't there. She wasn't required to be; she was the owner. Most business owners don't spend every day in their shops. But Prinny was almost always there, so it surprised Chelsea whenever she wasn't. Suddenly she felt like a kid who'd just realized she was home alone and could do *anything* but then didn't feel the need to do anything differently than usual.

She clocked in, turned on the OPEN sign, unlocked the safe, counted the drawer, put it away, and then turned on the fairy lights that were wound with copper wires around the entire store. Then she waited. There wasn't an appointment on the books for several hours.

Though she wanted nothing more than to curl up in a ball on the cozy chair-and-a-half that sat in the corner and sleep until the front-door bells jingled, she couldn't. Not only because if Prinny found out she'd kill her, but because she had lines to memorize. Another audition to prepare for. The results page to reload six hundred times.

She sat down in the chair and refreshed the audition results page for the production of *Finding Neverland* that she'd been waiting weeks to hear back on. For the first time, it did not read "Audition Results to Come . . ."

There was a cast list.

Chelsea took a deep breath and flipped the phone over for a second to collect herself.

It was okay if she didn't get it. She didn't quite have enough savings to travel like she would have to if she got it. It was going to tour up and down the East Coast. She still had rent to pay. She would have to put it on credit, which would not be ideal.

But on the other hand, she had felt good about that audition. Damn good about it, in fact. She'd been emotional and raw, and projected her voice to the back of the room. Not to mention the fact that she'd had excellent onstage chemistry with the guy who was already cast as J. M. Barrie.

And traveling up and down the coast . . . getting away from here, getting away from everything, that would be so good. She needed that. She really, really needed it.

She cracked her knuckles and then flipped the phone back over.

Sylvia Llewelyn Davies . . . Maria Kingston

Chelsea's stomach and heart expanded and then deflated completely. She didn't get it. The part was given to someone else. It didn't matter how many times she looked at it. The part wasn't hers.

The worst part was that it didn't just go to someone else, it went to Maria Kingston, of all people.

Maria Kingston had the same look she did. They could be cast in the same roles, and it seemed always to come down to the two of them. The difference between them was Maria's offstage personality. You'd love to imagine that this doesn't matter, but it does. She was flirtatious and charming. The kind of girl you had an inside joke with after one conversation. She won people over right away. She always did. She was confident in a way that, when Chelsea had tried to imitate it, made her feel like a fraud instead of like an actress.

She put down the phone and stared out the window. Of course it was cold, gray, and raining today. Exactly the kind of day that brings forth bad news. Sunny days were for celebrating. Rainy, gray days were for hating that bitch Maria Kingston.

The worst part about Maria was that she *was* good. The other worst part was that she *wasn't* a slut. She was a flirt, but only in a friendly way. She didn't sleep her way to the best roles. She was just good. She was just nice.

She was just better than Chelsea. She was just more charming than Chelsea.

It was as if Chelsea had been asking *Who's the fairest of them all?* And the casting directors had agreed for years that *she* was. *Of course* she was! She was the best! The fairest! The winner.

But now? *You're fair, my lady, it's true, but now there is another one fairer than you.*

Maria Fucking Kingston.

Was this how careers ended? Actors' lives changed? Would she, not quite thirty, have to begin auditioning for hag roles (apt, considering she was now envisioning herself as the old witch arriving at Snow White's door with a poisoned apple) until she hit forty and could play nothing more than a corpse or a mummy?

Was this business truly so unfair?

She had heard it all her life, of course, but how much could she possibly care as a young woman? Those warning stories were for other people, not for *her*. She was young, and she would be young forever and ever.

But she wouldn't. She already wasn't.

And suddenly that fact was hitting her full force.

After another twenty minutes of feeling sorry for herself, she pulled herself together. She was being stupid. Far from the plucky Katharine Hepburn type she idolized and wanted to cultivate over a lifetime. She'd lost out on one (more) audition. There would be a million reasons, personal or otherwise, but whatever they were, she couldn't allow this one instance to make her quit.

She would not do that.

So she took the stapled sheets out of her bag that she needed to work on for that next audition.

It was hard to focus. Her mind kept drifting back to her recent failure and the possibility of another one. *What if . . . ?* had become a scary question. She just stared at the highlighted lines—ones she had highlighted while actively thinking of this as a backup audition, back when she felt pretty sure she'd get the *Neverland* role.

What a fool.

The phone rang a couple of times. Chelsea—always the professional outwardly—answered with her dreamy work-voice and walked people through their rainy-day cancellations.

There were a handful of them, and with each one Chelsea envisioned a different corner of a cozy home that had kept that person from going out on a rainy Sunday.

She thought of a warm bed with a down comforter and the even warmer body of a beloved boyfriend, a Netflix queue filled with unwatched episodes of a favorite show.

She imagined a cooking mother and a happy, chatting child at the counter and a cup of warm, creamy coffee.

Even an empty house, a record player in the corner, a good book, and a chair with a glass of midday Who Cares, It's Sunday wine.

All of the things that could stop people from needing to leave the house and find out where they would be at any point in the future. Why would they need to wonder? Those imagined characters had time, love, security. They didn't have stomach-plunging misery to revel in or to unsuccessfully distract themselves from.

The door jingled, and Chelsea looked up to see Prinny coming in with a woman she didn't recognize.

She shot up, jumping into character. More

psychic in tune with the world, less *mopey, aging barely-was actress.*

Luckily, she got to be dramatic either way.

Chelsea rose and smiled at the two women. Both were soaking wet from the weather, and the stranger looked utterly miserable.

Prinny held out an introductory hand. "Chelsea, this is my sister-in-law, Diana."

Relaxing, Chelsea put on a smile. "Hi, Diana."

"Di," she said, with a tight-lipped smile that lacked even the slightest shadow of joy.

Chelsea was startled. "I'm sorry?"

The woman's face registered the misunderstanding. "Call me Di. Or Diana. It really doesn't matter. I don't even know why I said anything." She looked disproportionately distraught about her name, but it was obvious that wasn't really the issue.

It didn't take psychic ability to tell that this woman was in the lowest of the lows. It was so obvious that Chelsea wanted to simply ask, as she might have asked even a stranger in her bubblier days, *What's wrong? What's happened?*

But instead she sat back down in the chair and watched as the women took off coats and boots. Not only had she lost her bubbles lately, but she knew that sometimes people simply did not want to discuss whatever was making them feel noticeably bad.

"I'm not seeing much business for today," said

Prinny. "The streets are flooding. Fifty is closed under the Memorial Bridge thanks to flooding, and the GW Parkway is a mess. I would be amazed if anyone decided to stop and walk around M Street today." She stepped into the back and grabbed two towels. She handed one to Diana and then started patting down her long, damp hair.

"Yes, we've had a few cancellations and one missed appointment so far," said Chelsea.

Unlike back in her waitressing days, the idea of no business for the day sounded pretty appealing.

Di looked like she was in a haze. She moved slowly, drying herself off in such a vague way that she appeared almost to be in a trance, copying Prinny's movements.

Chelsea gave Prinny a questioning look, and Prinny raised her eyebrows in an expression that said, *It's a doozy*.

After the two of them were as dry as they were going to get, they sat down in the other chairs.

"Would either of you like some tea?" asked Di.

Chelsea was confused. That was an offer usually reserved for the hosts. Also, she didn't think they even had any tea. Perhaps she was hinting that *she* would like some.

"I don't know if we have—" she began.

"Diana makes teas and tinctures," Prinny explained. "I actually think she could be a really good addition to the shop. Remember how we were just trying to come up with something, Chelsea?"

Chelsea nodded. Of course she did. Suddenly Prinny not only had a magical herbalist but it was her gloomy Eeyore of a sister-in-law?

Seems like that would have come up during the original conversation if it was really a legit idea.

But it was none of Chelsea's business what Prinny did with the shop. As long as it stayed open, Chelsea was glad. It was the bulk of her income (a very sad statement, and the kind of thing Maria Kingston would probably never have to admit to).

"I think you could have a new career at hand, Di," Prinny went on with false cheer.

"I haven't had a career in God knows how long." *It'll never work . . .* Glum from *Gulliver's Travels* came to mind.

There was an awkward silence that Chelsea filled almost immediately from discomfort. "Well, what of it? No time like the present, is there?" *Was* there? What was she saying? She didn't even know what this woman was doing here.

Prinny straightened her spine. "I don't want to push, obviously. But you were saying you need to do *something,* so . . . why not give it a try? Can't hurt, can it? We're looking for cool things to do with the space next door. It's so small that it'll sit there forever, looking vacant and bringing down my own real estate here. A tea shop. An apothecary. Maybe we can make our own incense, wrap some sage. Get some palo santo wood." Prinny's eyes shut in a way Chelsea had seen only a few times but recognized at once.

She was seeing something. *Seeing* seeing.

"In fact, the roof is flat on that property, we could even"—she looked suddenly like she was puzzling something out—"maybe have a garden up there. Grow our own ingredients. Some, at least." She opened her eyes, then looked slightly embarrassed.

Prinny always looked apologetic after falling into one of these moments. Visions. Whatever you wanted to call them.

Chelsea wished she and her boss were closer so she could give her a look that told her it was okay.

Instead, she shifted her gaze to Diana, who had clearly noticed the slightly unusual brainstorm Prinny had just had.

"Leif told me about your . . ."

"Gift," Chelsea filled in when she looked for the word.

"Your gift, yes, he told me about it. I mean, I realize where we are"—she gestured around at the shop—"but I'm not sure if it's common knowledge that you are the real deal?"

Prinny laughed. "This would be a bad place to try and keep it secret."

Diana smiled. "True."

"If you're going to hang around, get ready to get freaked out sometimes, that's all I can say." Chelsea smiled. Her comment loosened up the room a little.

"Well, if you're serious, or thirsty, I've got a couple of things in my bag here . . ." She unzipped her purse, suddenly having a bit more energy and enthusiasm than she had walked in with. "Let's see . . . I have one for relaxation, one for energy, one for intense stress relief . . ."

"Last one sounds pretty great right about now. In, you know, life." Chelsea laughed.

"I don't know about that one. It's really strong. Strained kava. Think Xanax meets peyote. Not the sort of tea you drink if you want to function at high speed."

Chelsea looked at Prinny. Half asking permission, half communicating that their day was basically shot anyhow.

The rain got louder and heavier, as if on cue. It slammed into the storefront as if it were coming from a collection of fire hoses.

Prinny shrugged. "My brother is an asshole, and you look like you haven't gotten more than a couple of hours of sleep in the last month." This last part was tossed maternally in Chelsea's direction.

She simply shrugged. "And I didn't get *Neverland*."

Prinny stood to turn off the OPEN sign. "Honestly, too-intense stress relief sounds like something we could all use."

Twenty minutes later, they were all sitting in the chairs, clutching steaming ceramic mugs while the rain spit miserably onto the window and sidewalk outside.

They made small talk about things going on in town recently, but all the while Chelsea was dying to ask what exactly Diana was doing here and what her problem was.

She wasn't even halfway through her tea when she started to feel her muscles loosen and untangle. Stress seemed to scatter like tiny beads and then disappear. She felt slack and lazy, but peaceful and awake. Her brain was thinking efficiently and at a pace that didn't send her tension through the roof. Usually her mind was racing at ten miles a minute, thoughts coming at her in a useless fast-forward. Hard to understand, yet quick to tighten her nerves.

But right now her brain was ambling at an easy pace. She felt almost like she was floating on a cloud. She had to admit, the tea *was* strong. Or maybe it was the power of suggestion. Whatever it was, Chelsea really did feel a little drugged. Not in an unpleasant way—she could certainly have walked to the bus stop and made her way home, but she would rather curl up and take a nap. It had been a long time since she'd been this relaxed.

Whatever it was, she would be buying some.

Chelsea glanced at the other two. Prinny was staring at the ground, looking thoughtful. Di's eyes were shut, her brow knitted.

Chelsea's inhibitions began to abandon her. She took another sip and asked, "So what is going on, Di?"

Prinny stiffened.

Diana opened her eyes and tilted her head. "I'm sorry?"

"Well . . . I know the look of someone who's chewing away on a problem and can't let go, even in a crowd." She gestured around them and smiled. "Even a tiny crowd."

She certainly did know that feeling. She used to study it. Now she lived it.

"Chelsea, Di might not want to talk right now—"

"It's okay." Diana mustered a smile. "Are you a psychic as well, or something?"

Chelsea had to applaud her rallying to make the reference. "I've been taught by the best." She raised her mug to Prinny. "But you don't need to be psychic to see that you're seriously sad."

"I . . ." Di managed that single word with some strength, then pressed her lips together while her eyes filled with tears. She raised a shaky hand in front of her face.

Chelsea immediately felt bad for pushing. "I'm sorry. Look, I'm always wondering what motivates people, but I'm not always as sensitive to that as I should be. Forgive me, please. You don't owe anyone an explanation. Hell, I'm just glad you're here! This tea is great, and I bet it's going to ramp up business hugely." She was rambling now at full speed. That was her thing: overstep, freak out, then talk spastically to try to obscure the mistake, thereby calling even more attention to it.

"No, you know what, it's okay." Diana took a trembling breath. "I know you've probably never heard of me, and suddenly here I am and here, apparently, I'm going to be for a bit, and not only that, I'm this Mournful Mary being a total drag from moment one." She gave a dry, insincere laugh. "All I need to do is wet my pants to round out the image of being the kid no one was supposed to invite to the party, but . . ." She shrugged broadly. "Here I am!"

Chelsea gave her an encouraging look.

"And . . ." Diana set down her mug. "And like so many foolish women before me, I fell in love with the wrong man, married him, and I am having a hell of a time getting myself away from him even though he hurts me all the time."

"He . . . *hurts* you?" Chelsea shot an uncertain glance at Prinny. "Is this, like, kill or be killed? *Sleeping with the Enemy*?"

Diana shook her head. "Oh, I'm way more foolish even than that. I simply can't get myself to leave a man who doesn't love me." She shrugged, but tears filled her eyes yet again. "Nothing special about my story, it's just the same old, same old, same old. Cheating husband, pitiful wife, parade of who knows who."

"God," said Prinny, propping her forehead up with two fingers and looking at Diana.

"And what's worse is that I know he isn't just a jerk."

Chelsea braced herself to hear the slew of man-defending excuses she had heard—and given—before.

Instead, she got something worse. "If he was a jerk who lied because he didn't care or had gotten in too deep, that would be one thing. It's worse than that on both sides. I am completely in love with him."

Her gaze didn't lift, but her eyes widened as she stared at the ground. The small room was silent.

"I am completely in love with him, and he's somehow not quite human. He doesn't have the little"—she pinched the air with her fingers—"tiny thing that most people have that prevents them from being that deeply dishonest. It's not that he doesn't know better or doesn't care—although he doesn't seem to care, either—it's that he lacks whatever it is that makes human beings think that it *matters* to be good. He would never want to do the right thing, the good thing. If he did it, and I'm sure he has before, he'd simply find that he felt no differently if he did the right thing or the wrong thing."

She looked each of the women in the eye, but they were both struck dumb. Even Di herself seemed to be understanding the depth of this realization for the first time as she spoke it.

"Jeez," said Chelsea.

At the same time Prinny said, "Fucker."

Chelsea almost gasped. Not because of the word itself, definitely, but because of the mouth it came from. Prinny was so . . . well . . . prim. Proper. Not an F-bomb gal.

Di shrugged. "It's not like I'm an idiot—or at least not *that* kind of idiot. The kind that can't see what's right in front of her. I'm the kind of fool who weighed how much I loved him against how much pain I could withstand. Turned out I was exceptionally strong in an exceptionally weak way."

There was silence. Not uncomfortable. Just sad.

Diana shrugged, as if to dismiss the whole subject. "It's so discouraging how different a person can be when you meet them. Or how different they can appear, anyway."

But Chelsea, always in search of motivations, was fascinated. "What was he like when you met him?"

The question seemed to interest Diana. She thought about it. Pursed her lips and really thought for a moment. Then, simply: "He was everything I ever wanted. That's it. The big, fundamental things were there. The little things I would have never known to ask for cropped up as surprises. He got me right away, but I'm starting to think that was *why* all those things existed. He saw what I wanted. He became it. I just don't know why he even bothered. Or maybe I don't know why it had to be me."

"It would have been some other woman sitting here with us right now," said Prinny. "It would have been another woman in your place, but only if she was strong enough to get here. Otherwise . . ."

Thought filled the room, mixing with the spicy-sweet kava.

"Let's just round up all the jerks we've ever met," said Chelsea finally, "put 'em in a room, and let them fight to the death."

"And then we can kill the victor."

They all laughed, but in the dreamy haze of her mind, Chelsea imagined who she would want dead. She might not have been clairvoyant, but she just knew they were all thinking along the same lines.

Wouldn't it be nice to really get revenge?

Chapter Thirteen

Diana, Diary Entry,
Twelve Years Earlier

Tonight, I am the happiest I have ever been.

The middle of October, in the middle of the night, in the middle of a college campus is the height of perfection for me. The skidding of the leaves across the chalk-ridden sidewalks (Vote for So-and-So! Clothes Swap Saturday, 11 A.M.!) and cold wet grass are half the atmosphere, and the pounding bass pulsating from within the surrounding dorms is the rest of it.

I have never been happier.

Voices and laughter echo in the air, like I remember summer nights sounding when it was filled with conversations on the neighborhood porches. Except this is college, so there's a little more shouting, squealing, chanting, flirting . . .

Red Solo cups litter these perfectly manicured lawns. And on the wind, there is an undulating current of this beautiful, snaggable opportunity. There is a chill in the air that suggests impending change.

Ugh. I don't mean to get poetic on myself. It's just that every beautiful lyric from every beautiful song or poem I ever heard is coming to me now in full bloom. I keep imagining the beautiful lines—even the stupid clichés—and finally understanding their truth! Ahh . . .

See, this is why I have never really kept a diary. Every time I write anything, I end up looking back on it and criticizing it. It feels self-indulgent. Feels like it tries too hard. Why I give myself these criticisms, I'm not sure—it's not like I would *ever* allow anyone to read these entries . . .

So yeah, I rarely write in this thing. But—as I will obviously already know when I reread this cringe-worthy, love-goggled dribble later—it's a beautiful, red leather–bound book that sits on my shelf empty and really deserves to be written in. I am not even entirely sure where this book came from anymore. Maybe I got it for Christmas at some point? From someone? One of those nice but sort of "oh, wow, great" kinds of gifts.

Mom gave it to me, probably. She was always trying to make me more Virginia Woolf and less *Clarissa Explains It All*.

As little as I write in it, I do my best to put in my stand-out experiences. There are certain nights you want to remember every aching detail of, even if it makes you cringe to read later on. I feel sure that I will at some point, looking back on this one, because I am a giddy schoolgirl right now. Literally. I am utterly infatuated by a boy in a way that I have absolutely never been.

I have always been so distant with guys. Never

really felt that exquisitely painful pull toward anyone. Which is good, I have always thought. I've never been hurt. Never been dumped. Never been heartbroken by someone. I don't mean to brag about this—I feel lucky *and* a bit gypped, if I'm honest. Maintaining a steady *nothing* is ultimately as unrewarding as having intense highs and lows.

Either way, no guy has ever done it for me in a way that shook me to my very core. I have had boyfriends, crushes, dates, hangouts (particularly in groups), and (many) (very) meaningless hookups. I have delivered the lies that get me out of further interaction so many times. I have snuck out while they pee. I have been awkward and then left giggling with a friend even though it probably hurt a guy's feelings.

Some of my disinterest, ambivalence, whatever, comes from my confidence. I have a healthy amount of confidence. I think I have earned it, so I refuse to be the kind of girl who apologizes for having it. I have made an active effort to be intelligent and an active learner in and out of school. I have a beautiful family who have blessed me with healthy, thick blond hair, nice eyes, and a smile that looks real even when it isn't. I work on my insides and I care about my outsides. I think it's okay to love yourself when you're making the effort and not just complimenting yourself for something that was always out of your control.

I'm a good listener. I'm not big on "let's talk about me" conversations, even when people ask.

One of the reasons I believe I've never quite found myself sinking my teeth into a guy, so to speak, is because I've never felt *seen*. Again—maybe that makes me sound like a brat . . . but aren't we allowed to be brats about the person we end up sharing our lives with? Especially when writing in a diary?

I think so.

I want someone to see me for exactly who I am and get what's so great. I don't want someone I'm with to *miss* the things I think matter about me, and then I also want that person to tell me reasons I'm great that I wouldn't have known if it weren't for him. And I would love to care enough to do that for someone else in a real way. But so far, I have not been able to really, authentically provide this for my boyfriends, nor any of them for me.

Which has been okay. I get that I'm still young and silly enough to be arrogant and in no rush. I have listened enough to my mom and her friends talk to realize that I am young, silly, arrogant, and on a timed schedule for all of these things.

As they've all told me:

Your metabolism will catch up with you!

Enjoy it now! (This they apply to everything from romance to career to dinner choices.)

Eat up every experience life offers you—trust me, you will regret it if you don't!

NEVER. GET. MARRIED.

You'll remember the days when you had options!

To admit some weakness here, I have feared that lack of interest or enthusiasm was an actual missing puzzle piece within me rather than just a matter of time. But even if I am completely wrong and this guy ends up meaning nothing in the end, in the last few weeks he has shown me a side of myself that feels valuable.

Well, the last few weeks have shown me a guy that made me realize things about myself. Healthy, interesting things, because he's definitely no ordinary guy.

The first night I met him, I almost didn't even go out. (Ugh, can you believe that? Fascinating how one little choice can change everything . . .)

It was one of those nights where I had to decide to do it. I almost didn't. I almost stayed in with the essay that I had another week to finish, and a cup of my kava tea. Sometimes I feel I *need* to afford myself these nights, since ninety percent of my life is about social interaction. But on this night, I wisely made the choice to do what I "shouldn't" and sneak into the pool of a model home with thirty of my closest friends.

It was warm still—actually a bit warmer than the surrounding nights—and we had a keg of some cheap beer, two handles of raspberry vodka, and another of Captain Morgan. No food, but who needs it? Our parties don't involve crockpots full of meatballs served on toothpicks. At best, someone remembers they have a bag of potato chips in their car and everyone crowds around it and empties it like vultures with a carcass.

Real drunk vultures.

So anyway! I was in my black bikini with the gold fastenings, the one that always makes me feel good. I have no crush, I have no person of interest. (This can be such a relief, while all of my friends stress about unanswered calls, possibility of appearance/nonappearance of said love interest, etc.) My intention is to go out, have fun, and probably field interest from several different people. It's a high that I enjoy, one that I prefer to any drug-induced ones. I revel in the compliments or harmless flirtation and then go home feeling clean and happy.

(This is something that wins surprising favor from people. I don't do any drugs at all—simply not my thing. Not that I'm judgmental about it, because there are a whole lot of us with trouble getting through the night and I *get* it, I just don't get it.)

So this party. It was typical. Loud, drunk, music blasting, girls singing along to music, guys watching girls, girls watching guys. Except we were in an uninhabited pre-residential development with no neighbors to worry about. And in an exciting turn of events for me, there were actually people there that I didn't recognize. I feel a bit like I've run through my gamut at school (and come up with nothing but a few horror stories). So it was a nice feeling to see a group of guys I didn't know.

They were evidently athletic from their build, charming, destined for good jobs, big fans of beer. And I had enough self-assurance to walk over to the keg where they stood and just *be* in front of them before wandering back to my friends. One of them captured my attention right as I finished filling my cup.

He was sitting on a three-foot stone wall that held in the landscaping. He was in a gray T-shirt. His body was tan and sculpted—that is the word, because the angles of his body follow the meter of the word. Curved with sharp angles. He had straight eyebrows, piercing eyes that seemed to be x-raying me, and a beautiful ease in his relaxed stature. He was so obviously completely comfortable in his own bronze skin; that was something I couldn't realistically imagine.

I could tell he was a bit older; that his friends were a bit older. They had this "down to have a good time" but "thank God we aren't this age anymore" vibe about them.

And then, of course, there's the thing I couldn't quite put into words that had me wholly startled. I had smiled and glanced at the guys when I started filling my cup, but hadn't locked eyes with him until after I dropped the keg tap and was already walking away. He was looking at me in the way that told me he'd been staring at me the whole time. I wanted to turn back and look at him too, but you can't do that. I tossed a glance back to see him still watching me, but that was it.

No matter what anyone says, a person's apparent interest in *you* can be extremely appealing. Or irretrievably unattractive. But it really just depends.

For a while after this, I could feel his eyes on me. I felt his interest, and almost saw myself through another set of eyes. I laughed and talked, but I sat a bit straighter and smiled a bit broader knowing that he was watching me. Knowing it was only a matter of time until one of us had enough nerve to go to the other and say something. I was pretty sure it would be him, but knew that if it wasn't, I needed to make it happen.

In the end, it was him (thank God). I emerged from the pool and threw my head back to get some of the water out of my hair. As my luck had it, he walked up during this movie-moment. He had two cups in his hand.

"Would you like to do a shot with me?" he asked, handing me a cup.

I smiled. I could feel now the gaze of my girl-friends. Surely envious. Surely giggling. Surely they were going to be willing to dissect this later with me. (They totally were, we totally did, we talked about it for forever afterward.)

"Sure," I said, and took the one closer to him instead of the one that he held out. "You never know. You could be trying to drug me."

"Or maybe I'm pulling a *Princess Bride*, and I put the drugs in *my* cup."

"Could be. Or perhaps in both, and like Rasputin, you've made yourself immune. All I can do is try to be cautious. There are endless risks here."

He grinned. "Or I think you're stunning. And I'm a dumb guy who could think of nothing more creative than a shot of shitty rum to come over and start a conversation with you."

I laughed. It truly made me laugh. Especially because of the tiny hint of nervousness in his voice—a voice you could just tell was usually brimming with confidence.

It turned out he *was* a bit older. He was only there because he lived down the road and he and his friends had picked up the beer so his friend's little brother could be the Hero with the Booze Connection. When they got there, they decided to hang out and make sure everything was cool.

That explained why they were so much better composed than the other guys there.

I maintained my composure that night. I could tell *I* was transfixing *him,* and hid my own fascination as well as I could. I could tell that *he* could tell that I was different. We both knew that I wasn't the same as so many of the shrill, simpleminded girls that surrounded us. I could tell that he was on a slightly elevated level compared to his friends. We knew that we were the outliers. There was something the same that we spotted in each other, and I was so excited to find that in someone else for once. Especially when—as is always promised by the cliché—I was definitely least expecting it.

We talked all night, suddenly on a different schedule of drinking than our peers. We had shots and refilled cups in time with the meter of our conversation, as opposed to that of the party. It felt good. I don't even know what we talked about. I knew that he was funny and biting, with moments of truly insightful—unpretentious—observation mixed in with moments of being delightfully, relievingly *normal.*

He was the way that I always like to think of *myself,* or that I aimed to seem. Smart but not irritatingly so. Able to blend in with the crowd, but able to stand out to those who cared to notice. Funny without trying to be a calculated laugh-a-minute. Intriguing and nice without being sickly, saccharine sweet. I didn't care one bit about the rest of the party from the first second that we sat on that wall together, legs slung over the sides, facing each other.

The party didn't care too much about us, either, except for a few friends coming up to each of us and telling us to stop obsessing over each other and come hang out. Which of course fueled the mood of our conversation and kept us exactly where we were, on our own.

We outlasted everyone else, and fell asleep under the stars in a big sleeping bag he'd had in the back of his truck. He gave me his sweat-shirt to wear, and we used my clothes and a raincoat from his truck as pillows. He put his arm around me and didn't try anything. To be honest, I had feared that moment of truth. I have grown so tired of explaining why my answer is no that it felt wonderful to simply not be asked. The only thing he did was kiss the spot behind my ear after he seemed to think that I had fallen asleep.

It made my heart tremble with excitement. It lit my muscles on fire. It electrified my skin. I knew I was feeling what people say you feel. I knew I was knowing what people always promise you'll *know* when you know.

I'm not sure if I know that he's the one—it's only been a few weeks by the time I write this—but I know for sure that I would be happy if that's what he ends up being to me.

I've been a bit afraid to see him after that. I fear that the magic will be gone. I fear that I have put him on a pedestal and set myself up for disappointment. I have been pedestaled before . . . I have been disappointing after being interesting to someone. I have felt like I wasn't "on" enough to delight someone else, and I don't want that to happen to either of us.

But it hasn't so far. Magically, though a little less poetic and dreamy, every interaction with him has been something special. It's only been a month and a half since I met him, and already I've done more with him and felt more than I have in my life with anyone romantically.

I've danced with him to Johnny Cash in his shitty dorm room while the reek of weed clouded around us from his roommates. I showed him my favorite old movie, and he laughed in all the right places. I sat on his lap at a bonfire, his sweatshirt hood up and my hood up, both of us vanishing into a world that was only our own until one of my friends threw a stick at us. Our friends get along. He thinks my girlfriends are funny, even when they are speaking only in inside jokes and high-pitched voices. My tire went flat and he showed up at 6:00 A.M. to change it for me. We went out to a nice dinner, but both agreed that we had enjoyed the time we split twenty bucks worth of Chinese food on the floor in front of the TV just as much.

I fell asleep while he watched SportsCenter and felt like "such a girl" lying next to her very own "such a guy." He fell asleep while I watched a romantic comedy. He has come over to my dorm and not missed a beat before kissing me on the cheek, even though I was in no makeup and hadn't washed my hair.

He is real.

He is good.

He is everything I never knew I wanted.

He has shown me that I have the capacity for this, and for that I owe him endlessly.

And tonight, he told me he loved me.

I was dressed up like a cat. A black bodysuit, little ears, black on the tip of my nose, whiskers drawn on my cheeks. He was dressed up like Indiana Jones. I like that he's the kind of guy that will wear a costume. I also super-like that he's the kind of guy that doesn't go embarrassingly over the top.

He's asleep next to me now, lying on his side in my tiny twin-sized bed, his arm draped over my abdomen. He's drunk, but not as drunk as any other guy on campus (it seems). We just had sex for the first time. He was good. He was giving. He made me feel sure about the choice to do it, and gave me explicit freedom to say no. He knows I'm writing in a diary, because he woke up a few minutes ago and said, "I didn't know you kept a journal."

When I told him I didn't always, he gave me this sleepy half-smile and then squeezed my hip before falling back to sleep.

And now I feel a kind of contentedness I realize I never knew I was missing, but one which I always feared (on some level) that I would never reach.

I am in love, and whether it works out or not, I will never deny that I have fallen in love with Leif Tiesman.

Chapter Fourteen

Diana

I was embarrassed about my first impression on Chelsea. My small mothering instinct told me it was wrong to make everything seem so hopeless to a girl who had the optimism to believe she could still get it right. On the one hand, they were adults in that room when I'd spilled my soul all over the place. But on the other hand, I didn't need to be another woman lamenting the lost illusion of love. Maybe I could find a way to say something less hopeless to her the next time I saw her.

Then, of course, I also didn't want to come off as such a loser. But bigger than all of that, I just barely had a relationship with my sister-in-law. (Soon to be *ex*-sister-in-law, I guess; what would she be then? Would she even be a friend? Or just someone who was relieved as hell to get rid of the dead weight of her brother's ex-wife?) When I called Prinny it was because I could *literally* not think of another person in the world to turn to, partly because the last place he would look for me would be with her.

It was like an emotional hangover. At the time, spilling my guts to them had felt easy and comfortable. *Good,* even. But by the time I got to think for way too long about it, I was sure I had talked too long, been too wordy, been too raw. Been too *much* all around.

As far as Leif was concerned, that would be the definition of me sleeping with the enemy. He had counted on me for years to coo and caw and agree with him that life was horrifically unfair to bring That Woman (Prinny's mother) into his charmed life, steal his father away, and then make that loss irretrievable with the introduction of the Little Princess.

That's how Leif usually referred to her, by the way. As the Little Princess. Obviously their dad *did* call her Princess until it was shortened to Prinny, but Leif could not bring himself to refer to her in any way that was even remotely affectionate, so he managed to make every little girl's dream title into an insult, dripping with loathing.

Now, I also remember a time in life when I longed for the title of Mrs. Leif Tiesman so desperately that, honestly, I could practically *taste* it. In fact, I think in some ways I *could:* It tasted of blood and sweat and dark, leaden, metallic desperation. I was so sure that it would make me happy forever. That, once it was *accomplished,* the hardest part of my life would be over and there'd be smooth sailing forevermore.

I could stop being Diana Warren, and I could become the one and only Diana Tiesman. Mrs. Tiesman. Mrs. Leif Tiesman. Picture it scribbled all over a composition book.

Anything I didn't like about Diana Warren could be completely rewritten in my new, married life. The second act of my life.

Instead, I killed my old self, and that New Me I wanted so badly is being slowly poisoned. Now I didn't even know who Diana was to begin with anymore.

The bitterest part of me wants to say, *And he managed to ruin that name, too,* but there's a grown-up inside me who knows that if I grant him the power to have ruined that name—*my name*—then I will never have the power to redeem it myself.

Okay, then, life itself took me by the hand, gave me a new name, a new idea of myself, and then challenged me until I reached the point where I had to make my own name and create a solid self instead of perceiving some *idea* of one.

And that's where I found myself very late on the night I hooked up with Prinny, saw the store, met the crazy actress I was to work with, and got the dented brass key to the space upstairs that she said "was once an apartment but might not have much in the way of habitability now."

Those are daunting words in a neighborhood as old and trashy and beautiful and dangerous and undeniably rat-filled as Georgetown.

All cities are rat-filled. It's nothing against Georgetown, or the generous offer of a place that Prinny gave to me. I remember going to get a pedicure with my friend Crystal in Manhattan one evening, at a place so swanky and close to the New York Palace that even I probably could have hit a tennis ball from point A to point B. Good neighborhood, right? But just as I was relaxing into the massage chair while the manicurist did some magical reflexology on my feet, I watched Crystal's eyes dart left to right at some unseen (by me) object at the back wall; then her face went white.

"What?"

"Nothing." Utterly unconvincing.

"What just happened?" I looked behind me but saw nothing. No thug with a gun, no guy in a trench coat with bare feet, no spooky ghost, nothing. "Why do you look like that?"

"I don't look like anything," she said, still looking like she'd just been threatened with her life. The manicurist working on her nails filed down a little too close, and Crystal jumped.

"Oh, yeah, you're fine."

She gave me an exasperated look and stage-whispered, "I just saw a . . ."

"You just saw what? A what?" I realize now that

this was almost me asking *Why are you kicking me under the table?*—the kind of ham-fisted ignorance usually reserved for the dunderheads I dated, but we were in New York, as famous for its danger as for its glamour, and I didn't have time for her to be too *polite* to mention that my hair was about to catch on fire because the bright blue Macaroni and Cheese food truck outside the front window had just burst into flames.

"Rats," she hissed.

"Rats?" This time I looked down. I did not want rats underfoot, climbing up my legs and into my underwear.

Both manicurists carried on as if they hadn't understood a word Crystal had said, and for all I know they hadn't.

"Three of them." Crystal pulled her hand back. "Boom boom boom, and then they just *flattened"*—she smacked her palms together in a way that still gives me chills to remember—"and went through that space in the wall behind you."

A chill ran up my spine. Or was it a rat?

"Behind me?"

She nodded frantically and pointed, and now I saw that the cheap plaster wall—like the stuff elementary school ceilings were made of—was pushed in a little bit at the seam. Right behind me.

Right behind me.

"Are they coming back?" I asked nonsensically. As if Crystal had suddenly turned into Jack

Hannah, able to predict the behavior of wild, bubonic-plague-carrying animals.

"I don't know!"

It was the least relaxing pedicure I've ever had, possibly even more uncomfortable for me than for Crystal because the Imagined is often so much worse than the Reality (though, for the record, I've had various problems with both).

Since that time, I have stepped much more gingerly through city streets in general, and been grateful for my generous suburban home in Northern Virginia, where *critters* don't tend to be a problem.

So it was with a great deal of angst that I went to a big-box store and picked up every cleaning supply I could think of, as well as a rat trap I hated the idea of using but was determined to if there was evidence that I needed to.

I parked in the alleyway behind the store and used the back-door key Prinny had given me along with the apartment key. I didn't have a store key, though I would have preferred my first few steps in—and possibly my scampering steps out— to be through the pristine, beautiful storefront, rather than the cement stairwell that loomed darkly before me. Of course, beggars can't be choosers, and I was most definitely, at that point, a beggar.

And Prinny was a saint, because she didn't have any reason in the world to trust me or help me, particularly given how my husband had treated her.

I turned on the flashlight app on my phone and tried to remember, with every step up into the inevitable expanse of darkness, that this was a blessing.

It was.

It reminded me of those photos that showed up all over the Internet a couple of years ago of the Parisian apartment abandoned during World War II and discovered perfectly preserved and Gigi-esque lovely under a light coat of dust, but more complete, in a very compact way, than I had expected.

There was a large room, probably above the sales floor of the store below, with an old sofa (with cushion, so I was afraid what might be in there), flanked by two side tables with marble tops. A leather wingback chair that was probably worth a pretty penny sat in the corner with a matching ottoman. There was also one of those round dish chairs that Pier One sells, but the bamboo base was visibly broken, and even if it hadn't been, the cushion had probably been purchased by an acid fan at *least* two or three decades back.

That was it for furniture in that room. There was a nook of a kitchen off the back with a small built-in counter, but no stools. The two-burner electric stove would do fine if it worked; likewise the fridge, though I was sure that was going to be a big cleaning job. The bathroom, next to an unusually long, narrow closet that ran along the back wall, was just about what you would expect. Dirty linoleum floor, toilet too gross-looking even to puke into, and a shower/tub combination that I knew I'd never sit in no matter how clean I got it.

I began with the bathroom.

It wasn't half an hour into the task—worse than anticipated because sometimes what you think is just some calcium deposit in a toilet isn't—that I began to crave one of my newly invented energy teas, but given that it was 1:00 A.M., that was probably due to my overall exhaustion as much as to the daunting task before me, and if I had one now I wouldn't get an ounce of sleep even when I was finished. My drive to move forward, away from Leif, was stronger than ever, and the very thought propelled me on.

Until the phone rang.

I had turned off location services on my regular phone (versus the pay-as-you-go phone I'd gotten at the grocery store on my way out of Dodge) but had somehow neglected to turn off the ringer. Or maybe it was a subconscious act so when he called I'd be reassured that he cared, although I certainly hadn't been expecting the call, and the last thing in the world I felt was *cared about*.

My first reaction was to freeze in fear; my second, to flog myself for not having remembered to save myself from my first reaction by simply turning off the ringer.

My third reaction, which probably should have been my first and only, was a certain anger at the fact that it had taken him this long to notice I was gone and to have enough concern to call.

"Concern" might be the wrong word, but it's all I can come up with. Anything conjuring genuine *care* feels wrong, as Leif's first seventeen layers of reaction to *anything* are self-protective. Any reaction to my being missing would begin with his ego. Was I with someone else? Had someone else taken what was *his?* If I'd left of my own accord, had I told anyone and thereby embarrassed him?

I managed not to answer, and he didn't leave a message.

So I returned to my work and tried not to think about it.

Twenty-one minutes later, he rang again.

Again no voice mail, but this time it was followed immediately by a text.

Where the fuck are you?

Touching, isn't it?

I had been one hundred percent loyal to this man for *years,* yet when he came home from God knows what unholy activity in the middle of the night and found I was not there, his first reaction was *Where the fuck are you?*

It's embarrassing to admit that after the surge

of anger I felt, like the sudden and brief swell of pain when you stub your toe, I fell right back into the ditch of rationalization. My old habit. My old enemy.

He's scared, my mind tried to say. *People often manifest fear as anger.*

That would mean he was scared a *lot,* though.

I was pondering this when the phone rang again. Holding it, right there in my hand, made it harder to ignore. It took every ounce of will and determination I had, and my hand hurt from clutching the phone so hard when I set it down.

Another text: *I know you're there, answer the damn phone!*

A creepy feeling of being watched came over me, even though I absolutely knew he wasn't literally seeing me. It was an interesting reaction, though, because while I realized he was domineering at home, I hadn't quite put together that I felt so scrutinized that the feeling could follow me even into a space as small, dark, private, and unlikely as this.

It was like being watched by a ghost.

That was the thought in my head when the phone blasted again. I can't even say why (Habit? The need to stop the sound?), but I answered it. Before I said a word, I thought it was a mistake.

As soon as he spoke, I knew it was.

"Where. The fuck. Are you." A question, stated as a command, blurred slightly by Lagavulin, the sixteen-year-old single malt Scotch he drank—neat if he was in a hurry, with water if seduction of any sort was in order. He thought it was less ostentatious to go with the sixteen- rather than the twenty-year-old. In any event, tonight was a no-water night.

"I've left you, Leif." The words came so simply it was as though I were saying them in a play or something. They didn't sound true. They didn't *feel* true. They sounded silly and airy. Dumb. Not strong and biting, like I would have liked to sound.

His laugh proved that he felt the same.

The humiliation of that genuine chuckle went deep in me.

"I mean it!" I insisted, sounding like a child on the playground. *Yes, I did! Ask Mom!*

"Get your ass back here before anyone notices you're gone, Diana. Jesus."

"Took you awhile to notice I was gone."

"What?"

"It's"—I looked at my watch—"two in the morning now. What took you so long to notice that your wife was gone?"

"I was busy."

A million faces of *busy* floated through my mind. Any of the hot women who worked at his office; the woman who lived two doors down with the foreign husband I'd never seen in the three years we'd lived there; the barely legal bank teller with the red hair and green eyes who might have just stepped out of Ireland or the song "Jolene"; and, of course, there was the Plumber—and who knows how many more?

Yeah, truer words he'd never spoken.

"You are definitely busy. That's the problem."

"Get your ass home." He was having no more of this. Even the small veneer of niceness was gone. The courtesy of pretending to be a faithful husband even when the truth was more undeniable than gravity.

"No."

A pause. A menacing pause. Then a quiet voice that was more shocking than a shout could ever be. *"Now."*

"Why?"

"Because I don't want questions from anyone. You have a position here, and you need to fulfill it."

"A job to do?"

"If that's how you want to look at it."

"Then I want a raise."

"Diana." I hated his voice. It was like a movie villain's suddenly. "If you want to look at this as a job, then you probably don't want to be fired, do you?"

My chest tightened. "Is that a threat?"

"That's a warning."

"A little too late." I took a breath and worked up a little insincere bravado. "I already quit."

"You can't quit."

"I did."

"Where the fuck are you?"

"None of your fucking business." I never spoke to him that way. Part of me cowered in anticipation of retribution.

Another pause. I couldn't tell if it was him deciding his next move or him already knowing it.

"Diana." A weary sigh. "I don't have time for this. I don't have *interest* in this. You need to get back here, now, and stop this bullshit, or the police are going to get involved."

I gave a spike of laughter. "You're going to call the police and tell them your wife ran away from you? Somehow I can't see that. The great Leif Tiesman never admits anything is out of his control."

"I didn't say I was going to call the police and tell them my wife ran away," he said evenly. "I said if you didn't come back now, the police were going to get involved."

"Right, so obviously—" I stopped. Yes, obviously. But not *obviously he was going to call the police for help in finding his poor, lost wife and returning her safely home.*

No, his implication was far more sinister. And so subtle that I might have missed it. Yet even though he'd never threatened me outright before— he'd never had to, I was such a good little wifey— I recognized it almost as soon as I heard it.

The worst of all possible threats.

"You've got to be kidding," I said, my voice like a flat basketball, thudding on the court.

"Try me."

Man, that answer came so easily to him. After all our time together, after all the love I thought I'd built for (and from) him, all the bricks we'd set and mortared to build the foundations of a marriage, it was that easy for him to eliminate me if I became inconvenient for him.

Or at least to contemplate it.

I knew the difference between something he was saying for effect and something he was saying because he meant it deeply.

He meant this, deeply and easily.

He was a monster.

For so long, he had been the Leif I could make explanations for, and now it was so obvious that he was the horrible man I thought he was. I wasn't wrong. I wasn't imaginative. I had lied to myself and turned him into a reasonable person, not the other way around.

"Why not just let me go, then?" I asked, doing my damndest to keep my voice steady and strong. "Why the threats, Leif? Why go so low-rent? That's not like you."

"This isn't like you," he countered. "And, more to the point, it's not like me to have a live wire out there, about to throw sparks in any direction at any time with little or no provocation."

"Little or no provocation?" That was the wrong thing to say. Don't incite him. "I don't have any interest in tangling with you at all," I covered quickly. "I want to move on, get out of your realm. Will you give me a reasonable divorce?"

"No one divorces me."

I hesitated. Not because I was thinking about *obeying* him or going back, despite his incredibly *romantic pleas*. No, I was scared. Straight up scared. "Well, then, what on earth do you want me to do?" I asked, now allowing all the fear and hopelessness into my voice.

It was real, even though I wished it weren't, but it was also going to serve me a whole lot better than pissing him off with bravado.

"I will say this one more time." He expelled a long breath, and I could imagine him pinching the bridge of his nose. "You come back, you stay in, you shut up, you speak when instructed and at no other time."

I backed up to the dusty sofa and reached blindly behind me for it, then sat, dropping my forehead into my free hand. "What happened to us? When did you become my keeper?"

"The moment you became an escaped prisoner."

"And before that?" I couldn't help the tears that came. And, worse, the sadness that sank my heart. "Before I escaped, was I your prisoner then, too?"

"Was it so bad?" I could see him shrug. *Meh.*

Like it meant so incredibly little to him that my *whole life with him* had been a lie.

And that, goddammit, I cared enough, even now, to feel huge grief at its loss.

"No," I lied, and stood up, my legs moving like mechanical limbs or something driven by remote. "No," I repeated, going to the door and opening it quietly, thinking to throw the deadbolt on my way out, so it wouldn't lock behind me. "Obviously it hasn't been that bad. I love you, Leif." The words tasted like poison on my tongue now. In my whole mouth. Like when you spray disinfectant in the air and accidentally inhale it.

"And?" He wasn't sure about my sudden turn-around. He wasn't that stupid, and he wasn't that easy.

But when it came to his ego, he wasn't that smart or complicated, either.

"I need to know that you will never, ever cheat on me again," I said, because that was the first—and very least—demand he would have expected of me.

"Who said I ever did?"

This was chess, I reminded myself. I was playing chess. He didn't have that much faith in me, though; he thought I was a blind idiot, so he was still playing checkers. If I went too soft, he'd figure me out. I'd already gone off on him about cheating; there was no putting the smoke back in the chimney. So no, I had to go hard, but not too hard.

"You know you did," I said. "You know it, I know it, she knows it. In fact, a whole bunch of *shes* know it." I sounded more like myself now, even though I didn't *feel* like myself at all, going down the dingy, dark cement steps of my new digs and walking out onto the eerie quiet of wee-hours M Street. "I don't even want to talk about them anymore. I don't want to *think* about them. But there cannot be any more." I turned right at the corner and headed south two blocks.

"If you don't go fishing," he said, oozing confidence, "you won't find yourself with a bunch of fish."

"Likewise." I could have puked.

"So you're coming back," he asked, and it wasn't even a question. I could tell from his tone that he was sure he'd won, sure my tail was firmly between my legs and I was returning to the "safety" of his rule.

I sighed.

He chuckled. I gagged. "That's a yes, then." Not a question, a statement. Naturally.

"I suppose." I wished I could lie as easily as he could. "But I drove for hours and just got here when you called." I prayed my casualness was convincing. "So I'm just going to sleep first. I already paid for the night, after all. Or *you* did." Was I laying it on too thick?

"There's nothing on the credit card statement," he said. Because of course he'd checked.

"Cash, Leif. You think I wanted you to know I came down here?"

"Down—wait, you went all the way to Hilton Head?"

Hilton Head was one of my favorite vacation destinations. For a brief time I'd owned a condo there and had a lot of fun fixing it up and renting it out, in addition to going down whenever I could for my own time off. When I'd said "down here" to him, I only wanted to indicate I hadn't gone north, but he'd taken it and run with it, and I was going to let him.

And sickeningly, that weak woman inside me loved the fact that Leif Tiesman knew me well enough to know where I would be most likely to run away to.

But, the stronger person in me said, *I didn't run there. For once, I did something different.*

"Guess I'm not all that unpredictable, huh?" I gave a lame-sounding laugh. "No wonder you're bored with me." Just the words made me feel ill. I had *thought* that about myself, in comparison to his glamorous self, for so long, and now that I was starting to see his true colors, it absolutely sickened me to pretend to bow and scrape in comparison to him.

"You're good at what you're good at," he said, his monotone voice as complimentary as it ever got.

"And that is?"

"Being Mrs. Leif Tiesman."

"Ah."

"While you're down there?" he went on. "Maybe take a couple of days and go to a medispa or something to get *refreshed,* would you? You could use a little Botox on your forehead. You always seem to look angry lately."

Gee, why would that be?

"Good idea," I said. "Prepare yourself for a considerable bill." Because that's how it would have been if I'd been telling the truth.

He laughed. *That,* of all things, gave him a genuine laugh. "Bring it on. Just come home pretty."

Ew.

"I'll think about it," I said. He could never accuse me later of having lied, then, could he? He couldn't say I'd specifically promised to return to Virginia, as I had no intention of ever doing so.

In fact, he could never accuse me of anything again, because he'd never be able to find me. This conversation might have bought me a few days, but now I had to buy myself a whole new life.

"So I'll see you in a couple of days?" he prodded.

"Whatever you want."

"Thursday, then. I'll tell everyone you're on a girls' trip or something."

"Perfect." Like I had girlfriends. He'd success-fully isolated me from everyone. Funny, though, his own cover story showed how unlikely he was ever to figure out the truth. "Bye, Leif."

"Be good," he said, a command, not a playful comment.

"Right."

I left. I drove until I stopped at the edge of the Potomac River. There was a large harbor a few blocks west, at the end of Wisconsin Avenue, all lit up like a party all the time, but I was in a quiet little nook by a lock that ran parallel to the river. Laughter and voices carried out over the water, people having fun, enjoying themselves, enjoying each other. I used to be one of those people.

They had no idea this tortured, foolish woman was just a few blocks over, trying to get rid of a life she'd spent years building.

How many times had my bubbly voice risen above the group's din, or my own laugh spiked the nighttime loud enough for someone across the river to hear? Had a broken woman ever heard me, envied me?

I did, now. Broken Di envied the young, unbroken Di.

I took a deep breath, pressed the power button on my phone hard, to shut it down completely, just in case there was some sonar technology I was unaware of, and then threw it as hard as I could into the river.

Did I mention I used to be on the softball team in high school? Well, I'd lost quite a bit of talent, but at least the thing went far enough that, given its density, it would never wash up on shore.

And with it went Diana Tiesman. Twenty yards out and six feet down.

Better it than me. Hopefully he hadn't already traced it.

I got back to the apartment above the shop and discovered that no, the toilet was in fact *not* too gross to puke in.

Chapter Fifteen

Prinny

It had been a long, gorgeous, successful day at Cosmos. The weather had been beautiful, bringing lots of foot traffic by and into the shop. Even with Gail, the part-time cashier who was always ready to work in a pinch, Prinny had spent the entire afternoon feeling overwhelmed. Gail didn't know much about the merchandise, but she was fast and efficient at ringing up sales. Normally that was enough. But today they'd outsold their previous year's best by nearly threefold, and it was only 6:00 P.M. when *she* came in.

Prinny knew who she was immediately, probably could have sensed her without so much as a glance in her direction. As a matter of fact, she probably could have sensed her *faster* without a glance, since today she was sporting chunky platinum highlights in her light chestnut hair—a passé look that she somehow managed to rock—instead of the glossy dark lion's mane she wore in the picture on Alex's desk.

The picture of them on some beach at night, their happy faces illuminated by the camera's flash.

It had always struck Prinny as odd that he had chosen a low-quality snapshot to frame instead of the usual wedding picture or otherwise posed shot, but looking at the woman's face now—a serious, sexy, narrow blend of aristocratic features—she knew exactly why he liked the picture he'd chosen: They looked happy.

This woman, beautiful as she was, didn't look happy. She had the sort of chronic Resting Bitch Face that rarely looked happy.

"I want a psychic reading," she said.

Prinny reached for the book under the counter. "I can schedule an appointment for you with Ada. When would you like to come in?" *Anytime but now,* she thought frantically. *Say you'll come back.*

"Now," Britni Spencer-McConnell said. "I'm here now." She waved an arm airily toward the sign on the door. "It says walk-ins welcome." There was nothing bitchy or argumentative about her tone at all, yet the commanding air of it made Prinny recoil inwardly.

Thank God she didn't reach out to shake hands

or something, Prinny thought. She was positively repelled by the woman. Not her fault, of course. She didn't marry Alex with the plan that it would someday break Prinny's heart.

"I'm afraid our system is down and we're only accepting cash this evening," Prinny tried, hoping to stave her off that way.

"No problem."

She wanted the reading and she wanted it tonight and there was no changing her mind. She was impulsive, spent a lot of money this way. The less available something was, the more she wanted it.

"Oh." Prinny straightened. "Okay, then." There was no winning this one. She signaled to Gail. "I'm going to do a reading in the back. If you could just keep an eye on the register?"

"Sure thing!" Gail chirped, like nothing in the world was wrong.

Like Prinny wasn't about to see a whole lot of stuff she really shouldn't see.

Prinny didn't usually do readings. Weirdly enough, she got a kind of stage fright and sometimes just froze up and seemed fake. Or she thought she must seem fake. Who believes in a seer who is all nervous and sweaty and *um* this and *ah* that?

It wasn't just that she was extremely self-conscious, though that was a considerable part of it. One of the things she remembered most clearly about her childhood, though she couldn't explain it, was that she had hidden a lot. Found hiding places in every single room. Behind the large drapes in one room; in the cabinet beneath the bookcase in another; behind her headboard, which was tricky, but under the bed was too obvious; she'd even literally hidden inside the dryer, just like so many urban legends had warned against. But no one had turned it on, and she was positive that even if they had, she would have been able to kick it open.

Anyway, yes, she was self-conscious, and yes, that contributed to her problems with being "onstage," even in front of one single person for whom she was doing a reading.

But even more than that, she was acutely aware of how important it was that she get it right. People counted on this. Admittedly, there were many false psychics out there—far more fake ones than real ones—because it was easy to prey upon a person's need for validation in any or all areas. *You're doing great, just keep going* or *Sit it out, the good will come, the bad will pass* . . . Those two statements were usually true, but there was an important distinction between them, and when faced with an emotionally vulnerable person, Prinny was always afraid she was going to overcompensate one way or the other to make the person feel better.

That's why Chelsea was such a great reader.

Way better than she thought, by the way. She'd spent years trying to understand what would make a character act a certain way. That was what made her readings so wonderfully raw and real. Every satisfied customer felt like a triumph for Chelsea, Prinny knew. And was that a bad thing? If it validated her passion for acting *and* genuinely served those who came in for help, was it wrong to let her think she was a faker even when she wasn't?

That was the kind of crazy moral question Prinny was faced with every day.

Like now. Reading Alex McConnell's wife.

"This way." Prinny led Britni to the small room in back that she'd embellished so warmly for readings. The peach walls glowed softly under indirect lighting, and the room smelled of a strange mixture of peony, rose, and tobacco from the candle Diana had recently made as an experiment in the use of spent herbs and essential oils.

"This is sweet," Britni murmured, taking in the surroundings. "Very quaint."

Quaint. Sweet. The words niggled, even though, from anyone else, they would have been a perfectly nice compliment. As it was, Prinny had to force herself to sound gracious. "Thank you so much. Please have a seat. Would you like some tea?" A wicked little joke crossed her mind about hemlock tea, and she chastised herself for even thinking it.

Though, could something like hemlock tea be made? Not that Prinny was serious, but was it possible for a person to just buy hemlock and soak it in boiling water and serve it to someone? And if so, would that be truly fatal, or were the stories of Aristotle and the so-called hemlock brew exaggerated for the sake of drama?

"No tea," Britni said. "I don't suppose you have wine."

"No, sorry." Not for public consumption. But why not? Why on earth didn't they? Lord knows she got that question all the time.

She was tempted to offer Britni a glass of the wine she *did* have in the back, just informally, but she wasn't sure that was legal.

"That's all right." Britni sighed. "Dean and DeLuca is my next stop. I suppose I can make it a few more minutes." She gave a small, unamused laugh. *I'm kidding but not really.*

Prinny found herself wondering why anyone who was fortunate enough to be married to Alex McConnell—to get to see him all the time, last thing at night and first thing in the morning, if she wanted—would have such a seemingly urgent need for wine.

Definitely not a happy woman. Not depressed, either. Bored. Terminally bored. Prinny got a flash of the feeling, and it choked through her ribs. *Nothing could give Britni McConnell pleasure even though she kept on trying to buy it.*

"What brought you in here tonight?" Prinny asked.

"Oh, I don't know. When I saw the sign out front tonight, it felt like fate or something. I have a . . . friend . . . who has mentioned this place a few times."

"Is your friend a customer?" Prinny's question was sincere. The connection to Alex was obvious, but she couldn't quite see him chatting about Cosmos, or Prinny, around the house.

"Not really." She didn't elaborate, and there was no good reason to ask her to.

And there was nothing beneath it to pick up on.

Prinny took out her own tarot deck, as opposed to the one Chelsea usually used, and set it on the table. "Shuffle."

She was nervous suddenly. Afraid of her truths, the ones she knew and the ones she didn't know.

A lot of people got that feeling. It was like waiting for a doctor to give test results—even though there might be a hopeful outcome, the fear of disappointment was always there.

She took the cards and shuffled them in silence. The air in the room seemed to thicken, and Prinny longed to open the door, but they were too close to the rest of the store. She and Chelsea never did private readings with an open door.

Yet still Prinny felt somehow deceptive doing this. As if she should make some admission to Britni, tell her she knew Alex or that she was likely the reason Alex had mentioned the store, or that she wanted Alex and that she hoped with all her own little black heart that she was going to read a divorce in the cards, which went against every standard and principle she had for reading.

But Britni shuffled on, oblivious to Prinny's frenzied thoughts; she was just trying very hard to sense the right time to stop. She wanted this to go well.

When she'd finished, she set the deck down.

"Cut three times to the left."

She did.

Prinny put her hand on top of the deck and closed her eyes. "Now say your full name."

"Britni Marie Spencer. But people call me Brit."

Prinny frowned, opened her eyes. "Spencer?"

"That's right."

"But I thought you were married." That was stupid. Why did she even say that? Maybe Britni went by her maiden name. Or maybe that "was" her married name, for all Prinny knew. Prinny was letting her personal knowledge get in the way of things.

Britni—Brit, now—apparently didn't notice anything weird about the comment and simply gave a laugh. "I am. Wow, you picked up on that fast."

"No, it's just—"

"That's one of my big questions. What's going to happen with my marriage."

Ask who Roberto is.

"Who is Roberto?" she asked, though usually at that point she would have asked if Roberto was the husband because she wouldn't have known otherwise.

Brit looked at her with shock, her face draining of color. "I—I beg your pardon?" Her immediate instinct—to bluff, to lie, to come up with any other answer—filled the room like fog.

"Who is Roberto?" Prinny asked, though the answer was coming clear to her. *Roberto is the boyfriend. Unclear if Brit can love, but she wants him. She wants to marry him. He excites her. She wants to know if she's going to marry him.* "He's not your husband."

Will be. Will be.

Cold washed over Prinny. She'd read for friends before, so it wasn't normally a problem to know a few personal facts about her questioner, but she'd never had the experience of knowing far more *facts* than the questioner realized.

Would it have been more ethical to say right up front that she recognized Brit from the picture on Alex's desk and therefore couldn't be impartial? Maybe. But that would have opened a whole new can of worms and possibly even gotten Alex into hot water for something he didn't do or have any knowledge of.

"I want to know," Brit began carefully, "if I have a future with Roberto."

Yes.

"Yes." But what happens to Alex? Prinny couldn't see that. No obvious answers came to her about that. She could see, and hear, and sense, only the things that Britni was so intently focused on three feet in front of her. Britni's energy superseded everything else. As it should in a reading. Prinny really shouldn't have done this. But now it was too late to do anything but press forward. "I see a ring."

Three large fine diamonds, each encircled with smaller diamonds, set in platinum.

A pretty flush crept into Britni's cheeks. "I've seen it, too. He doesn't know I've seen it, but I suspected . . . Do you know if it's the Tiffany one?"

Prinny concentrated. "No, I can't see that." And she couldn't. She just saw the diamonds and the band. The eternal circle. Easily broken when the two people weren't right for each other. Usually they weren't. "But you have a husband now."

"Yes." Brit sighed. "I don't know *what* to do about that. If my husband finds out there's another guy, he'll flip out."

"I don't think he's the flipping-out sort."

Something like surprise flickered briefly across Brit's expression. "Actually, you're kind of right. It would be a very quiet flip-out. The kind that would lose me a lot of alimony."

She didn't love him.

Had she ever loved him?

Prinny asked but couldn't get an answer.

"Should I leave my husband?"

Yes, everything inside Prinny said. But it wasn't a psychic answer. She didn't get psychic advice herself, only facts. It was up to her to wrangle it into advice when needed. The *yes* that was yearning to come out of her now was personal, self-serving, and completely unfair.

"I'm sorry," Prinny said, gathering up the cards. "I can't see anything more."

"What? That was barely, what, five minutes?"

"No charge."

"I'm not worried about the charge, I wanted a whole reading! Why are you quitting?" Fear gripped her posture. "Did you see something terrible? Is there something you don't want to tell me?"

This was always the fear with clients; one always had to be very, very careful not to inadvertently lead them to believe they were doomed.

"No," Prinny said quickly, then faked a laugh. "It's not that at all, I just don't have the full"— she gestured blankly—"psychic energy tonight to do this reading."

"You have a sign right out front that says otherwise."

"Well, technically, it doesn't guarantee—"

"Come on." Britni gave Prinny an impatient

look. "You know damn well this is terrible customer service."

"I'm sorry. I was getting crossed signals for some reason." True, though she knew the reason. "I wasn't going to be able to give you what you were looking for."

Neither will Roberto, a sarcastic voice in her chirped.

"That's clear." Britni braced her hands on the table, and for a moment Prinny was afraid she might flip the whole damn thing.

"You are welcome to come back and get a reading from Miss Ada. On the house." She probably shouldn't have added that, but part of her was morbidly fascinated by seeing Britni in person.

"No, thanks." Britni stood up and hefted her purse over her shoulder. "I don't think the vibe is right for me here."

That was for sure.

"I'm sorry," Prinny said helplessly.

But as she watched Britni huffing out of the store, frustration pouring from her, almost like a cartoon character with smoke shooting out of its ears, she could see the same woman, the same stride, walking away from her husband.

Alex McConnell.

Something bad was about to go down.

The teas were going to be a hit. A big hit. It was just the "something extra" they'd been needing.

Diana was an absolute magician with herbs. Prinny had tried her teas several times over the years, though they'd just been flavored ones, rather than medicinal. She had a blood orange and clove blend that she'd used for iced tea during one summer visit three years ago, and Prinny had been dreaming about it ever since. The aroma, the ethereal light green glow of it, the way Diana had served it in tall bubble glasses with sugared rims . . . it had all added so much to the ambiance of that summer afternoon on Leif and Diana's beautiful wraparound veranda.

For Prinny, socializing with Leif was rare, of course, but her father had wanted to go and visit, and he was too infirm to drive by then, so Prinny had volunteered. Now that she thought about it, that was the last time she'd been to Leif and Diana's house. It had been uncomfortable, even with her father there, though she'd been awfully grateful for Diana's calm demeanor at that time, as Leif, even then, had been strong-arming their father regarding his will.

"There should be a trust," she had overheard Leif saying to him in the other room while she was in the kitchen with Diana, chatting about little butter cookies or something equally innocuous. Exactly what men like Leif would expect women like Diana and Prinny to discuss.

"I've already spoken to my lawyer about it all," her father had said, noticeably weary.

"Are you sure that Prinny is"—there had been the slightest hesitation—"taken care of?"

"Of course."

"Perhaps you should assign me as the executor."

"Leif." It was only the one syllable, but it held a strong warning tone against continuing the line of conversation.

And so it changed to the coming Redskins season and who was in what starting position.

When Prinny turned back to Diana, her sister-in-law was looking at her thoughtfully.

"I'm sorry you had to hear that," Diana said, looking down and busying herself with arranging the cookies on the plate.

"Hear what?"

"Leif. I'm sure you don't like thinking about your father's will, or the need for it, much less your brother's ideas about it."

Prinny had to laugh. "You're right."

"For what it's worth, he's like that about everything. Everyone. He's always worried about getting what's due him."

"If he got what was *due* him . . . ," Prinny began.

Diana caught her eye and nodded. "I know."

Prinny could read into the moment that Diana knew much more than she did about what was *due* Leif. In fact, Prinny could see, hear, feel, almost even *taste* the fact that Diana was being lied to and cheated on and that it was pounding her self-esteem into a tiny block of steel.

"Any way to make this a Long Island Iced Tea?" she asked Diana with a smile.

"Better. A French Sixty-nine." Diana poured the glasses about three-quarters full, then took gin off the shelf and poured a dollop in each, adding a squeeze of lemon juice and a sugar cube from the tea supplies. Then she went to the fridge, took a bottle of champagne from the door—already opened, Prinny noticed, and ignored the thought that Diana had been drinking alone—and topped the glasses with it. She took a couple of strawberries off the beautiful tray of cookies and dropped one in each drink before holding one out to Prinny and saying, "Cheers."

Prinny clinked her glass against Diana's and took a sip. It was delicious. She'd never had anything like it; citrusy and bright and bubbly, yet with that distinct caffeine hit of green tea. "Where did you learn to make this? You are a genius."

"I'm not," Diana objected. "I'm just a bartender at heart. A bartender and a witch doctor."

"Where did you learn to concoct the teas themselves?" Prinny asked. "It would never have occurred to me to do anything but buy it."

"But it's better fresh, don't you think?"

"Oh, definitely."

"The herbalist at the acupuncturist's office where I work was retiring, and I managed to convince them all it was a brilliant idea to teach me to carry on the job. Incredibly, they did."

That was when Prinny had learned that Diana could make medicinal teas as well. Actually, *medicine,* Diana had pointed out. "Medicinal tea" implied something you could get from the grocery store and safely help yourself to without regard to quantity, but the teas she made were sometimes quite potent.

There had been many sleepless nights when a stressed-out Prinny had wondered what kind of tea Diana could make to knock her out, but they weren't that close. Though they got along when they saw each other and there was that hum of sympathy between them, it was always understood somehow that Leif wouldn't like it if they were close, and they wouldn't like it if Leif was pissed off about one more damn thing, so they had kept a cordial distance from each other.

So when Diana had arrived at the store and needed work, it was easy for Prinny to jump right into the idea. Especially when Diana had explained that her ingredients came from a prominent distributor who was very stringent about quality control. Prinny had been surprised when she talked about control over herb distribution until Diana had pointed out, obviously, pot.

"That's the least of it," Diana had said. "A well-stocked tea cabinet could literally kill you."

"Literally?" Prinny had a horrible vision of

some hapless puppy getting into a kitchen pantry and consuming some horrible herb. "Or do you mean if you add rat poison and poisonous mushrooms and whatnot?"

"Literally. Seriously, Prinny, never piss your homeopathic practitioner off. It could be deadly." She'd considered for a moment. "If only because of allergies. You should make sure you have a waiver for people buying medicinal. You don't want someone suing you because they got the sniffles."

Prinny wasn't as business-stupid as people sometimes seemed to think she was.

Alex was the only one who took her seriously enough to bat her ideas around with her.

She probably asked too many questions and lingered too long over his concerns, but that was only because she wanted to spend more time with him. Not *probably;* it was *obvious.* It was just really damn unfortunate, because he was married and that was that. Unhappily, yes, but married nonetheless. And nothing could ever come of them together.

Yet even so she enjoyed her moments with him; the repartee, the back-and-forth, and sometimes just the reassuring sound of his voice. Actually, *often* it was the reassuring sound of his voice that she needed. Because *often* she was up against the wall in terms of proving herself.

Over and over again.

"So I signed the lease for the place next door," she said.

"Good," he said. "Good."

"And I had an idea." This was probably going to be a tough sell.

"Did you?" He looked interested.

"I did. Today. It hit me suddenly, but I am absolutely sure it is the way out of all of my problems. To make the business grow like nothing this town has seen in a long time."

"You certainly have my attention."

He was playing with her. She amused him. He liked this; it added levity to his life that wasn't usually there.

Her heart both broke at the idea of his heavy life and bloomed at the idea of lightening it.

"You might think it's crazy," she said, smiling.

He smiled back and shrugged and gave his familiar mantra. "It's your money. Now tell me. What have you decided? As I recall, it was workshops."

"Well, yes, workshops. That was the plan initially. And I still want to do them," she hurried to add. "But I came up with a little extra something that's going to make the business take off."

"And what's that?"

"I want to get a liquor license."

"A *liquor* license." He frowned. "And open, what, a bar?"

"Actually, it began with tea. I wanted to sort of turn the place into a teahouse."

"I'm sorry." *He was concerned.* "Did you say *tea?* Like you drink?" He mocked drinking a cup of tea, pinkie out and all. "That kind of tea?"

She nodded. "Yup."

"Not edibles, at least."

She laughed. "Nope. I have a person who makes medicinal teas, and I've been enjoying them for a few days. It's really amazing how well they can work. But then it occurred to me—there are metaphysical shops and there are bars, but there's no place doing *both.*"

He leaned back and steepled his fingers in front of his face for a moment, then sighed, returned his gaze to her, and said, "This is going to set Leif into orbit, you know."

That was another thing she loved about Alex. He understood Leif. He understood the kind of selfish man he was, and the kind of muscles— legal, financial, and emotional—that Leif was willing to flex in order to crush her.

In fact, maybe most important, Alex understood that Leif wanted to crush her.

Prinny knew it, too, of course, but that was where her resources left her. She knew that he wanted her to go down, but she wasn't sure where he was burying the land mines.

"Do I care?" she asked Alex. "I mean, there's nothing he can do. I could invest every penny into a miniature horse farm in Monaco and he wouldn't have a leg to stand on, right?"

Alex grimaced. "He'd try. He'd make an argument about your sanity, and then, as your next of kin, he'd probably try and get power of attorney."

"I should get married," Prinny commented.

She didn't really mean it, but she was struck by the way Alex stiffened when she said it. His reaction to the very word sent a shock of negativity into the room.

"Has someone proposed?" he asked, just a little too casually. He tapped his fingertips on the desk three times. "I didn't know you were with anyone. I apologize."

She laughed. "I'm not, but I can see the advantage of a marriage of convenience!"

His shoulders relaxed fractionally. "So no fiancé."

"Nope."

His face colored slightly, and he quickly added, "And no miniature horse farm?"

She shrugged. "Never say never, but so far it's just Cosmos." She slumped back in her chair and regarded him. He was just so cute. There was such a charming boyishness under his tailored suit and serious visage. "What do you think of the tea bar idea? For real."

"For real?" A smile played at his mouth. She knew he found her charming. That was one of the many things she found charming about *him*.

He seemed to see who she really was, and he seemed to like it. "I think it *could be* a great idea."

She hadn't been expecting that.

"Please tell me you're not pulling my leg," she said.

He shook his head. "Not at all. If your new person is as good at this as you say, and word gets around about it, I think it's a very reasonable segue into retail for you. If you're mixing teas and spirits, I see the possibility of doing that retail as well."

"We already do retail!" she objected.

He waved that off. "Four, five thousand bucks a month. You're not a serious presence."

But they needed to be. She now had two employees, plus her own salary, and her rent was going way up. And she had absolute faith that it would be worth it, because of the tea and the added room for workshops, but even for a psychic *absolute faith* sometimes wobbled. "We will be."

"You can be."

His phone rang; he looked at it, and she noticed a tiny muscle twitch in his jaw. He pushed a button, and the ringing stopped.

"No calls after hours, huh?" she joked, noting that she'd been sitting there half an hour past the time when his secretary usually left. They were alone in the office.

A shiver ran through her.

It was her. Britni. She'd been trying to have a

talk with him for some time now. He was avoiding it. Everything was a fight between them. He was avoiding her.

"Some conversations are better had through voice mail," he answered, and she noticed the light was gone from his eyes. His tone had changed, and the playful air between them had gone stale.

Not only did he not want to talk to her, but probably the only reason he was still here, spending his valuable time talking about miniature horse farms and gypsy teas, was because he didn't want to go home.

She wanted to prod him on the subject, but it was none of her business, and the last thing in the world she wanted was to let her stupid crush on a married man get out of hand.

It was one thing to admire qualities in him and hope to perhaps one day meet a man who possessed some of those same qualities, but it was quite another to be glad at signs that he might be a bit less than in love with his wife.

"I'd better go," she said, because a moment longer and she'd be asking pointed questions that were none of her business. She stood up. "I'll look into the liquor license and e-mail you the ratified lease as soon as I have it."

"And the information on the new employee," he added.

"The . . . ?"

"The tea girl. The one who's making the teas.

Send me her information and W-4 and whatnot."

"Oh. That." Prinny sank back into her seat.

"Prinny?"

"Yeah, I have a nonstandard arrangement worked out with her. I'm compensating her rent in the unit upstairs from the shop and then paying the rest under the table."

Alex sighed and his chair squeaked as he leaned back, templing his hands before him. "And why is that?"

"Because it's easier?"

"For whom? It's illegal to pay *or compensate* over a certain amount without filing a 1099. I don't suppose you were planning on filing a 1099?"

Prinny shook her head. "She needs to stay somewhat . . . anonymous." There was no way he was going to let this slide.

"Don't tell me you're handing Leif an immigration cupcake to bite into."

"Worse, I'm afraid. It's his wife."

Alex looked at her for a moment in stunned silence, then laughed. "His *wife?* His *wife* is working at Cosmos now?"

Prinny nodded, but she wasn't sure what his laughter meant. "She makes the teas."

"How on earth did he let that happen?" He frowned thoughtfully. "Maybe your problems with him are over if he's letting you employ his wife in what I believe he last referred to as 'that patchouli-scented, idiot-filled box of magical rocks.' "

Anger rose in Prinny. "He *said* that?"

"Oh, come on, you know he always says that kind of thing." *Guilt filled him. He didn't think highly of Leif but he didn't want to hurt her with Leif's words.*

But, yes, she knew. Of course she knew. In fact, Leif often even brought her mother into it, talking about her "voodoo" and, yes, the "magical rocks" and various other weird little insults about her interest in spiritual things.

Alex cleared his throat. "I guess he's had a turn-around, then. At least as far as respecting the fact that the business has legs. That's refreshing news."

"He has?"

Alex shrugged broadly. "He must have, if his wife is working there, right?"

"Oh. Yeah, no, he's not. He doesn't know she's there. In fact, that's why I don't want her pay to be traceable. Actually, that's why *she* doesn't want her pay to be traceable. She doesn't want him to find her."

"You've got to be kidding."

"I'm afraid not." Prinny looked at him imploringly. "And she's got a talent that she's finally able to use, with confidence, without that jerk breathing down her neck. I know it's *ironic* that she's working with me—"

Alex scoffed.

"—but it's obvious to me that it was meant to be. She needed a place where she'd be welcome and understood. And since she and I both have no desire to incite Leif, it works out perfectly."

"Unless you consider the fact that you're handing Leif added reason to want to blow you out of the water and added ammunition with which to do it."

"He doesn't even know she's there!"

"If his wife has disappeared without an apparent trace, he's going to find her. Or have someone find her. Come on, Prinny, that's child's play for a man with his resources."

"I'm not so sure. In a way, she's hidden right out in the open. Just in a place he'd never look. He hates me; he'd assume his wife is aligned with that viewpoint, and always has been. He definitely would never think she'd come to me."

"Did she ever call you from her phone?"

"No! She has a TracPhone."

"Car?"

"I don't know. I think she dumped it somewhere."

He started to say something else, then stopped and shook his head. "This is a ridiculous conversation. Suddenly I'm plotting a movie. Look, it's none of my business what you and she do; there are no legal implications that I know of. But Prinny"—he leaned forward and looked so deep into her eyes that her breath caught in her chest—

"he is a powerful man. A powerful, *spiteful* man. And that makes him a powerful, spiteful enemy for you."

A ripple of fear corseted her. "He'd never take a chance on actually *harming* either of us."

"I hope not," Alex said. "I really and truly hope not."

Chapter Sixteen

Chelsea

"Please," Andrew whined from his "work recliner," a leather study chair that was really closer to a stiff, sleek leather torture device. It was about as far from a La-Z-Boy as humanly possible. "If I sit around this place one more night, working until my fingers ache, I'll die. My fingers are starting to permanently look like they're doing spider impressions."

"You were just out night before last!" Chelsea said, laughing. She'd seen the pictures of him with his other girlfriends. She knew he liked her best, but part of her had envied the carefree fun the rest of them were all out having. The high heels, the tight dresses wrapped around still-hot bods, the actual makeup. The energetic music that blasted from bass-heavy speakers. The pregaming bottle of champagne that kicked off a night of Vodka Cranberrys out on the town. She remembered that fun fondly, but as if she were small and feeble, remembering the glory days.

"Yes!" said Andrew. "And it sucked! Jason bailed early, and I was stuck talking to a bunch of weirdo sycophants."

"Oh, I'm sure you loved it."

"Yeah, I would, except none of them were the *least* bit interesting. Not even, like, douchey-but-hilarious or anything. And it was disgusting out, so I wasn't really trying to go bar to bar. Do you see all this?" He gestured at the expanse of hardwood floor, completely covered in neatly lined pieces of paper. Andrew said he couldn't rearrange his work on a computer; it stressed him out. So he printed it out so he could hover over it physically while he panicked. She knew part of the reason he did it was for his blog and social media, where he posted Extremely Artistic pictures of his Extremely Artistic process.

"Yeah, you're right. You have a lot of work to do. You should probably stay in."

"Yes, Chel, that's why I need a break from it."

Chelsea slouched on the floor, leaning against the hand-shaped chair, and pushed slowly with her bare toes at one of the papers. "Soo much work . . ."

"Seriously, it'll do you good to get out and actually do something. You've been mooning around over Mike for what feels like forever."

"It does feel like that." She put a hand to her

head and a hand on her hip. "It's not about him, though. I'm over him. Really. It's the general malaise that comes from breaking up with your soul mate. That's all. No big deal!" She shouted the last part at him dramatically.

He raised his perfect thick eyebrows and rolled his chair over to her, picking up the open bottle of Cabernet on the way. "Glass, lady."

"It just seems so ridiculous now," she said, picking up the conversation they'd been having before Andrew decided that the remedy was going out.

"What seems ridiculous, this moping? You're right."

"No." She pushed his chair, and he rolled back a few inches. "That I broke up with Mike. I mean, I loved him. He was my best friend. Diana's over here hiding from an abusive man who's obviously compensating for some . . ."

"Shortcoming?" Andrew filled in.

She couldn't help giving a laugh. "Sure. And I'm just this midtwenties brat who broke up with the perfect guy two years ago and still isn't over it. And I broke up with him because we were too happy. Too settled."

"Don't rewrite history, love." He cranked open a window and sat by it with his cigarette. "You left him because he wasn't enough. You left him because you wanted a big life with a big love."

"Yeah, and what am I doing? I'm failing at

my craft, or whatever you want to call it, and struggling to make ends meet. Working twenty-four/seven, complaining as often, and definitely not having a better life."

"You have no idea what your life would be like now. You could be miserable. And *pregnant*. Count your blessings."

She sighed. "I know."

"Plus, how do you know this Leif guy isn't Diana's Mike? Maybe she loved him only enough to marry him, and she should have kept looking."

"No . . . you should have heard the way she talked about their beginning. That sounded like real love."

"Well, I didn't hear her. But I can tell you that if you want to talk about rewriting history, that is exactly what you've done with Mike. Whenever you talk about it nowadays, it's all got this pretty pink lens on it. I was there, don't forget. You two fought like stray cats and had sex like—whatever the opposite of a rabbit is."

"Oh, come on, our relationship wasn't bad."

"I'm not saying it was. But what I am saying is that when you broke up with him and your acquaintances started making you seem like Ross and Rachel or Cory and Topanga, I saw it differently. As someone who saw your best and your worst together, I *got* why you broke up with him."

Chelsea stared down at the brick-colored wine, struck a bit dumb by what he'd said. He took silent drags from his cigarette for a few minutes, letting her ruminate on it.

"You're right."

As if he'd known exactly when she'd say it, he said, *"I know I'm right,* Chelsea."

She laughed again, then let out a groan. "I hate when that happens."

"I know you do."

Andrew's phone rang, and he held up his middle finger at it with a scowl, then held up his pointer finger to Chelsea as he stood and took the call. It was some business contact he'd been waiting for hours to hear from. "Of course *now* he calls." He walked into the next room, sounding professional, fifty percent more masculine, and not at all tipsy.

At that moment, Chelsea's own phone buzzed, and she looked down to see a text. She slid open her phone and read:

> Chelsea, it's Diana. I apologize for being such a downer! Don't listen to what I said. They're not all jerks. I didn't want to seem like a No-Hope Nancy to you.

She didn't quite know how to respond, so she set it down and had another sip while she waited for Andrew to return.

Two minutes later, he returned. "I positively hate that guy. What happened while I was gone? Why do you look like someone just told you you're pretty?"

"What?"

"You look pleased but confused, like you always do when you get a compliment. What happened?"

She held up her phone and watched his eyes scan the words. When he reached the end, he said, "If that's not a sign, I don't know what is. Now let's get your ass out on the town. We can go to Saint Marie's first, then maybe——"

"I know you want to say Gin Bar."

"No, tonight is about you!"

"Look, I'm not trying to, like, *meet* someone tonight. Honestly, just going out with you is a good step. Plus, at Gin Bar I can just dance without feeling like everyone there is hitting on any chick that moves and/or has a pulse."

"What about that guy you met at work?"

"What guy?" Jeff. He meant Jeff.

"Hunky statue guy. Michelangelo's David."

"He wasn't David. But"——she shrugged and smiled——"he was Jeff. Why? What about him?"

"Why don't you call and ask him to meet us there? I'd love to get a gander at him."

"No way. I can't just call and ask him out!" Could she?

"Why not? He asked you out and you turned him down! Seems like it's your turn, chickie."

"No, no, no."

"Yes, yes, yes." Andrew reached into her purse and took out her phone. "You call him or I will. I assume you still haven't locked this thing." He pressed a button, and the screen flared to life. "Nope."

"Come on, Andrew!"

"Call him!"

"Okay, okay, okay." She'd had just enough Chardonnay to convince herself that she was feeling risky. But the truth was, she wasn't feeling risky; she'd been wanting to go back and rescind her refusal to go out with him more than once over the past few days.

"You got his number, I assume."

"I did manage that, yes." She looked through her contacts and found *Jeff guy from work.*

"Do it," Andrew urged. "Just do it."

If she didn't, she'd never live it down with Andrew. She knew that. He was relentless about wimpiness. She should have just claimed not to have the number. Now that she'd admitted she did, she was stuck.

So she pressed it.

It rang two times before he answered. Her heart leaped to her throat. "Jeff?"

"Yeah, who's this?"

"Chelsea? From work? At Union Station?" God, she sounded like an idiot. Like she wasn't sure of even one fact about herself. "So listen, my friend Andrew and I were going out for a drink, and we thought you might want to join us."

"Your friend Andrew?"

"Yes, he's a playwright. A really good one, very, very talented." She looked over at Andrew, and he gave her the thumbs-up sign. "Once he almost had a date with Andrew Lloyd Webber even!"

"Don't tell that story!" Andrew hissed, but he was smiling.

"We'll tell you all about it if you meet us."

There was a long hesitation.

Long enough that Chelsea thought they'd lost the connection. "Hello?"

"Uh, yeah." Jeff cleared his throat. "Look, I appreciate the offer, but I'm just . . . I'm not interested. I hope you're not offended."

Her face burned, positively *burned*. "No! No, of course not." She felt sick. Her stomach twisted. She could *not* let on. She did *not* want Andrew to see her disappointment or have any idea how soundly she had just been rejected. "Another time, maybe."

"I'm gonna run now," he said. "See you at work."

"Oh. Okay. Well. Bye!" There was no way Andrew was going to miss how flushed her face was, so she had no choice but to just gush. "His voice makes me so hot!" She hoped she wouldn't puke. She really hoped the humiliation would let go of its grip on her gut and not make her puke.

"I can *see* that!"

"So. Gin Bar?"

Her act seemed to have worked. Andrew smiled. "Well, maybe we can just go there for one drink."

"Okay. So I'll just go home and change."

"No, no, *hell* no," Andrew said. "If that happens you're never coming back out, and I know that."

"I will! I just—"

"Need to get your bearings, need to recoup—|no. Not happening. I've still got that dress of yours I spilled wine on a couple of months ago. You can wear that, and you're already in heels. And God knows you carry around emergency liquid liner and red lipstick wherever you go, since you are not an idiot."

It took an effort to keep up the conversation normally. "Hey, I forgot about that dress—did you get it cleaned, or am I just going out looking like the mess I am inside right now?"

"I got it dry cleaned, obviously. I just forgot to ever *tell you* or give it back."

"Oh, perfect. Helpful." She had more wine. *You know what? Screw Jeff.* He was a jerk. Who was that rude? No one she wanted anything to do with, that was for damn sure.

"Um, are you not about to wear it out? Seems sort of like I saved the day." He started off to his room. "Text the lady back and tell her she got you out of your funk and that you're going *dancing!*"

She finished her wine and formulated a response.

Di, your sorry was not necessary, but it worked out. My friend's been begging me to go out all night, and I just decided to go for it. :) He's convinced dancing at Gin Bar will get me the man of my dreams. Ha. Doubt it, but going anyway.

Diana answered after only a moment:

Ha! I remember the Gin Bar from my own days out on the town. Have fun, I'll see you at work soon!

Chelsea smiled, wondering if she could be talking about the same Gin Bar, since it was primarily a gay hangout. Maybe it didn't used to be.

Fifteen minutes later, her lips and eyes were painted, her dress was on, and she was kicking her leg back and forth, waiting for Andrew, who always took an age to get ready.

When he finally emerged, Chelsea said, "Y'done?"

Andrew laughed. "Shut up. Let's go."

With nothing but his keys left to be momentarily forgotten, they were on their way.

Chelsea had walked, so they took Andrew's car—a shiny, new Mercedes-Benz that looked like a prototype set to release in about five years.

They turned on music, which Chelsea turned down three times before accepting that Andrew was not going allow her to have a quiet night whatsoever.

This was always Chelsea's problem lately, and she knew it. She took life so seriously, despite historically being a fun and excited human being. Since she was little, she was so energetic. For the last year, getting her to loosen up took a magical alignment of the planets.

Andrew had full say in his car, so he turned up the nineties station on Spotify. A little nostalgia never hurt things.

He looked over at her, and when he saw her on her phone he asked, "Seriously, how can you not get excited when Britney accidentally does it again?"

"No, I'm sorry, I just have to check the audition page again. Just real quick."

Andrew rolled his eyes. "If you stay on that thing all night, obsessing over Mike's Facebook, I swear to God I will take it."

"I'm not on his Facebook!" She hid the face of her phone so he couldn't see the essay of texts Mike had indeed sent her.

But Andrew's ability to read a concealed phone screen was like a superpower. "Oh my God. Chels, it really is Mike. You cannot sit here and do this all night. Ignore him. Ignore it. What's he even saying?"

"He's just upset. He's really going through so much, and he just needs someone to talk to."

Andrew made a face that meant he thought she had learned nothing.

"No, I'm sorry, you're still right. I'll stop."

For the first time in God knows how long, she felt her shoulders release their tension. Her resolve needed to be stronger than her silly emotions or her body's physiological manifestation of stress. She needed to Get Out There.

Andrew smiled at the strength in her voice. Chelsea tossed the phone into the backseat. "I'm not even going to bring it with me." It wasn't like it actually had happy connotations for her at the moment.

"Hell yeah, girl."

They made their circuit around town, grabbing a shot or two here, and a martini or two there, before winding up pretty early at Gin Bar.

The bar was practically hidden from the main drag, but she knew about a million people who said it was the best.

A large bouncer in all black, wearing an earpiece, let them in and guided them to an elevator, which let them out into an underground bar lit entirely with ultraviolet lights. It looked as if a bar had been formed out of a radioactive igloo.

Every girl who *was* there was in a bandeau dress and sky-high heels. Lots of engagement rings—

girls just out with friends to have a good time without getting hit on. She knew the type. Most of the guys were dressed impeccably, all with tailored clothes. A gay bar in Northwest D.C. was practically like stepping into the pages of *GQ*.

When Andrew and Chelsea had met, she was the chatty one, the loud one, the one who could tell a dirty joke at a table full of guys. When they were younger, Andrew was the workaholic (even in school), the one in the shadow, the one who got ill from one cigarette. In the last couple of years, he'd loosened up and turned into a million different people's Favorite Friend. For a while, overlapping, they had both been this way. They'd been total partners in crime.

Now Chelsea was the wet blanket, and she was sick of it.

"What do you want? First round's on me!" Andrew shouted over the crescendo of the song.

"Um!" She glanced at bottles behind the bar. "Tanqueray Ten gimlet, please!"

"Rocks or up?"

She gestured upward with a thumb.

The bartender gave Andrew a nod when he ordered, then turned to make the drinks, taking Andrew's Chase card with him.

Chelsea took a deep breath and decided that a night at a bar in Dupont Circle was not the time to have a deep, existential look at herself or to do any real reconsideration. There was time for that tomorrow, or any other day.

The drinks were handed to them, and they made their way into the crowd to look for an empty booth.

It was an extremely small space. Everything was dark at the same time as being blindingly lit, and you could tell immediately that with the lights turned all the way up the place would be unrecognizable. The atmosphere was built around its shadowed corners and well-lit cheekbones, and bottle service that included shining steel champagne buckets and a lineup of expensive vodkas. It was built around strangers sitting on strangers' laps, and subtle rendezvous in the bathrooms with shiny, brassy, unnecessarily golden toilets, whether for drugs or sex or just an uncomfortable exchange.

They sat in an empty corner of cushioned vinyl for a while before an extremely handsome guy came up to Andrew. He invited them both to the VIP table behind the DJ booth.

Andrew looked at her, giving her the look that said, *We don't have to, but oh my God, did you see his beautiful face?*

"Um, free booze," she said, gesturing to get up.

He gave her arm a squeeze and said, "I love you."

After a few more minutes of listening to Andrew flirt, Chelsea went to the bathroom. Both stalls were filled, and she was next in line. A moment of leaning against the wall, and she noticed there were two inverted sets of heels in the closest stall.

So no hope of that one emptying out anytime soon.

All she could hope was that the other stall contained a girl who was not vomiting into her own bare lap.

Luckily, a girl looking feeble on a pair of pumps emerged soon, arms out and supporting herself against the plastic door and partition.

"Thank youuuu," said Chelsea, slipping in after her and beginning the bathroom-bar protocol:

Flush the toilet with one foot, since it wasn't effectively flushed before. This wasn't exactly *not* a challenge, especially in stilettos after a few drinks.

Gather three long rectangles of toilet paper and lay them on the toilet seat in a way that her mother had taught her ages ago.

Then use thigh muscles like a jockey to keep a good distance from the toilet seat anyway.

Finish, check heels for stabbed white flags of surrender/toilet paper trails, and head out to wash hands and check makeup.

"Fuck" came a voice next to her at the other sink.

The girl was probably around five foot eleven, and beautiful. Her brunette hair was pinned and curled in a way that reminded Chelsea of 1940s cigarette girls. She wore a deep scarlet V-necked halter top that Chelsea recognized as a leotard from American Apparel. Her high-waisted black shorts were short but cute. The girl was trying to get hold of herself, clearly not in the habit of crying in bar bathrooms.

Chelsea got her attention with a tap on the forearm, and the girl turned.

"You okay?"

"Yes, sorry, this asshole just . . ." She shook her head and wiped black away from under her lower lashes. "I'm just an idiot." She laughed and smiled.

"I'm sure you're not nearly as stupid as he is. I mean, that's just odds. Guys are wrong so much more often."

She nodded and then tilted her head. "Certain guys, you just feel like you should have known better with, you know?" Her tongue tangled in a way that is indicative almost always of heavy intoxication.

"I feel like that's my actual life, so yes." Chelsea washed her hands and didn't try to console the girl anymore. She knew she didn't need that, and Chelsea knew she wasn't any good at it anyway.

On her way out, she said, "Fuck him, seriously. Forget him," and then checked her heels for toilet paper once more—always her biggest concern when leaving the bathroom.

The girl smiled at her.

Andrew was still in the DJ booth when she emerged.

She gave Andrew a look of encouragement when he looked her way, then crossed the busy dance floor to the bar, chugging the rest of her drink.

She wasn't sure exactly what it was she hoped to get out of going out, but almost every time she did it she thought, *Not this*.

"Can I have a Hendrick's Tonic?" They'd only had whiskey and Cîroc vodka in the VIP, both of which gave her a headache. The whiskey because she didn't do dark liquors, and the Cîroc because it was made from wine grapes and *always* made her sick. She'd already had wine earlier—too much and she'd really regret it.

"Cucumber or lime?"

"Cucumber."

The bartender, who looked about fifteen and had an Afro that added at least four inches to his miniature build, winked at her. "You got it."

Once her drink was ordered, she had almost no choice but to lean against the bar backward and look around the room without letting her eyes land anywhere. The only other option was to use her phone, but she didn't even have it.

"You bored, too?" came a voice next to her.

It was a man, older than she was, whom she had evidently ordered her drink next to and hadn't noticed. He was attractive, she saw now.

"Well, my friend got hit on the second we walked in, so it's not like we got the chance to really hang out before I had to give them space, you know."

"That's the worst," he said. "My buddy did the same thing. He walked in and started bullshitting with some guy, they started talking about some Bravo TV show, and then they were off." He gestured vaguely out into the crowd.

Chelsea laughed. "Not much of a reality TV guy, huh?"

He made a straight line with his mouth. "Not so much. Although I have been known to spend a summer watching *Big Brother* and denying it to everyone I know. I had a girlfriend who was into it."

Girlfriend. Huh.

She'd binge-watched enough *Sex and the City* and been friends with Andrew for too long to believe this meant the guy was straight.

"Hi, I'm Lee."

"Hi, Lee."

He waited a moment before giving a concessionary smile and asking, "And what is your name?"

She smiled. "I'm Chelsea."

She searched his face, trying to make sense of the effect it was having on her. He was part generically handsome, part familiar and comfortable, and part unique. The only thing she knew was that he was immediately appealing.

"What a pretty name. Like the area in London?"

"Most people guess New York!" She was amazed. "But yes, London. My mom went to college there and named me after her favorite part of the city."

"She gave a very pretty name to a very pretty girl."

"Thank you!" Chelsea felt her hopes surge; earlier, she wouldn't have believed that possible.

Maybe Andrew had been exactly right; maybe this was her night. Despite the whole clusterfuck with Jeff earlier. She had thought that was a really bad omen. Certainly it had been embarrassing.

Maybe everything was going to change, finally, starting now.

Chapter Seventeen

Eighteen Years Earlier

The occasion was Leif's twenty-first birthday.

Prinny was eleven and so thrilled to be able to be there for the small family dinner and the cake she'd helped Cook to decorate ("help" basically meant she'd put the two candles, 2 and 1, in the center where Cook pointed).

But Leif's mood was off. It was usually off, she found. He was frequently mean, and when he wasn't, he was chilly. But Prinny knew that was because he'd always been upset that she and her mother had come along and, as he saw it, ended his Original Family.

But Prinny wanted to be his family now. She didn't understand why he was so resistant to it.

So she got him something she knew he'd like, even though it was just a small version.

She handed him the box she'd wrapped herself and sat back, her hand on the back rail of her father's chair, watching in happy anticipation as he opened it.

He threw the paper aside, knowing someone else would pick it up, and looked at the box in shock. It was a model of the car he'd been wanting, a 1965 Mustang convertible. She knew it because he thought about it all the time and had spent a ton of time trying to find one nice enough for him, since apparently there were a bunch of *clunkers* and *pieces of shit* out there, but very few *mint-condition vintage* Mustangs.

This one, at least, was mint condition, as it had never been owned before. How could it have been? It was just a toy from the model section of the toy store.

So why was Leif looking at it like she'd given him a hot potato with hot lava on top?

"What's wrong?" she asked nervously, and felt her father's hand come to rest reassuringly on her shoulder.

"How did you know?" Leif asked, only it wasn't

in that tone of wonder people used when they were thrilled with something. It was accusatory. As if she'd read his diary or something.

She shrugged. "I just . . . *knew.*"

"There's no way you could just *know.*"

"Son," Charlie cautioned.

"What?" Leif shot back. "You know what this is." He picked up the box. "We all know what this is!"

It was a toy car.

Wasn't it?

"And you know where she got it. She got it from her mother. You brought this into our house and into our family!"

"No," Prinny objected, thinking maybe she could clear this whole misunderstanding up and then she'd get that happy smile she'd been waiting for for so long from Leif. "It's from Sullivan's on Wisconsin Avenue. I bought it. I can prove it, Maria was with me!"

Leif gave a mean laugh. "Yeah, *that's* what I meant."

"Leif!" Charlie boomed.

Suddenly Prinny felt like she shouldn't have done this but she didn't know why. She'd been so excited to give him something she knew he wanted, but now it was clear that was *exactly* the wrong thing to have done. *Exactly.*

But why?

"Stop hating me!" she cried. "It's not my fault Mommy and Daddy fell in love."

Leif shot her a look, then transferred it to his father, pointing at her. "See that?"

"Nothing remarkable there. Everyone knows I loved Ingrid. I still do."

Leif nodded in a way that communicated that he did not agree at all. "Everyone knows. Everyone knows. Except not everyone *knows*."

"I don't understand!"

"Shhhh. It's okay," her father soothed her, patting her shoulder. "Leif just has other plans and is feeling a little grumpy because he's running late. Run along now, Leif."

"Me."

"Yes, you. If you can't behave in a civilized manner, you don't need to be here."

Leif looked at her with what seemed like sheer hatred, but Prinny knew that wasn't all there was to it. It was fear. "Don't be afraid," she said, hoping that would, at last, soothe him. Maybe the more she made him understand that she knew him, the more comfortable he'd be. "You're going to have a great night in Georgetown. Can't you just stay with us a little longer?"

Leif rounded on her. "What did you say?"

"Can't you stay—"

"Before that."

"You're going to have a great time in Georgetown." She concentrated. "At Rumors. Right?" She beamed. "That's where you're going, right?"

He shook his head. "This is sick." He didn't look at her again, just at his father. "You know this isn't okay."

"Everything is fine," Charlie said, but Prinny knew he was also rattled, though she didn't know why.

"Yeah, *great*." Leif turned and left the room, leaving the box with the car in it on the chair where he'd dropped it.

This wasn't an ordinary grown-up fight. This was something to do with her. Something to do with Leif's fear of her and her father's . . . she hated to see it, but her father's embarrassment.

But what in the world had she done?

Chapter Eighteen

Chelsea

"So is this the kind of place you frequent?" he asked her. The Gin Bar was still hopping. In fact, it seemed to be getting more and more rowdy as time wore on.

The song changed, suddenly louder.

"Not really."

She watched his lips. He mouthed, *"What?"*

"Not really!" she said, loudly enough this time.

"Yeah, well," he said, speaking closer to her ear, close enough to show that he wore good cologne, "first of all, I'm straight, so." He gave a *there's that* gesture. "But in general, I'm not really about the kinds of places where you feel like you're in the middle of a full-fledged nightmare."

"Oh, going blind and deaf isn't your thing?" She smiled and held a hand up at the startlingly white lights that strobed over the crowd now. "That's so weird of you!"

"Man," he said, drawn out. "This is hell."

Chelsea laughed, the sound drowned out in the repeating beat. Too much for a small space.

She glanced over at Andrew to make sure he was okay, but he looked fine.

"You want to do a shot?" He shouted it at her, and Chelsea heard him, but he leaned closer as if maybe she hadn't. "I feel like the only thing that's going to get me through this is a shot or two."

She nodded. "Sure!"

A few seconds later, a bartender was pouring deep brown liquid from an ornate round bottle into two shot glasses. *Dammit,* she thought. She should have specified.

Lee took both and handed one to her. "What should we cheers to exactly? Hating our lives right now?"

"Um"—she looked around—"the last night of our most useful senses? Saying good-bye to hearing, voice, and vision?"

He laughed and clinked his glass against hers.

She let the liquid trickle and burn down her throat, then set the glass down on the counter, trying to show no reaction whatsoever. God, she hated that stuff. It always seemed to get her drunker, too.

His eyes did a quick flick from hers to somewhere indistinct on her body. "You're something."

She shrugged. It wasn't actually so bad, she thought. Getting attention, even just a little flattery, might be just the thing to bring her out of her funk.

"I'm sorry," he said, surprising her. "I don't want to make it seem like I'm hitting on you or anything, because I'm really not. You just seem awesome, and I'm here to kinda, you know, babysit my idiot friend more than anything else." He pointed.

A balding man was dancing with a younger guy probably breaking into his thirties. He was narrow and looked like he might have a Thing for older guys.

"Looks like he's doing okay," she said.

"Yeah! I'm glad; he's been in a rough spot."

There was something in his expression then. Something that cued Chelsea in to thinking he had a lot of consideration around the situation. There was a kindness there.

"How about another shot?" she asked. "This one's on me." That way she could make sure it was vodka.

"Another shot, sure, but on you, no."

She started to argue, but her voice was lost in the noise. She pulled on the back of his shirt as he reached over the bar to order, but he ignored her. She laughed. The last shot was starting to go to her head in a blissful, freeing way.

Two shots were placed in front of them. This time they were pink and fruity-looking. She looked him right in the eyes and had a moment to appreciate the smile playing at the corners of his lips.

"To this not being whiskey," she said, holding up her glass. "Let's keep it that simple."

He laughed; they clinked. Again they drank.

The night evaporated for a bit then. Chelsea lost track of Andrew. She lost track momentarily of her clutch. She couldn't find Andrew. That asshole, he really left her?

Not worth being upset over, she decided. She could get home.

She emerged from the bathroom, thinking at first that the guy she had been talking to—Lee, right?—was also gone. But he wasn't. He was standing against the pillar where she now remembered she had left him.

"You feeling okay?" he asked.

"Oh, no, I'm fine." She heard her own tongue tangling now, and recalled the girl from the beginning of the night. The one she had felt smug and sober in front of, even though she liked her.

"Do you want to get some fresh air?"

She nodded yes, meaning it.

Once out onto the street, in real lighting, she could see that he was actually better-looking than he had seemed in the bar—almost never the case.

He had good bone structure and a broken-in face that told you exactly what he'd look like for the rest of his life, but also told you what he'd looked like before age began to take hold. She pegged him for late thirties.

They got food from a taco truck, which surprised her. He rolled up his sleeves and enjoyed every bite of the dollar-fifty taco that his suit would suggest he might not. He sat with one leg slung over each side of the picnic table bench, with a healthy distance between them.

After that he offered to walk her back to her apartment.

"I'm at least four Metro stops up. Really, I'll be okay. I'll probably just Uber—*dammit*."

"What's wrong?"

She slapped a hand to her forehead. "I left my phone in my friend's car." What a stupid gesture that had been.

"I would be happy to call you an Uber if you want. Otherwise, I'm staying in a hotel right around the corner."

She gave him a look.

He held up his hands. "No strings attached. I'm probably getting a pay-per-view movie and having hangover breakfast in my room tomorrow morning. If you want to come, there's no expectation. But you're a good girl, I wouldn't mind spending more time with you. Tonight or some other time. Whatever you want."

He was hot, she decided then. A crooked smile, honest eyes . . . she couldn't deny that she was attracted to him. And he was nice. There was something about the way he looked at her, the way he spoke, that made her believe him.

"No funny business," she said after considering, with a pointed finger and a set of narrowed eyes.

"No." He laughed, and she felt comfortable. He seemed more in control than she felt. Honestly, the risk of her trying to get home on her own in this state was probably worse.

The fact that she was so completely hammered was a whole other issue, of course. But it had been awhile, she hadn't eaten much, and she'd had drinks all over the spectrum. That was a conversation she'd have with herself in the morning. She downed the Mexican Coke she'd gotten from the food truck while he got her a water, too.

Their walk in the slightly chilly fresh air, mixed with the caffeine, food, and hydration, made her feel infinitely better. Not stumbling. Not sleepy. Drunk and silly, yes. But she also didn't feel like going home with him was all that big a deal. She was glad sobering up hadn't made her aware that she was making a huge mistake.

It turned out that he was staying at the Paramount. The big, grand hotel right downtown that she'd always walked past and wondered about. Ornately carved pillars, golden light pouring out of the lobby, expensive cars in the roundabout, and doormen who looked straight out of an old movie. She was suddenly thrilled at her choice to stay with him. She was probably going to hook up with him (could you say "hook up" when he was that much older?), but that was fine. She hadn't done something this foolish in awhile. Why not live a little?

And at the Paramount, of all places?

They went in, passing the check-in desk, and went to the elevators. She got a little flicker of pleasure when she saw their reflection together in the mirror. He looked like a real man, and he made her look slender, pretty, youthful. She hadn't felt that way for some time. Something she knew was stupid.

He asked her if she'd drink a glass of champagne if he ordered one, she said yes (she knew she probably shouldn't, but a few sips couldn't hurt), and he called room service and asked for a bottle of Moët & Chandon.

He was practically Cary Grant, she thought, as she reclined on the luxurious king-sized bed.

Some silly part of her felt like she was just acting. Like they were in a scene, and he was her husband. They were just getting home from a night of entertaining. All he wanted was to unbutton his cufflinks, and all she wanted was to unsnap her garters . . . the dreamy sort of vision she secretly had of men and women together.

She smiled as she leaned back on the pillow, laughing at her imaginary scenario. Her ever-outlandish mind.

When suddenly imagination became reality. He was upon her, his weight depressing the mattress at her side, just a little. His lips kissing her shoulder, her neck, and her jaw.

She laughed again and let it relax her even further.

It felt like no time until the knock on the door came. Yes! The champagne!

When had she pulled down the straps of her dress? Had she not worn a bra tonight?

She rolled over so the room service guy didn't see her. Something Lee didn't seem to be worried about.

"Champagne?" he asked, bringing over two glasses.

She had never had Moët. She'd always wanted to. How could she say no?

"So good," she said, but all she noticed was that it quenched the thirst of her dry mouth.

"I'm glad you like it."

Some gap in moments passed, and then he was asking if she wanted him to help her. She became aware that she was trying to pull the zipper down on the back of her dress. She nodded.

It was off.

Then she was on her back. He kissed her. It was amazing. The kiss was incredible. Practically morphine. She could have done it all night. But that didn't seem to be up to her . . . Was she being driven by him or by her desperate desire?

It was like being a teenager again. Racing hormones. The tearing at each other's bodies. She wanted to kiss him, kiss him hard, pull at his shoulders, but then, no—

No . . .

She had pushed back on him, to flirt a little more. She didn't want to go tearing into this part of the evening already, even if she *did* end up doing it. Right now, she didn't want to go that far, maybe not at all. She pushed back on his chest with her palms, and he held her down with his forearm, right across her breasts.

Whoa.

Chelsea struggled to remember his name. "Wait, no, please, I don't want—"

He kissed her, and she kissed him back, because that part was okay. That part was fine, it wasn't that part . . .

She pushed back on his lower abdomen—bare, she noticed now with a gasp—his muscles were strong, and she still tried to rationalize, noting that his body was better than she'd expected.

She tried to get into it, but she couldn't. This

wasn't desperate passion. This was force. But he couldn't know that, surely. He must think they were *both* feeling this into it.

And yet when she pushed back or tried to speak, he pushed *her* back and covered her mouth.

The words to express what she needed to would not come. The bubbles from the champagne filled her head, and the pain between her thighs became something she couldn't bear, as she slipped off into unconsciousness.

Chapter Nineteen

Diana

I have to say, I really loved the store. Almost right away. "Almost" because it was initially daunting to have such a change of lifestyle. Don't get me wrong; I was so grateful to Prinny for the apartment and for the opportunity to make something of the hobby I had been indulging for so long, but it was a far cry from the comforts I had become used to.

The comforts I had, in fact, come to rely on as the only real "good things" in my life. It's an age-old story; I'm hardly the first and sadly not the last to live it: One's love life is unsatisfying, so one acquires *things* to make up for it. Sometimes the *things* are lovers, sometimes the *things* are children, but most of the time things are *things.*

They certainly were in my case. I would go to Nordstrom or Simon's with a blank mind, and *whoosh,* I could buy into every fantasy they tried to sell me. A beautiful, colorful serving tray? I could immediately see my funky martini glasses on it for a party I would never have, so I'd buy it.

A new perfume *from Paris* (probably by way of New Jersey)? One spritz and I was imagining myself on the Champs-Élysées, Audrey Hepburn hat in place, tasteful Hérmes Kelly bag hooked over one forearm, a rack of iconic shopping bags on the other.

Leather riding boots? Preferably predistressed, thank you very much. I could see myself at the point-to-points in Middleburg, at the Clyde's tent, sipping fine champagne, nibbling shrimp cocktail, betting twenty-dollar bills on sleek Thoroughbreds.

The softest Belgian linen sheets? I could even picture having sumptuous sex on them, despite the fact that it would not just be the *cure* for my emptiness but, more important, was the *cause.*

Well, none of that was part of my life anymore, and even though time had yet to tell what our division of assets might end up being, chances looked good that I would remain as I was, with nothing. And, truth be told, that was ceasing to seem like such a horrible thing.

After all, I had *satisfaction,* and that was

something I had *never* had in my marriage. It had been a long time since I'd felt productive or important, or like anything I did or thought or achieved made a lick of difference to anyone else in the world.

Yet just yesterday, Prinny and I had come up with a gorgeous, simple logo for the Cosmos tea. A little shower of herb leaves like stars spilling into a steaming mug that had the Cosmos logo on it. We were even going to start producing the mug.

And I was *part* of that. I was a big part of it. It was an exciting new venture, and I was in. It felt great.

So that put me alone, working, feeling content in the shop. I was listening to music that had made me happy as a teenager, the lights were dim, except for my workspace, and I was alone in the store, ten minutes before closing, concocting away when the bells on the door jingled.

A young man with a flushed face and hair that had clearly been repeatedly raked back with his fingers stumbled in.

I knew this story. It had already happened multiple times in the short while I'd been here.

He looked around, confused. "Ahh, where's the bar?"

"This isn't a bar." People always thought it was. Cosmos. Like the drink. "Sorry."

He came closer, and apprehension moved over

me. "This"—he pointed at the counter where I was working—"looks like a bar."

I shook my head. "Only if you want tea. Did you want tea?"

"Tea?" He looked as if he'd never heard the word before.

I laughed. "No alcohol. Sorry."

"Ahhh." He rolled his eyes and waved me off with his hand, turning from me. "You're a tease."

I squinted, trying briefly to figure out if he had misunderstood the word "tea" that completely.

"I think you'll find plenty of other options on M Street," I called after him. "Good luck!"

Perhaps it was fortuitous that he'd come in, because it gave me the idea to come up with a hangover tea, maybe with some detoxing dandelion for the liver. I was jotting the idea down on a pad when the bells rang over the door again.

Oh, no, he was back.

I looked up, ready to usher him out and lock up early. But it wasn't him. It wasn't him at all.

My stomach lurched.

It was Leif.

"Mrs. Tiesman," he said easily, ambling in. He stopped and turned the lock on the door and moved the sign from OPEN to CLOSED. "Fancy meeting you here."

Everything froze for a moment, my body stiff, my ears ringing with blood. And then I decided to be calm. Or my body realized it had no choice.

No amount of panic, fury, anger, nothing could make him go away or control the situation.

"Took you long enough," I hedged.

He laughed. "So it *was* a game all along. To get my attention."

I shrugged, as if flirting. Hopefully he didn't know how my heart was pounding. "I didn't say that."

I remembered the breakup games of my teen years. I remembered driving off into the night, only so I'd be chased, ignoring phone calls to make my boyfriends worry. If he wanted to believe that's what this was like, maybe I could be convincing.

He came over and leaned on the counter in front of me.

And *dammit,* my body reacted, just as it always did around him. My body wanted to angle an eyebrow at him, pull him in to me, like this was all some elaborate role-play. I had no control over my desire whatsoever. It was so infuriating.

"You have *really* pissed me off." His voice was low and smooth and unmistakably threatening.

The only way to deal with it, I decided, was to fight fire with fire. I couldn't let him know he was rattling me.

I leaned down in front of him, our faces just inches apart. "Ditto," I said.

He drew back and slammed his hands so hard on the glass counter that I was amazed it didn't break. "I could kill you for this. In fact, I *should* kill you for this." He splayed his arms. "Who'd know? Who'd *care?* Here we are in this dumpy little shop late on a weeknight. It's busy enough to be unsuspicious out there, but deserted enough for almost complete privacy. Tell me, Diana, why should I not strangle my estranged, betraying wife right now?"

"Oh, I don't know. Because your chances of getting caught are better than you say, as you well know, and you don't want the great Leif Tiesman going to jail? You know that would be a bad way to go."

He scoffed at the very idea.

Did he mean it? I had no idea. This might be a shop full of psychic paraphernalia, but I didn't have an iota of talent in that arena. Not one little bit.

"Tiesmans don't go to jail." He shrugged. "At least not this one."

"Oh, come on, Leif, cut it out. You shouldn't talk this way. Someone might take you seriously." Oh, I was taking him *very* seriously. But as long as he didn't know I was, there was still a chance I could get out of this unharmed. "You've caught me. You're pissed. What is my punishment, dare I ask?"

"I'm not sure." He started walking around the store, eyeing the retail items with disdain. "Look at this shit." He took a handful of quartz crystal and hurled it in my direction. I put my hands up in front of my face just in time, as the crystals pinged against my palms painfully, then clattered onto the glass counter and floor.

"Leif!"

"She's as crazy as her fucking mother." He continued his perusal of the store, tipping books off the shelves as he read them off. "*Magikal Kitchen, Herbalism for Her, Fly to the Moon Without a Broom, The Magic of Stones, The Single Witch*." He took that one in hand and laughed. "You might be wanting this one." He winged it at me like a Frisbee.

I was scared. I didn't want him to know it, but I was *so* scared, how could he not?

"Yes, Leif, I wanted your attention! So what? What did you expect me to do when you were running all over town with other women? Touching *other women?* I hated you for that, but I wanted you anyway. You talk about killing me? You *are* killing me!" The tears that sprang to my eyes came naturally, but they were not for the reason he thought. It was because the truest thing I had ever said to him was that he really was killing me.

He was. Being with him was killing me. Being his wife was killing me. Killing. Me.

His expression softened fractionally, while my resolve strengthened. I *would* rather die than go through this anymore, if those were my only two options left.

Somewhere inside, he must have sensed the shift in my energy, because his tactic changed. Predictably. "Baby, I told you there's no one else for me."

"Yes, you said that."

"I meant it."

"Tell Eastern Shore Plumbing, or whatever it was you had her listed as in your phone."

"What are you talking about?" He was so good at this, so good at sounding convincing, genuinely baffled.

But I knew. I *knew*. I'd read it all myself. Saw the call logs. I knew beyond the shadow of a doubt.

And he knew I knew. But only he could make me wonder if I really did.

I shook my head. "How many have there been, Leif? Can you even count them?"

"One." He reached for my hand, which I knew was as cold as a corpse. His was hot. Comforting. Of course. "I married only one woman. And it's not just because you ticked all the boxes that looked good for me in business."

"It's not?" That hadn't occurred to me, actually. But it answered some questions my ego hadn't wanted to ask.

"No."

I pulled my hand back. "I want some tea." I went to the back counter and turned on the electric kettle.

"Of course you do."

I busied my hands, taking out a strainer and moving to the glass pots of herbs. "You used to like my teas," I commented with a tiny smile as I moved along from container to container, taking out what I wanted. "Or you *said* you did. I realize you have some trouble with the truth."

"Yeah, yeah, you're ace at tea making. I just prefer something stronger."

A little chamomile, a smidge of lavender, a bit of foxglove, and a pinch of kava, then a fruity hibiscus base. The kettle was close to a boil, and I poured the water into the strainer and let the mixture steep.

"My teas are pretty strong."

"They are when you put vodka in them."

I looked at him, shocked.

"Did you think I didn't know?"

"Yes," I said honestly. "I did think you didn't know."

"Baby, I don't trust anyone in this world. Our security cameras showed everything."

Everything? I wondered if there was an infrared one with the embarrassing image of me pressing his finger to his phone and sneaking into the bathroom to read all of his private messages. Was there a camera in the bathroom, too, disguised, perhaps, as one of the shower spouts? Had he watched me sitting on the floor, flipping through everything, crying like a fool?

What about him bending me over the counter and taking me as he had after I'd accused him of infidelity? Was that captured on tape somewhere? Would that be a recording he'd keep to *use* later on, or one he'd ditch in favor of something hotter with someone younger and more interesting?

Why did he even *want* me? Was it only to win?

I looked in his eyes and saw my answer. Yes. All he wanted me for now was to win.

And, equally important, to not let *me* win.

I poured the tea into a cup, then paused. "Do you want some?"

"What are you going to do, poison me?"

I continued pouring my own. "Scared of *me,* are you?"

"Pour me some," he said, and I did.

Ha! The playground taunt had worked. The "scared of a *girl*" line had *worked* on this over-grown child.

"Maybe this will calm you down. I'm sure you've got some Scotch in your left breast pocket as usual," I said, handing him the cup. "Slip some in this; maybe it'll make you see things a little clearer."

"Oh, I see things plenty clear."

"And what is it you see?"

"That we need to figure out the terms of your return. And you need to obey them."

Obey. Nice.

"Who says I'm returning?"

He laughed heartily and took a flask out of his inside pocket, right where I knew him well enough to predict. Probably single malt Scotch. He was a Scotch snob, so if there was one thing he would have on him, that'd be it.

He never offered to share. Tonight was no exception. He poured some into his own cup and put the flask back in his pocket.

It was just as well. I would hate to waste a good Scotch.

"We're going to tell people you went to a spa," he said, drinking, then making a distasteful face. "Bitter," he said.

"It steeped too long," I said. It had. That made almost anything bitter.

Nice of him to point that out, though, wasn't it? Even in the middle of his dictator act, he had to interrupt himself to point out where I had failed.

"Anyway," he went on. "We're going to tell everyone you went to a spa. So you're going to have to get some Botox, maybe a little filler here and there so you look refreshed." He appraised my face with a sneer—his, not mine—and added, "You can use it."

"Thanks so much."

He drank more tea. "Then you're going to be under house arrest."

The words were horrible. "What on earth do you mean?"

"I mean, you're not leaving again. I'll hire

a housekeeper to accompany you if you go shopping or something. Otherwise, you stay in unless you and I have an engagement."

"You've got to be joking."

"Do I look like I'm joking?" He slammed his cup down. What was left of the tea splattered in a constellation across the floor.

Shit!

God, he'd made a complete mess of the place. How was I ever going to explain this?

I grabbed a paper towel, doused it with hot water, and ran around the counter to clean up the spilled tea, but the moment I put the towel to the spill, he grabbed me by the hips and threw me several feet away, into a spinning wire display rack. "What are you *doing?*" I cried.

"A lot less than you deserve."

I ran to the door and fumbled with the lock. Normally it was so easy, but it felt like my hands were made out of Play-Doh. I had just managed to grab the deadbolt and started to turn it when he grabbed me again, this time throwing me against the bookcase, knocking a large amethyst geode off. It struck the top of my head and crashed to the ground, breaking in half and scattering smaller bits around it. I bent to pick up the large pieces, thinking one of them would make a decent weapon if I needed it, but then I felt a warm tickle on the crown of my head. It quickly grew, and the next thing I knew, warm blood was pouring down over my forehead and spilling onto the floor.

"What the fuck!" Leif yelled. "I didn't do that!"

"Who the fuck *did,* then?" I screamed back. At this point, I didn't even care what he'd do to me. He was going to kill me or I was going to kill him; there was no in between.

He backed off, looking at me in horror.

I have to admit, it was almost funny. I knew he had a blood phobia, but I didn't know it was this powerful. He was making his way slowly to the door as if I were holding a gun on him.

"Proud of yourself?" I demanded, and pushed my hair back, knowing it was smearing the blood across my forehead.

"Clean that up," he said, and gingerly reached for the paper towel I'd started to clean the tea with. He picked it up and came at me with it. "You've got to stop bleeding."

"No!" I knocked his arm away, sending the paper towel flying. "Don't touch me with that." I'd as soon have let him stab me as swab up my wound.

Which, from the looks of it, had to be a terrible gash.

I reached for the phone on the wall and dialed 911 before he could stop me.

He made a noise of anger and lunged toward me, but I held the receiver up. "It's too late. I already dialed. Even if you manage to hang up this call, the police will be here any second. You'd better get out of here, Leif. You'd better get far, far away from here and hope I don't decide to press charges."

"You can't charge me, I'm your husband!"

One of the stupidest statements he had ever made.

"Let's see what kind of settlement you come up with, huh?" I was getting woozy.

He glanced at the phone, then at me. "This isn't over." But he didn't wait for a response; he turned and left the store, a lot more frantically than he'd entered it.

"Yes, it is," I said, watching him go. Then I put the phone to my ear, steadying my voice. "Yes, hello, this is Diana over at Cosmos in Georgetown? I've been hearing a lot of loud voices in the alleyway behind the shop and my apartment here. I wonder if you'd mind sending an extra patrol our way now and then tonight?"

The place and I were nearly entirely cleaned up when Prinny walked in. The bleeding had stopped—revealing a shallow cut less than a centimeter long—and I'd rinsed the blood out of my hair. I was just picking up the quartz pieces from the floor when the bells rang.

I jumped.

She looked at me, alarmed.

We were both the deer in the headlights and the person looking at the deer in the headlights.

"What the hell happened here?" she asked.

"Leif," I said.

"He did this?" She looked around, but the worst of the evidence had been cleaned up already.

"We had a little visit," I said. "Yes. He did this."

"That is so weird. I just saw him at my place and had a bad feeling he'd come by and set the place on fire. That's why I'm here."

"No fire," I said, then thought about it. "Can't say that's out of his wheelhouse, though."

She came over and helped me pick up the little stones. We dropped them back into the basket one by one. There must have been a hundred of them.

Then it registered what she'd said. "He went to your house?"

She nodded. "He said he knew you were here." She gave a dry laugh. "He knew you were here, and he was going to take me down for betraying him that way. He said he'd be back. He loves to\ do that, to hang punishment over my head. To ratchet up my fear that he will ruin me or what I love."

"Like he hasn't been trying to take you down already."

"Yes, well." She shrugged. "I didn't know if he'd somehow gotten to you and . . ."

"Sweet-talked me into somehow testifying against you, literally or figuratively?"

Her face went pink. That meant yes.

"It's all right," I said. "I understand why you'd

worry about that. When you see someone betray themselves as many times as I have, it's hard to imagine they're going to have any loyalty to anyone else. At least anyone who isn't swinging an ax over their head."

"That's kind of how it seems.

"Well," she said, resolve set in her jaw. "He definitely didn't get me this time."

Chapter Twenty

Seven Years Earlier

Prinny had a sip of Chardonnay. Leif had announced to the table at large that it was something extremely expensive. He never could let an opportunity like that pass. Chateau Montelena, whatever. He seemed to be the only one who really cared about the *prestige* of it.

He was red in the face at the head of the table, being loud, commanding the room, and telling raunchy jokes.

> Two men are out fishing when one decides to have a smoke. He asks the other guy if he has a lighter. Other guy says, "Yes I do!" and hands his buddy a very long Bic lighter. Surprised, the first guy asks, "Where did you get this?" The second guy says, "Well, I have a personal genie."

The first man asks, "Can I make a wish?" "Sure," his friend tells him, "but make damn sure you speak clearly, because he is a little hard of hearing." "Okay, I will," says the other as he rubs the lamp and a genie appears. "What is your wish?" the genie asks. The guy says, "I want a million bucks." The genie waves his hand, and immediately a million ducks fly overhead. So the other guy says to his pal, "Your genie really sucks at hearing, doesn't he?" His friend says, "I know. Do you really think I asked for a ten-inch *Bic?*"

How was that poor woman going to marry him? Prinny didn't know Diana. She was pretty and seemed nice, but all she could imagine was that she must be stupid. How could any smart woman marry him?

Maybe it was unfair of her to ask that question, since she'd spent her entire life hoping that just *once* he would act like a brother to her. When she was little and she'd asked him time and time again to play, he would respond either by destroying one of her toys or by pushing her to the ground. How long had it taken her to learn that his version of playing had a lot more to do with destruction and a lot less to do with sitting calmly and pretending there was real tea in the teacups?

He wouldn't even play tag with her when she

was that age. Well, he would, but when he caught her he would push her to the ground. Tag stopped being a chasing game and turned into the reality it mimicked: running from the enemy.

How about when she was older, and he couldn't do what she needed from him then? She asked for help with homework, and he refused. Except for the one time she'd frantically asked him for help with a take-home test at the end of a semester, and he'd reluctantly done the work for her. He'd done it all wrong. On purpose. And she'd had to repeat the class in summer school.

And what about when she went out on her first date and had called him desperately from the pizza place asking for a ride? She'd snuck out for the date and didn't want to call home because she might get in trouble. The guy she was on the date with had started to give her the creeps (and made her pay, because she was "rich as hell anyway"), and Leif was in town, not near enough to walk, but close enough to not be a huge inconvenience.

She'd told him she was afraid of the guy. When he asked why (Should he have had to ask? Or should he have just shown up, *for once?*), she had told him she wasn't quite sure. Just a weird vibe. He hung up on her. She ended up walking three miles home in the middle of the night. Then he told on her anyway.

It was impossible to explain to anyone. First of all, everyone loved him. For whatever reason, everyone fell for all of his crap. Whenever she *tried* to explain it to anyone, all they did was laugh politely or roll their eyes, as if this were just normal sibling stuff. He was just being an older brother. He was just being a teenager. He was just being a good brother, telling their parents about her sneaking out.

Right.

And now she sat here at his rehearsal dinner, drinking Who-Cares-How-Expensive Chardonnay, wishing she could crack the bottle over his stupid head. She knew she was being childish, but that's what he turned her into. He treated her like a bratty, precocious child, and she got as angry as one.

All of his friends looked like complete jerks, too, she noted. And if her intuition meant anything, she could see where they were all headed. She could see what kind of people they were.

Best Man: Looks at gay porn in the bathroom at work, then pretends to be "just not that sexual" with his wife at home.

Best Man's Wife: Cheating on him with no one in particular, but whomever she wants, whenever she wants.

Groomsman #1: Leif's longtime best friend. They buried a rabbit in the ground once. A live rabbit.

Groomsman #2: Kicked a homeless man on a dare—but would have done it without the dare.

Groomsman #3: Is only friends with Leif for the money.

Disgusting. Everything about Leif and the world he had created was horrific.

Diana. Prinny stared at her.

Diana was good. Diana loved Leif and saw nothing beyond what he wanted her to. But she would.

Prinny got uncomfortable chills thinking about it. She hoped to God it wouldn't be bad. Hopefully he was just a regular jerk, and she'd pick up on it and leave him high and dry when she realized it.

It won't be like that. It'll be bad for a long time. And then it'll be worse. Then it will be over.

She took another swig of wine and stood up from the table. They had taken a limo to the restaurant, which he had rented out, so she couldn't escape yet. But she could at least get some fresh air while that awful, disjointed party sat around getting too drunk and talking about *nothing*.

At least nothing good.

Prinny wasn't outside more than five minutes before the hairs stood up on her neck. She felt him before she heard the door open.

Lo and behold, preceded by the stench of Marcassin Pinot Noir and Lagavulin, Leif had arrived on the front porch.

Why? Why did he always have to follow her? Poking her, prodding her when they were kids; finding a way to do it now, too.

"Good evening, Princess." He walked over to her on the top step and leaned on the opposite post. Smiling at her, he pulled a cigar from one inside pocket and an expensive lighter from another.

When the air wafted toward her, she could smell that it wasn't, in fact, just a cigar.

"Are you smoking *pot* right now? Seriously?"

Gripping it between his teeth, he put out his arms. "What?"

"You're a grown man, and this is your rehearsal dinner! You're going to get high, like it's some, what, basement frat party?"

"Fuck off," he said, still with the thing between his teeth. He lit the end.

"Me? I was out here first."

See? He always made her sound like an impatient little kid.

He inhaled, holding his breath, squinting, and then coughing the deep, unhealthy coughs she'd heard so many times through their walls. In fact, that's why she knew the smell so well. It used to creep like noxious gas from his window into hers. That was one of the deeply inherent differences between the two of them: She might open her window in the summertime to let a breeze in, or in the wintertime to look out and smell the coming snow, and he opened the window so that he could blow smoke outside.

"So, you having a good night?" he asked, as if he hadn't just been a dick.

"Yes, it's very nice, Leif. A seriously wonderful night you've put on for us all."

He didn't miss the sarcasm. At least he wasn't too stupid to miss her jabs completely. That would be less satisfying.

"You like Diana?"

"She seems nice." This time she meant it. "I don't really know her that well, of course."

"She is nice. She's a good cook. She wants to be June Cleaver. And I'm just the guy to let her do it. Though ol' Mrs. Cleaver didn't seem like she had much NC-17 in her."

"Oh, ew, Leif. God." Prinny had a gulp of her wine.

"She's not really my type, though."

"No? I thought your type was 'willing.'"

He laughed. "Good one, Princess."

She hated it when he called her that. It had a sick, poisonous undertone when he did. So different from when her father said it. Even though she could do without the nickname all together.

Then she got the vibe. She might have expected it. He was marrying Diana because she was good. Not *too* good. She didn't outshine him in any ways. She wasn't even prettier than he was. But she was good, and the longer he had a history with a good woman, the better that was going to make him look as he got older.

Many men just wanted arm candy, someone to look hot and make them look like they must be good with the ladies. Not Leif. His ambitions were far reaching.

Poor Diana was playing checkers, and Leif was playing chess.

"If she's not your type, you shouldn't marry her," Prinny said. "Let her off the hook."

He ignored her and continued his thought. "My type is more blond hair, blue eyes."

"Creative." Prinny looked out on the lawn, already wishing there was more wine in her glass. She could escape and go in to get more, but then he'd just follow her there, too. All she wanted was for him to lose interest in the fresh air he was decreasing and to go back inside to the party on his own.

"That sort of old-time movie star look, you know?"

She made a face. "What does that even *mean?*"

"Your mom had what I'm talking about." He inhaled again, the next part of his sentence coming out from a tight, held breath. "Your mom was smokin' hot."

Ew didn't even begin to cover it.

With an icy, nauseating chill, she felt something coming off of him.

He wants you.

She felt like a bag of slimy, wet, diseased, dirty rats had just been dumped on her head. She wanted to throw up, run away, scream, something, anything.

"Yeah, your mom was *good*." He dragged out the word in a way that made her feel even sicker. "You look just like her, you know. I've seen pictures. In fact, I've seen a few pictures you probably haven't."

She shot a look at him. He winked at her and then looked her up and down quickly.

That couldn't be true. How . . . No, she had to believe he was making that up.

"Yeah, you two look *just* alike."

His implication made her take a step forward and smack him hard in the face. The cigar, joint, blunt, whatever it was called, fell from his mouth to the ground. He looked at it and then at her in stunned silence for a second before picking it up and putting it back in his mouth.

She was frozen as she watched him. In the blink of an eye, he grabbed her by her shoulders and threw her down the three steps into the grass.

Prinny was so surprised that for a moment she didn't react at all. Then suddenly, like a child who'd skinned her knee, she wished she could burst into embarrassed tears. But she couldn't. She *wouldn't*.

All he did was inhale again and then give a nod at the ground next to her. "That wineglass break? Too bad. Riedel crystal. And good wine. Damn." He shook his head as if his team had just missed a field goal. "What a waste."

Another moment passed of Prinny just hoping to God he'd go inside.

And then he put out his cigar and gestured at the glass again. "You should really clean that up. Someone could get hurt."

Chapter Twenty-One

Chelsea

It was a couple of days before Chelsea was able to recover herself enough to go back to work at the store and several weeks before she could muster the courage to go stand in public again, where anyone and everyone could observe her with or without her realizing it.

The very idea spooked her now in a way it never had before. She felt on display. Wasn't it part of her intrinsic self to *crave* that?

She blamed herself for overcompensating for her humiliation with Jeff that night. If she hadn't been on such a *to hell with men* tear, maybe none of that would have happened.

It was going to be tough to face him again.

She would have liked to stay in bed forever, but that wasn't happening. She couldn't afford that. She couldn't afford to miss work, and she couldn't afford to dissolve into a pool of misery from which she could never climb out.

Besides, she was putting a burden on her co-workers by not showing up. She knew that already, but when she got to Union Station for the first time after her . . . experience . . . the first person she saw was Jeff.

"Hey, we missed you!" he said with bright enthusiasm.

He had no idea what she'd been through, and part of her wished he did, while the other part wanted to hide it completely. He had no idea how damaged she was. That she was a different person now than she had been when she'd last seen him.

"Oh, hey, sorry."

His entire face changed, from open happiness to concern. "What's wrong, Chelsea?"

"Wrong? Nothing. I'm just tired." God, could he read it all over her face? Was it that obvious? Was he remembering that night, too, her pitiable attempt to ask him out and his rejection?

She wanted to turn and run and never come back. Dye her hair, change her name, start over in another state.

Not New York. Not California. Her acting dreams were diminished. She couldn't even *act* like nothing was wrong now, in front of one virtual stranger. No, she would move to Cincinnati or something and be an administrative assistant in a company no one had ever heard of.

Then she'd be safe.

Except.

Except she'd thought she *was* safe and it turned out she wasn't after all. Maybe that state didn't exist. It wasn't Ohio.

It might as well be Narnia.

"Chelsea." He didn't get closer, but something about his energy shifted and it felt as if he did. "There's something wrong."

"I'm fine."

"Really?" He said it as if he knew just how big a lie that was.

"Really."

"I hope . . . I hope that I didn't do anything to offend you."

"Not at all." *Except totally. But that doesn't matter anymore. Much more important things came to matter instead.* She gave a smile so unconvincing that it probably came off as weird.

"Okay, well, we're on together today. So I hope you're okay with that?"

Act normal. Get it together. Be professional. Stop being like this. "Sure, what's the pose?"

"A painting by some guy named Maxwell or something. Maxfield, maybe?"

"Maxfield Parrish?"

"That's it!"

Once upon a time she had dreamed of stepping into a Maxfield Parrish painting. She wasn't going to let that asshole Lee take that away from her. She was going to dive right into this.

At least the best she could. Because she had to.

They turned their backs on each other and put on their bodysuits, then opened a can of the greasepaint they had to use to cover their bodies.

"Could you get the middle of my back for me?" Jeff asked, looking a little shamefaced under the white curtain of makeup between his skin and the rest of the world. "I forgot the stick I normally use for that."

Chelsea swallowed. "Yeah." She didn't want to touch a man right now, that was for sure.

He handed her the paint and turned his back to her.

She took the sponge brush they used and started smoothing it over his skin. And she was amazed at how sensual and yet *not* sensual it felt. The warmth from his body was comforting, kind; it didn't have uncomfortable sexual overtones. There was no sense of threat from him at all. Just his own vulnerability in his smooth, bare skin.

Huh.

She finished and set the can down. "You should stand in front of the fan for a few minutes. I put it on a bit thick."

"Thanks." He moved to the fan and stood with his back to it. "So, tell me, what do you plan to do after this?"

Now he was going to ask her on a pity date? Where he could either try to subtly toss in a bunch of hints that he "just wanted to be friends," or where at some point he would "get everything out on the table" and tell her he just wasn't into her? As if she didn't get that yet?

No thanks. She did *not* have the time or inclination for that.

She bristled at the very idea. "Oh, I'm just going to go home and get some sleep. I'm really tired." She made a show of yawning, to prove it.

He laughed. "I mean after this job. Are you planning to go onstage or into movies like so many people here, or what?"

She was surprised at his question. It wasn't like it was so easy to just *decide* to go onstage or into the movies. If she could have just *decided* that, she would have done it a long time ago, and she wouldn't have this bullshit job as a statue in a train station.

"I think I'll go ahead and be a movie star," she said. "But I haven't decided for sure yet."

"That's awesome."

She looked at him. "Are you serious?"

"About what?"

"About thinking *I'm* serious. Do you know how hard it is to get onstage or into movies? Even in a tiny role, much less something major and starring."

From the way his shoulders slumped, she imagined he was blushing. She'd been too sarcastic. Apparently he really *didn't* know. Now she was being a shrew. Probably making him really, really glad he hadn't gone on a date with her after all.

"I don't really know that much about it all," he said. "I'm an electrician."

"Wait, what?" That was not what she'd been expecting. This pretty boy, here half naked in a job that was typically something *real actors* used as a stepping-stone, was actually an electrician? "What are you doing here, then?"

"Aw, it's such a stupid story," he said. "Let's just say I needed money fast and someone recommended me for this job. It's been a life-saver, honestly."

"Why?" She was interested, and for the first time her mood lightened and she wasn't thinking about *her situation*.

"I bought a truck three months back and got the wrong insurance for it. I asked for comprehensive when what I needed was collision, and it's a stupid, boring story but basically at the end of the day I had a collision."

"But no collision coverage."

He shot a finger gun at her. "Boom. And I owe the guy who fixed it. If he hadn't given me the credit and let me pay him back, I'd have missed a hell of a lot of work."

"Wow. So you're not a model?"

"Me?" He gave a genuine laugh. "Hell no!"

"Not an actor."

"If I were, I'd have come up with a better

story than that and somehow made you believe it."

She laughed. Her heart lifted. "We'd better get out there."

"Here are the pictures." He reached for prints of three beautiful Maxfield Parrish paintings. "They have a set out there, and all we have to do is stand about twenty minutes at a time. Much better than the usual."

"I don't know." She pointed to a picture where she'd be bent backward and he'd be holding her, bent over her as if about to kiss her on the throat. "That looks a little challenging."

"It'll be totally relaxing," he said in a way that she could almost believe. "Don't worry, I won't let you fall."

He was beautiful. Yes, he was covered in white greasepaint. Yes, they were in a public place where everyone was staring at them, so there was nothing like what you'd call sexual tension, and she was glad for that. She would have thought that, having been so unceremoniously rejected, she wouldn't be able to muster desire for the guy, but apparently she was wrong. She would have thought that after that night, the awful, awful night, she would remain gun-shy—not that she'd wish, suddenly more than anything, that she didn't feel so damaged. And she didn't know him well enough to feel this, but she wished that he could take away the pain.

So many girls depend on Band-Aids and crutches to get past the tough stuff, Chelsea thought. *They seek out someone to fix it for them. They seek out someone to fall into, so they don't have to be their own person. My problem has always been that I won't ask for help. Ever. Yet something about this person makes me want to be saved.*

How unhealthy was that? She'd *just* found out how untrustworthy, how evil, human beings can be, and here she was letting herself lean completely into somebody she didn't even know.

The first position they had to hold *would* have been hard on her, but, true to his word, he held her up easily, seemingly without effort. And as weird as it seemed, being in his arms like that was very comforting to her. She had no choice but to let go; otherwise everyone would have seen the shaky strain of her effort. So she let go. Completely.

And that made all the difference.

She couldn't help it. She couldn't say no just because she "should," or because it was "too soon," or even because he'd already turned her down. When he asked her out at the end of their shift, she couldn't say anything but yes.

And so they did go out for that drink, finally. At Madhatten down off Potomac Street. It was small and quiet and there was no crush of people, as there was at so many other places in Georgetown.

"So do you really want to be famous?" Jeff asked her, sliding her second Schlafly ale to her across the wood table they were sitting at.

"I used to think so. Now, I'm not so sure. Fame is one thing. Success is another. I think I'd rather have success. A lot of people have fame and aren't happy."

He smiled, and she loved the way his mouth turned up at one corner. He really was cute. Wavy brown hair, tawny skin, denim blue eyes. He was a little bit cliché—she'd certainly thought so when she'd first met him—but now she realized he was less of a cliché than she was.

Out-of-work actress trying to make it in an impossible dream, mourning her passing youth and losing roles to a younger actress she had no right to loathe so much.

Wasn't there a Bette Davis movie like that?

Chelsea had to accept that a lot of things in her life were good right now. She had to stop trying to become Halle Berry and accept that if she was incredibly lucky and worked incredibly hard she might become a Maggie Smith sort of character actress.

That would be fantastic.

"A lot of people with success aren't happy, either," Jeff said. "Look at all those lottery winners who end up blowing their fortunes and becoming destitute. Miserable."

"It's true."

"But you know who *isn't* miserable?" he asked. "Across the board, the happiest people there are?"

She smiled. "Well, lottery winners would have been my guess, but you just nixed that one."

"Nah." He waved the notion away. "Money won't do it. Fame won't do it. The only thing that makes people *really* happy is actual love."

Chelsea heard herself make an involuntary noise of surprise. "Wow. That's a good attitude. A little sappy for an electrician." She smiled.

"Ha. Yeah, I know, I grew up with sisters. But it also . . . it also kind of leads me to something a little awkward."

Uh-oh. That was never a good intro. "What's that?"

"Do you remember that night you called and asked me to meet your friend Andrew and you for a drink?"

Did she remember that night? Hm. It would take a little thought, but, God help her, yes, she *probably* remembered that night.

She'd never forget that night.

"Yes?"

"I'm just wondering. Not offended or anything, but just wondering. I'd been trying so hard toask you out. Why did you think I was gay?"

"Gay?"

300

"Yes?"

"Why do you think I thought you were gay? Of *all* things!"

"You were pretty insistent on me meeting Andrew, and you were saying how he almost had a date with Andrew Lloyd Webber once . . ." His face colored.

"Oh my God."

"I'm not saying there's anything wrong with that, it's just . . ." He shrugged. "I guess my male pride was a little wounded. Or at least confused."

She shook her head. "I was so self-conscious that night. *I* was asking *you* out, but I was so nervous that I think I bungled the whole thing." She shook her head, thinking how very thoroughly the whole night had gotten "bungled."

"Aw, man." He raked his hand through his hair in that way he did. "I'm sorry I wasn't clearer. Man, I had no idea. I thought . . . I mean, it seemed so obvious."

"It seemed obvious to me, too," she admitted. "Now I totally see your point. Ugh." Stupid, stupid misunderstanding. How could she have let that happen?

More to the point, why did she let it break her down so much that she allowed herself to be so vulnerable?

Well, she wasn't going to let her experience make her vulnerable with men again. She couldn't afford to waste a bunch of her life in therapy because of some random awful thing that had happened to her.

"So we're just two people who tried to ask each other out and refused to see it?" He shook his head with a laugh. "Remember those sisters I mentioned? They would be smacking us both in the back of the head right now."

"I'd say we deserve it."

"Well, how about this. How about we just start over?" Jeff suggested, raising his bottle. "Hi. I'm Jeff. I'm an electrician, not an actor. Certainly not a model."

"I'm Chelsea. I'm an actress and the least psychic psychic the world has ever known. Nice to meet you."

They clinked their bottles together, and, for the first time in weeks, Chelsea had the feeling that everything might actually end up being all right after all.

Chapter Twenty-Two

Prinny

Prinny had not been expecting Leif to show up at her door again.

Even more, she had not expected him to be there to blame her for "taking his wife away" and "filling her head with crazy notions."

He was a madman at this point. Flushed, sweaty,

raging. Prinny had seen him angry many times before but this was a new level.

Leif Tiesman was not pleased that a woman had left him, and so he blamed the only other living woman that he hated as much as, or more than, his wife.

"Send her home," he said, referring to Diana. "Send her back now before anyone realizes she's left of her own accord."

"I don't have the power to send her home!"

"You took her away."

"*You sent her away!* This was nothing to do with me, this was all you. It's always you. You make everyone hate you! It's no wonder your wife left."

It was curious how his face registered acceptance but not regret. Somehow it was clear that he knew it was his responsibility even though they both knew he'd never *take* responsibility for it.

He was either diabolically evil or just plain insane.

She had no idea which.

"If you wanted her, you should have treated her with respect," Prinny said. "And that's not her talking, it's me. It's me, knowing that ever since you were a little kid, the one thing you were never able to muster for anyone else was respect. It's disgusting."

"If you or your mother had earned my respect, you would have gotten it."

"Don't you bring her into this!"

"How can I not? She brought *you* into this! And *you,* little sister"—he spat the word—"are the problem with *everything*."

"Meaning what?" She straightened her back and hoped she sounded braver than she felt.

"Meaning you need to *stop*. You need to stop or be stopped." He took a step toward her. "And your big brother is here to help you with that."

That was when Prinny knew that he was even worse than she'd feared.

"How dare you!" she shouted at him.

"How *dare* I?" He stopped. He stopped dead in his tracks and didn't move one more step forward.

Prinny summoned all of her internal resources and hurled them at Leif like some swirling, filmy ghost made of anger. "Yes, how *dare* you threaten me! You have been a monster to me my entire life, and I have never, ever done anything to you!"

He laughed, but she knew he was scared. And she finally fully understood why. He was terrified that she'd be able to see his terror of her. He was terrified she'd be able to see *everything* inside him.

And he was right.

She could.

The thing was, there just wasn't that much to see.

"You're scared of me," she said to him. "You always have been. Since I was little. I had no idea what your problem was. Remember when I gave you that toy Mustang for your birthday? I thought you'd be *so fucking happy,* and that finally— *finally*—maybe you'd smile instead of being such a dour old prick, but nothing could crack your veneer except the *truth.*"

"What truth?" he asked, then cleared his throat. She noticed he straightened his back as well.

"That you can't hide from me. You can't hide *anything* from me. You couldn't hide from my mother, either."

"You don't know what you're talking about, little girl," he snarled. "You'd better stop now."

"I'm not stopping! Not now, not ever. You made my mother's life miserable all because you were a horrible little toad with a lot to hide and you knew you couldn't hide it from her or from me. God almighty, imagine the stress that must have put Daddy through!"

Leif's face went scarlet. "*Dad* was fine. In fact, he was better before he ever met *Ingrid.*"

"Oh, please. She made him happy. I'm sorry that was so fucking *agonizing* for you."

"It was . . ." He straightened his back and cleared his throat again. His face remained red. "Everything was ruined when you and your witchy mother came along. I was glad when she was gone, and I'll be glad when you are, too."

"*Fuck* you!" she spit at him. "Fuck you, Leif. I *hate* you. Are you happy now? Is that what you wanted? Because that's what you got. I *hate* you!"

"Go . . . to . . . hell . . ." He put a hand to his chest. Then his other hand, and he coughed again. This time it was a raspy cough, odd.

And before she could even think, he had fallen to the ground.

Being in the waiting room was as impersonal and uncomfortable as sitting at a metal fold-down table in an elementary school cafeteria. Why buy such cheap, squared-off chairs for people who would inevitably be waiting a long time—and very tensely—for news, good or bad? They might as well have been hanging from monkey bars for all the comfort those seats provided.

And why was there always a fuzzy station playing some sort of foreign sports on TV? Was that *cricket?* Every time Prinny had been in the hospital, she could find only three channels, all local news, seemingly all the time. Why did the waiting room seem to have the boring upper 900s of cable?

Was the cafeteria ever open? Not as if hospital cafeterias ever had food worth bragging about, but here the only thing available to eat or drink came out of a vending machine. It was deplorable. So far all she'd had was a Butterfinger and half a Diet Cherry Coke, and she felt completely disgusting.

If there was one place that should be filled with easy chairs, spa music, and chamomile tea—or, on second thought, maybe a full bar—it was a surgical waiting room.

Prinny and Diana had been sitting there for an hour already with absolutely no idea what was going on, no idea what they were even waiting to hear. To say nothing of the fact that they had no idea what to hope for.

That was a tough admission Prinny never wanted to make.

She'd done this. She knew she'd done this. She never fully knew her power before and now . . . now it was too late to harness it.

Finally a nurse came out and, after stopping at the desk for long enough for Prinny to think she wasn't part of Leif's team, looked in their direction and came over to them.

"Ms. Tiesman?"

They were both Ms. Tiesman, of course, but Prinny knew that the nurse meant Diana, and indicated her. "This is his wife," she said, and then swallowed, a new and unexpected fear gripping her throat. Was this about to be some sort of *it* moment?

She wasn't feeling anything intuitively. The adrenaline was too distractingly high. All psychic energy was cut off, and she was running solely on nerves. She was too invested to see it omnisciently.

"What's going on with my husband?" Diana asked. "Is he going to live?"

"We're still working on figuring out exactly

what's going on. Mr. Tiesman presented with an apparent arrhythmia—"

"I thought it was a heart attack," Diana interrupted, and Prinny noticed her forehead knitted. Disappointment? Was arrhythmia worse or better?

The nurse, whose name tag identified her as Shannon C., was patient with the interruption. "The symptoms are very much the same: He had palpitations and was short of breath and diaphoretic."

"What's diaphoretic?" Prinny asked.

"Sweaty," Diana shot at her, then turned her attention back to the nurse. "So what is his condition now?"

Diana was absolutely panicked. Her voice was coming out in quick, breathy bursts. Nervousness radiated off her like heat waves. And talk about diaphoretic—a sheen of glistening sweat was appearing on her forehead. She was kneading her hands in her lap, too, scratching the skin next to her thumbnails. It was like watching someone in a full-on panic attack. Or, more specifically, Prinny *was* watching someone in a full-on panic attack.

Then, as she viewed the scenario with more distance, she started to pick up on something.

She literally believes her entire life depends on whether he lives or dies.

She believes her life lies in the balance of his. Whatever they say, that is her fate.

Prinny would not have expected this of Diana.

She thought her sister-in-law had grown far wiser than this in the time since leaving Leif. After all, she'd *left!* She'd gotten fed up with terrible treatment and had washed her hands of him. She'd been doing so well, even! She'd done an amazing job cleaning up the little apartment over the shop, and she'd come up with the tea logo and had already made several dozen ready-to-go kits.

Prinny knew Diana wanted to be self-sufficient, and she believed she had become so.

The panic coming from Diana became stronger, pulsing at Prinny almost like a fist.

Was she strong only because she knew he was out there, ready to bail her out if things got too hard? That wasn't the person Prinny had thought she was.

Was she really so dependent on a man that she couldn't see a way to live without him?

"I'm sorry," Diana said, taking a quick, deep breath. "This is all just so unexpected."

The nurse smiled, clearly trying to reassure her. "We're waiting for the labs to come in, as well as X-ray and EKG results, but there is reason for optimism."

"What is the treatment right now?" Diana persisted anxiously. "Are you doing anything at this time?"

"We're just trying to get him stabilized with some digoxin." She must have felt Prinny's question coming on, as she added, "Which is the standard medical treatment for arrhythmia."

Diana's shoulders slumped in apparent relief. "Thank goodness," she murmured. "Hopefully that will do it."

"What does it do?" Prinny asked, looking from Diana back to Shannon C. "That medicine, I mean. Is it a cure or just an emergency stopgap or what?"

She felt Diana shoot her a look and hoped she hadn't made things worse for her by prolonging the conversation.

"It helps the heart beat stronger and more regularly." She gave Diana a gentle pat on the shoulder before saying, "If you don't have any other questions, I'm going to get back into the ward. I'll let you know the moment we know anything more."

"Thank you," Prinny said. She took Diana's hand in hers. "Are you okay?"

"Yes." Diana blinked once, then turned her eyes toward Prinny. "This is all just so unbelievable."

"I'll say." The words "too good to be true" crossed her mind, and she silently chastised herself, ashamed to think that way in front of a woman who was so clearly devastated by the potential loss of the very person Prinny was having a hard time rooting for now.

But he'd asked for it. He'd asked for everything he was going through now. She didn't want to say it out loud, but if called to court, before God or anyone else, she'd have to say it. He'd asked for it and he got it.

This was his own damn fault.

"Do you want me to go try and hunt down some coffee?" Prinny asked her.

"No thanks."

"Or maybe a soothing tea? Something without caffeine? It won't be as good as yours, but maybe it would help calm you down some."

"No, it wouldn't be as good as mine," Diana said, then gave a laugh. Then another. And suddenly she was giggling like the proverbial hyena, clutching her stomach and bending over, unable to catch her breath.

Prinny felt her own face grow hot. The last thing she wanted was to be the center of the attention this was bringing from the nurse's station. She looked guilty of mirth by association.

Then again, maybe they were used to this in her family. Gallows humor, Prinny's father had always called it. The phenomenon of laughing at a funeral or at some other wildly inappropriate place. There was probably even an official name for it. Some sort of clinical diagnosis.

But that didn't make it okay.

"Shhhh." Prinny patted Diana, as if she were crying, not laughing. "It's going to be all right."

"I'm sorry." Diana wiped tears from beneath her eyes. "I'm so sorry."

"It's okay, Di, I understand."

"No, you don't. No one does. This is really messed up. I don't know what's wrong with me."

"Nothing?"

Diana shook her head. "The strain of all of this is taking its toll on me."

Prinny couldn't explain the relief she felt. "Of course it is! Who could expect anything else? This has been one hell of a night for you! Actually, a hell of a month. More!"

"I'll say."

She started thinking about what Diana had been through. "In fact, maybe we should take you down to the ER to get checked out while we're here."

Diana waved the notion away. "I'm fine."

"It didn't sound like it when I got to the store." She remembered the quartz scattered all around, and the broken geode. "And it sure as hell didn't look like it. How's your head?"

She reflexively lifted a hand to her head but remained resolute. "I need to stay here and find out how Leif is."

"I understand that, but if he were to skip out of here tonight, I'd be worried about what's going to become of you."

"Me? I don't think I'm the one in danger right now."

"Maybe not at this exact moment, but listen." She lowered her voice. "I don't mean to sound insensitive, but if Leif comes out of this like he does everything else and wants to come at you for some sort of vengeance, you really should have a hospital report."

"Mm." Diana nodded and thought about it. "I did take pictures. Bloody selfies."

"Those can be faked." That sounded harsh. "I mean, people could *accuse* you of faking them. I certainly don't think you did. It's just much better if you have an actual medical report."

"I know that, but why bother? Why even waste the time? You know Leif. Do you really think I could win against him under any circumstances?"

"Not if you don't try."

Diana dropped her head into her hands. "Then so be it. Let them think I faked them. I just can't face doing one more thing tonight. I don't even know how I'm going to get through the next ten minutes, much less *handle* things like medical reports and police reports."

"Okay, I understand." Prinny decided it was best not to push the matter, no matter how strongly she felt Diana was making a mistake. "I'm going to go try to find something to eat other than the crap in these vending machines. I'll be right back. Just let me know if anything happens in the meantime."

"I will." Diana nodded.

"Oh God, I should have asked—how are *you* doing with this?"

"Don't worry about me, I'm fine. Really, don't worry."

"I will." Prinny gave a short laugh, then left the waiting room and stepped onto the wide elevator just as someone else was stepping off. The doors closed, and it smelled like stale coffee inside. Stale coffee and sadness. Apart from the maternity ward, not a lot of really happy things happened in the hospital. Only positive relief after potential negatives.

As soon as the doors opened to the lobby, damp, hot air rushed over her. The lobby doors to the outside were open, and the tinny sound of pouring rain was louder than anything else.

That's when she saw Alex.

He was coming in from the rain, like a movie character, holding a newspaper over his head. As soon as he was in, he shook it off, threw it in the trash, and swatted the rain off his jacket.

Then he looked up and met her eyes.

There weren't even words for what that one look did to her whole physiology. Heart pounding, chest tightening, her breath shallow, she had every symptom in the book.

Which still didn't explain where she got the gall to run over to him and throw her arms around him.

Luckily, he welcomed her, pulling her into a strong embrace. For a long moment they stood there, holding each other, chest to chest, heartbeat to heartbeat. She felt her soul drain out of her and into him, then back again. This was *it,* she knew this was *it,* she'd always known.

Now, with this first touch, she had no doubt. The bliss of his touch was indescribable.

Even though they were right in the middle of a public hospital lobby, this felt, in a way, like the most intimate thing she'd ever experienced.

"Why are you here?" she asked against his shoulder. "Please tell me this isn't a horrible coincidence."

"I heard about Leif," he said. "I thought you could use some moral support. And maybe a lawyer."

She drew back and looked at him. "Moral support, yes. But a lawyer?"

"I'm kidding," he said, then removed his hands from her shoulders. "Gallows humor, I apologize."

"Gallows . . ." She smiled faintly. What a fool she was to take even that small expression that had just made her think of her father as a sign that Alex was the One for her. Especially at a time like this. "No, I don't think I need a lawyer, but thanks for the vote of confidence."

"Anytime. So what's going on up there?"

"They think it's something called arrhythmia, which they don't sound all that worried about, and they're treating it with some sort of medicine that sounds like it should take care of it."

"So he will live to torment you another day?"

She gave a nod. "Indeed he will. He always will. I think we know by now that he's immortal, don't we?"

Alex pressed his lips together in a grim line and didn't comment further.

"I was just on my way to find some alternative to the vending machines."

"Want to grab a bite of actual food?" he asked. "There's a diner across the street. They might at least have something *resembling* real food, right?"

She paused. How was it that sometimes things could be so good and so bad all at once?

"That sounds perfect."

They walked side by side through the rain—though it had lightened to a drizzle now; occasionally their arms bumped, and one or the other of them would draw back as if they had done something wildly inappropriate. There was a palpable tension between them that seemed so obvious that she almost acknowledged it.

She wanted to hold his hand. Such a silly, small desire, but she wanted to hold his hand.

In the diner, they found a booth by the window and took half an hour or so to enjoy good, strong java and, for Prinny, a toasted Asiago cheese bagel with veggie cream cheese. She hadn't realized how famished she was until she saw that on the menu.

After toying with the idea for a bit, alternately deciding to say something and deciding *not* to say something, she finally came out with it, surprising herself. "I saw your wife the other day."

He looked taken aback. "Did you? Where?"

"Georgetown." She didn't reveal that Britni

had come for a reading. That was a confidence she wouldn't break, but she wanted to open the subject. "It was only in passing, but I'd have recognized her anywhere." He looked puzzled. "That picture you have on your desk."

"Oh." He nodded.

They've already broken up. Whatever scene she had anticipated coming had already happened now. The marriage was over.

The picture was no longer on his desk.

And it wasn't Britni he was thinking about right now.

It was Prinny.

She blushed under his gaze, which caused him to blush as well, and suddenly she had no idea what to say.

"She always did love to do her shopping on that main drag," he said awkwardly. She didn't need supernatural intuition to know that he had put his wife in the past tense to communicate something specific to her.

Suddenly Prinny felt stupid for even bringing it up. Granted, doing so had brought out good information for her. If they were going their separate ways, that had to be a good thing, if only because Britni didn't love Alex, and no one should be stuck in a loveless marriage.

Diana could testify to that.

"I didn't mean to raise a sore subject," she said. "It was just such a coincidence."

He shrugged. "Honestly, I thought she'd go to your store. She saw your file out the other day and was asking about it. Not private information or anything, just the plans for expanding into the space next door."

"And how would you feel about your wife going to a metaphysical shop?"

He looked genuinely puzzled. "What do you mean? Should I feel negatively about that?"

"Oh, you'd be *amazed* how many men complain about their wives having readings or buying crystals."

He laughed. "Well, yeah, I guess I can imagine. Or maybe I've just had to intercept too many Leif calls."

"We know all about how Leif feels about the shop," Prinny went on. "But I never knew just what *you* thought of it."

He looked at her for a moment, his eyes so warm that looking at them made her have to fight back a giggle.

"I think the shop, like the owner, is absolutely charming."

She couldn't stop the huge, goofy, stupid puppy dog smile. "Oh, go *on*." She laughed. "Most people think it's a little weird and kind of . . . eccentric."

"That, too," he said. "Definitely that, too. But *charmingly* eccentric." He looked at her very seriously. "It's you, really, that makes it. You're what's so good about it."

She didn't know what to say. Of course she wanted the moment to last, but it couldn't, and even though it called for her to say something graceful in response, all she could do was grin like an idiot.

"Thanks." It was all she could muster, but it worked.

He gave a small smile in return. "We should probably go back to the hospital," he said. "See what's going on."

"Of course." What was she thinking? Flirting away while poor Diana had been sitting there all alone. "Di hasn't called, so I guess that's a good sign."

Alex left cash on the table, waving away her reach for her wallet, and together they walked back across the street. The rain had stopped now, but the damp was rising off the still-hot pavement of the street in waves. They went into the air-conditioned lobby and boarded that stale coffee-scented elevator and went back to the horrid little waiting room where seemingly nothing had changed.

Prinny introduced Alex and Diana, and Alex expressed his sorrow over meeting under these conditions. Then they all three sat, barely making conversation, watching snatches of golf on TV.

When the doctor came out, it wasn't like on TV. He wasn't taking off his cap and wiping his brow, with a sad look in his kind but wise old eyes.

He was all business.

"I'm sorry," he said, without compassion.

Then he went on to explain how Leif had died at 11:52 P.M. of cardiac arrest, just as they had been hoping to get the arrhythmia under control. It wasn't unheard of, he explained.

They did all they could.

They tried.

Diana's expression had grown distant while the doctor spoke. She looked numb. It wasn't even clear if she was hearing anything anymore. Prinny put an arm around her and squeezed until he had finished and told them there would be paperwork shortly.

Leif had come in alive, and now only paperwork would be leaving. It gave her the chills in a way that the news itself did not.

As the doctor walked away, Diana let out a long, slow breath. Almost like relief. At this point, with the tension of the past couple of hours, it wasn't surprising that both of them were finally breathing, even if it wasn't exactly a comfortable situation.

Prinny glanced at Alex, and he nodded back toward Diana.

"You're going to be all right," Prinny said to Diana, giving her another squeeze. "I swear you are."

Diana turned clear eyes on her. "He was so awful to me, yet he's been my life for so long that

I almost . . . I don't know who I am now. He's . . . gone."

"You're the same person you have been becoming since you left him, Diana. You are talented and starting a new life, a new business. I know this is hard"—she felt an unexpected pang of loss for the brother Leif had never opted to be—"but life will go on."

"Yes." Diana closed her eyes for a moment, and her shoulders sank. "Life will go on."

She did not cry.

Chapter Twenty-Three

Chelsea
One Year Later

Of all the nights when Chelsea really needed to get some sleep, it was that one. But instead of sleeping deeply and waking up with a dewy glow and energy for the day and more, she was half awake all night. Her feet writhed; she bit her lip so hard she tasted blood rising to the surface beneath the skin. She looked at the clock a million times.

But for once, she wasn't tossing and turning from anxiety. She wasn't longing for a drunken haze to put her to something resembling sleep. No.

Not anymore.

She couldn't sleep because she was so. Damn. Excited.

It was like Christmas Eve as a kid, with those glances up at the electric candle in the window, just waiting for the sky beyond it to lighten. So the day could begin. The half-eaten cookies could be found, the presents opened, the marathon of holiday movies begun in the living room.

Today, though, it wasn't Christmas Eve. In fact, it was almost just like any other day. Her happiness probably could have kept her awake even if tonight *wasn't* The Night.

Chelsea's alarm went off at eight—she'd looked at the clock every one to five minutes in the last forty-five minutes, waiting for it to go off—and she pushed herself up in bed.

"Up, up, up!" she said, not bothering to contain her Christmas-morning excitement.

Jeff groaned, but smiled when she laughed. "It's gotta be too early, doesn't it?"

"Nope!" she said, draping herself over his torso.

He yawned and put his free hand on her waist. Blinking, he looked at her. "You look pretty."

"You don't have your contacts in, you can't see anything," she said, but grinned anyway.

"Actually," he said, pinching her side, "I do, because somebody wouldn't let me out of bed last night to go remove them."

She made a *who, me?* face. For one more minute, she relaxed on his chest. His heat enveloped her and was almost enough to make her press snooze again.

But she couldn't—there was too much to do today. Brunch, primping, practice. Then tonight.

She did a quick drumroll on his chest, "Okay, let's go, I'll put coffee on."

"Make it so strong that you're pretty sure it'll be undrinkable."

"Will do!" she shouted over her shoulder, heading into his kitchen. Stainless steel, wood, marble, and clean. She loved waking up here.

"Hey, babe?" he called to her.

"Yep?"

"Do we have any of that what's-it-called spiky energy tea of Di's left?"

She smiled yet again. She loved when he asked if "we" had any left, she loved that he called her friend Di, she loved that he liked her teas as much as she did.

"Spike. I brought some back from work yesterday," she said, and waited for the response.

He was walking into the kitchen. "You're literally the greatest thing to ever happen to me." He walked up behind her, tilting her head with his own so that he could reach her neck to kiss it. "You, and then that tea is second. A very close second."

After making just enough time for a tussle in the sheets, getting ready for the day, and hopping on the Metro (where they were totally *that* couple, her with her legs slung over his, as if they weren't on the grimy earthworm version of transportation), they arrived at Medicini's, her favorite place in town for brunch.

Prinny, Alex, and Di were already there, and they waved at her from the best table in the place. Courtyard view, never any weird ice-cold drafts from the ceiling.

They all said their hellos, and a few minutes later, Alex and Jeff were talking about the Redskins' chances at the playoffs this year, and Prinny, Di, and Chelsea were on their own conversational island.

Prinny's arm was extended a little away from her body, still maintaining subtle contact with Alex's hand. They were always like this. Even when they "fought." This being said, their fights were somehow even more adorable than the times they got along. She was the wild-minded one with her head a bit in the clouds, and he was the logical one with his feet solidly on the ground. So their arguments usually sounded something like:

P: "What on earth is so ridiculous about having a goat farm?"

A: "Everything."

P: "You love goat cheese. Plus, we could make soaps and infuse them with things!"

A: "Do you know how to care for goats?"

P: "Don't they eat . . . trash? I mean, how hard can it be to keep something alive if it'll settle for *garbage?*"

Alex would then give her a look, and she would nod. That's about as rough as it got between them. They also threw extremely fun barbecues that tended to go late into the night and always ended in raucous laughter. Jeff had—affectionately— called the women the Three Witches on more than one occasion. Hearing themselves cackling together over mulled wine on a stove, even they could kind of see it. Which, of course, only made them laugh more.

Chelsea hadn't known Diana before the end of her saga with Leif, so she didn't know how she was before. Regardless, she could tell Diana was doing extremely well. She seemed happy. Content. The picture of independence. In fact, that had been part of what had helped to heal Chelsea after what had happened to her.

After the night at Gin Bar, when Chelsea had awoken hungover, sore, naked, and alone, she had realized she had a choice to make. The night before, she'd had plenty to make as well, until one was made for her. But now she had to decide.

Sink or swim.

She'd let a breakup with the wrong guy bring her down for far too long. And now she had to decide if she wanted to stay down and fall further into the pit of misery she'd been digging, or if she wanted to get herself together against the odds and climb out.

Chelsea lay there, head spinning for a few

minutes, and then got up and checked the room. There was definitely no one there. Then she locked the manual lock on the door and climbed back into bed. And she cried. She cried hard. Because she was completely entitled to hate herself but hate that man more, and the crying felt like doing something.

Once she was empty, she decided that she would never give her power away again. She resolved it to herself, knowing that intention and declarations meant nothing until they were followed through on. She would find out the guy's name if she could, and if not, she would move on.

She called down to the front desk and asked the name of the man staying in the room, and they wouldn't give it. Against policy to release. Chelsea, though not psychic like Prinny, had a feeling that it had more to do with his frequent stays at this hotel and less to do with hotel policy. If she could, later, she would figure out what her legal rights were.

In the meantime, she was ordering breakfast on his room charge.

She ordered pancakes *and* waffles, because she could never decide, bacon, sausage, hash browns—pretty much everything on the menu. She ate everything she *never* ate for breakfast. And she enjoyed every bite. With every chomp, she thought: *Fuck. You.*

She even ordered a bottle of champagne, and

requested to pop it herself. She put the bottle in her purse, after taking a hot shower, and walked out of the room. She knew she would have to deal in a very real way with what had happened to her. She knew that vindictive pancakes could go only so far, but she also knew that it was a good start. She was going to be strong now. She was going to stop feeling sorry for herself. Because the only place that had gotten her was rock bottom.

Chelsea told Andrew everything when she arrived at his place later that night to get her phone. He had fumed at the idea of "that asshole," yelled at her for leaving the bar (apparently he had never left—she had just been too drunk to realize he was there still, right where she'd left him), and then brought her in for a hug that was so hard she thought she couldn't breathe for a moment. Then he talked a bunch of legal talk and said he knew a friend he could ask advice from for her, and then he made her stay over. Which she didn't quite mind. She might have wanted to be stronger on her own, but some-times you need a crutch, even just for a little bit.

Later that morning, she got the call that Diana's husband, Leif, died. At first she was shocked, horrified, but then she wondered what she was supposed to feel for her. Diana hadn't seemed happy, of course, and he'd seemed abusive and horrible. And Prinny didn't sound like they were midcrisis over there. Still, she sent her best wishes.

It wasn't until she volunteered to help Prinny and Diana clean out Diana and Leif's house that she knew exactly what to feel.

They'd been mostly packing up kitchen stuff, makeup, clothes, things that Diana wanted to take with her. She wasn't messing around with junk drawers or old Halloween decorations. She was having a sale, letting people pick through her things for anything they might want; besides that, she was hiring someone else to deal with "all that crap."

And if Chelsea hadn't glanced at the mantel and unflipped a facedown photo, she would never have known.

Leif. She knew Leif. Well, no.

She knew "Lee."

There was no mistaking that face. The smile lines, the tan skin, the nice eyes with devilish cruelty hiding extremely well within them.

No wonder Diana had always seemed so haunted. No wonder she'd been such a mess, so cynical, the night Chelsea had first met her. Look at who she'd been dealing with.

Living with!

An extremely illogical part of her heart felt sadness that the man she thought she'd met was *dead* now. The guy who had sat next to her laughing and eating tacos was . . . completely gone.

Of course, that man hadn't really existed.

Everything made sense. Poor Diana. Chelsea had seen, even just in her one night, a slice of the spectrum she'd had to deal with. She saw the charm, and she saw the brutality. No wonder Diana was so completely conflicted.

Over the coming months, it was hard not to tell Diana or Prinny what had happened to her, and who the guy had turned out to be. The last thing either of them needed was to have Leif's actions stay alive with one more revelation. She didn't need to lead to even one more pang of betrayal, heartache, or anger on behalf of him. He might have wanted everyone in his life to be miserable, but she didn't.

She told Andrew, so that he called off the dogs. And after she and Jeff became friends, and then started dating, she had eventually told him. Both men had responded with kindness and an appropriate measure of sympathy. Neither had judged her for her own part in it—and they didn't need to. Like any other woman who has been through it, she did enough beating up of herself for her foolish actions that night. She didn't need anyone else to mention it, and the only two people she told weren't going to condemn her.

Diana and her fierce independence since the loss of her husband had been a huge inspiration to Chelsea. Not only was she happy and capable on her own, but she showed that the biggest mistake was in allowing the misery to run your life. Whether misery was tangible enough to be a human being or remained a green, toxic mental ether, it needed to be cut out of your life. Once you did that, you could be okay.

And now, Chelsea could look around the table at the other four people there with her and think how, whether that jerk liked it or not, he had finally done something good for every single one of them.

He had died.

They left brunch almost two chatty hours later. She hugged each of them good-bye, and they said they'd see her later on.

Jeff insisted on walking her home, so they held hands and talked all the way there.

"You nervous at all?"

"Not really. It never really bothers me to be in front of people when it's a stage. Put me in a party where I don't *know* anyone, and I might be freaking out on the inside, but you know. It's different."

He smiled. "Good. That's not totally what I meant, though."

Jeff looked at her. He knew her so well already. He knew how to communicate with her and when.

"I think it'll be okay."

"I know it'll be okay. But that doesn't mean you might not be having a couple of nerves about reliving some of this stuff."

"It's not a direct translation, you know that."

"I know, I know."

"But yeah, a little, anyway." She confessed. "I know it's cathartic. And I mean, I've felt pretty disassociated with it during rehearsals. It's just going to be a bit different with everyone there tonight. I think it might be a little hard for everyone . . . but in a good way, you know?"

"I do."

She knew that it would even be hard for Jeff. As she said, the play wasn't completely based on her own life. It was mostly about a terrible man and the effect he can have on so many different lives. Chelsea played the wife.

When Andrew had become so vigorously, angrily inspired by everything Chelsea had told him, she had talked to Diana. She hadn't revealed her own secret about the situation, but she had asked if it was okay if a bit of reality was used in a play.

Di had told her to go ahead. In fact, Di had said, *The more times that sonofabitch dies, the better.*

She'd even let Diana read the script beforehand. All she'd had was extra details to toss in. No cuts. No offense taken.

That night when she was onstage, she had given a performance that felt emotionally sapping and got glowing reviews from every critic in town.

Andrew, the play, and Chelsea, were a hit.

Which meant that, against all the odds, and despite all the genuine hardships Chelsea, Diana, and Prinny had been through, their *lives* were, in fact, a hit.

Chapter Twenty-Four
Diana

I don't like the designation "widow" much.

In fact, I never understood why the Merry Widow was a cocktail. I suppose if you drank enough of them you might *become* merry. Mostly "widow" is a downer, though. You'd be surprised how many forms have that box to check. Most people check "single" or "divorced" and never even noticed "widowed" there.

I never used to.

But for a little more than a year it's been a very real part of my life. In fact, being Leif Tiesman's widow was a full-time job for a while. There was so much paperwork, so many administrative loose ends to tie up. Fortunately, he had a good lawyer who helped guide me through the whole process, but still . . . once the worst of it was over, I had to take time off to go away and just be alone for a couple of weeks.

I chose a place in a corner of Fiji that I'd seen on some terrible reality show. And, believe it or not, it did the trick. I don't know how other tourists enjoyed it with a film crew there, but it was almost completely private when I was there, and the solitude was as healing as a medical treatment for an illness.

Now my life back in D.C. again is filled with work, and I couldn't be happier. I still have plenty of solitude, but I also have enough company in my friends and co-workers to keep me from going bonkers.

Every once in awhile I do miss that companionship I once imagined I had with Leif. Don't get me wrong: I don't miss Leif himself; he burned that bridge so well that even once he was dead and gone I was hard-pressed to have a kind or tender thought about him. But I well remembered the feeling I had when I first met him and all the things I imagined my life was about to become.

I missed that optimism.

I missed believing in love.

Now? Forget dating. The prospect of going online, posting my smiling pictures as an advertisement to come try me out . . . well, I would rather be alone. And so I will remain alone, at least for now. I don't see a crazy "meet cute"— like Chelsea and Prinny each got—in my future.

The last relationship was still just a little too fresh.

Would it always be?

When the doctor came to tell us that Leif had

passed, it was sincerely the worst moment of my life. I had so many feelings, and none of them felt appropriate. Plus, I was sitting there with Prinny, who seemed genuinely sad, and her husband (well, not her husband then), whom I'd only just met. Some stubborn, polite part of me felt like I had to be, I don't know, the hostess or something. Like I had to keep it together so as not to make Alex and the doctor feel awkward.

So I did keep it together.

I believe everyone saw that as odd.

The funeral was huge, though I recognized at least fifteen men there as guys Leif had vowed to take down in business, so I'm not sure they were there to pay their last respects so much as to make sure he was dead. No one took a mirror out and held it under his nose, as in the movie *Charade*, but I would wager more than one wanted to.

The will? Well, for a guy who spent so much time and energy—and *money*—trying to take Prinny's inheritance away, I'm sorry to say he didn't have a will. That meant the state got to take a bit of his estate for "administration," but who cares? Like I said, it took a long time and a lot of effort, but we worked through probate and got everything in order.

I would like to say that I distributed many of the funds to causes he cared about so that his energy could go to something good, but there were no causes I could think of that he cared about as much as himself, so I decided there was no harm in picking a few myself: Children's Hospital, the Red Cross, the American Humane Association, and a few more that have come to my attention as I've gone along.

I didn't move back into the house we shared. It was too big for two of us, so it was definitely far too big just for me. Besides, I had always felt it was haunted in some way. With Leif gone, it could only feel more so.

Instead I just kept the apartment in Georgetown, and I pay Prinny a good rent. She didn't want me to pay her anything, but I know she donates the proceeds, so it all works out. And I like being in that little place. It feels much more like *me* than the big McMansion ever did.

Plus, it's right there where I work. Within two months of starting Cosmos Medicinal Tea Co., we designated the expanded second half of the store entirely for that purpose and hired two new employees. I make the teas upstairs, and the downstairs is retail. It's doing so well that it looks like we might hire a third employee, someone to apprentice with me and learn the craft. The demand has been high from walk-ins, but our online business is booming, too.

The key for finding someone to work with and to teach is that I have to find someone very, very responsible. It's extremely tricky and dangerous dealing with herbs. They are not candy, to be consumed without regard for safety. Even one leaf of a particularly potent herb—say, digitalis (aka foxglove, a beautiful purple flower you can find growing on roadsides all over)—can create symptoms of arrhythmia or worse. Someone who is hospitalized with those symptoms and given the standard course of treatment—digoxin, a derivative of digitalis—might well end up suffering from digoxin toxicity, which leads to cardiac arrest and death.

Yes, one must be very, very careful.

Diana's Drinks
30 Recipes to Make You Feel Superb

Kava Tranquili-Tea

A very relaxing, magical tisane blend sure to bring peace of mind to even the most troubled soul.

    1 ounce chamomile leaves
    1 ounce kava
    ½ ounce lemon balm
    ½ ounce rose petals
    ½ ounce lavender
    4 cups boiling water

Place all herbs in a teapot, cup, or jar and carefully pour the water over them. Steep for fifteen minutes, then strain and serve hot or cold.

FOUR DRINKS

Let Him Eat Humble Pie

A spiked soda with a boozy layer of orange on the bottom. Make the blood orange reduction by simmering blood orange juice down to a thick syrup. Alternatively, use orange vodka, like Amsterdam or Skyy blood orange.

1 ounce vodka
1 ounce Aperol
1 dash triple sec
¼ ounce freshly squeezed lemon juice
½ ounce blood orange reduction
3 ounces club soda
Garnish: slice of lemon

Fill a cocktail shaker with ice and add vodka, Aperol, triple sec, lemon juice, and blood orange reduction. Shake and pour into an Old Fashioned glass filled with ice.

Top with club soda and garnish with lemon.

ONE DRINK

Marry Me Mimosa

The key to a great mimosa is to use freshly squeezed orange juice. Cheap sparkling wine is okay, though a good brut champagne is best. Top with a dash of Grand Marnier if you like it sweet.

This is not a breakfast drink only. Enjoy it and celebrate all day.

Since this is a drink that requires no ice, chill your glass in the freezer—or by filling with crushed ice that you pour out—before serving.

2 ounces freshly squeezed orange juice
½ teaspoon grenadine
dash orange bitters
4 ounces sparkling wine
dash Grand Marnier, optional
Garnish: orange slice

Pour orange juice, grenadine, and bitters into a chilled champagne flute and top with sparkling wine. Add a dash of Grand Marnier, if you like, and garnish with a slice of orange.

ONE DRINK

Lavender Lemon Balm Tisane for Nerves

This is a soothing, cheering tisane, excellent iced or hot, and will lift even the dullest of spirits.

6 sprigs lavender
6 sprigs lemon balm
4 cups boiling water
1 ounce gin, optional (preferably a more
    floral gin like Nolet's)
Garnish: sprig of mint

Place lavender and lemon balm in a teapot, cup, or jar and carefully pour the water over them. Steep for fifteen minutes, then strain into a pitcher. Add gin, if you like, and mint. Serve warm or chilled.

FOUR DRINKS

Black Satin Sheets

This is a simple, sexy cocktail, much more sophisticated than it seems. It's traditionally served in a Collins glass, but it's never wrong to use a champagne flute.

Since this is a drink that requires no ice, chill your glass in the freezer—or by filling with crushed ice that you pour out—before serving.

1 part nitro stout
2 parts brut champagne

Fill a chilled flute three-quarters full with champagne. Sink nitro into the bottom.

For additional chill, use iced whiskey rocks or wine beads, but not ice cubes as they will melt into unwanted water.

ONE DRINK

Old-fashioned Girl

There's nothing wrong with being old-fashioned. Some of the world's most desirable men have been won over by a good old-fashioned girl: Prince Rainier of Monaco got Grace Kelly; Prince William got Kate Middleton. Prince Charles, whose desirability is decidedly questionable, won over Diana Spencer.

This drink got its start as a morning cocktail—what better start to the day?

1 lime wheel
1 orange wheel
1 dash agave nectar
3 dashes Angostura bitters
2 ounces añejo tequila
1 ounce sparkling mineral water

Drop fruit wheels into an Old Fashioned glass, then drizzle with agave nectar. Add bitters. Muddle until sufficiently blended.

Hold the glass up and rotate it until the contents cover the bottom and climb the sides of the glass.

Add ice (this is a great time to use a single king-sized cube or ball) and top with tequila. Stir. Top with mineral water.

ONE DRINK

Maple-Rosemary Remember-Me Tisane

A spicy warm concoction, perfect for fall. The
ultimate nightcap.

2 sprigs rosemary
4 cups boiling water
1 tablespoon maple syrup
2 teaspoons freshly squeezed lemon juice

Place rosemary in a teapot, cup, or jar and
carefully pour the water over it. Steep for ten
minutes. Strain into a pitcher and add maple
syrup, then cool and add lemon juice. Serve cool
or warm up, if you prefer.

FOUR DRINKS

Sour Grapes

The traditional whiskey sour calls for a garnish of
lemon or a cherry, but why not use both? Sweet
and sour is always a good combo, and visually it's
beautiful!

2 ounces freshly squeezed lemon juice
½ ounce lemon simple syrup (see below)
2 ounces good bourbon
Garnish: Maraschino cherry or lemon wedge

To make lemon simple syrup, melt 3 ounces sugar with 3 ounces water, squeeze an entire lemon into the mixture (discarding rinds) and stir. Let sit overnight.

Add the lemon juice, simple syrup, and bourbon to a cocktail shaker and fill with ice.

Shake until well chilled, then strain into a glass over ice.

Garnish with a cherry and/or a fresh lemon slice.

ONE DRINK

Magic Lemonade

You can spike this with vodka if you want to, but it's a perfect virgin refresher as is. And sometimes we all need a virgin refresher.

1 can frozen lemonade concentrate,
    preferably pink (if you like pink)
1 2-liter bottle club soda
1 handful fresh mint

Make lemonade using club soda rather than plain water, add mint, and stir.

Serve over ice.

EIGHT DRINKS

Bug-Off Barbotage

This is a variation of a mimosa, only with more kick from the fresh lemon juice, grenadine, and cognac. For more kick and fewer bubbles—and therefore more "bug off!" attitude—double or triple the cognac.

Since this is a drink that requires no ice, chill your glass in the freezer—or by filling with crushed ice that you pour out—before serving.

½ ounce cognac
½ teaspoon grenadine
½ ounce freshly squeezed lemon juice
4 ounces brut sparkling wine
1 teaspoon Combier Liqueur d'Orange (the original triple sec; you can use another brand or Grand Marnier, but Combier is lighter and less sugary so is preferred)

Pour cognac, grenadine, lemon juice, and Combier into a chilled champagne flute, then top off with sparkling wine.

ONE DRINK

Damn Him Daiquiri Citrus Cocktail

The inexperienced will think of a daiquiri as the frozen fruity concoction served on the Lido Deck of the Love Boat. And that's totally legit; that's a great drink! But sometimes you need something a bit stronger—more sting to take away the sting. That's where this comes in.

Since this is a drink that requires no ice, chill your glass in the freezer—or by filling with crushed ice that you pour out—before serving.

2 ounces light vanilla rum
1 ounce freshly squeezed lime juice
½ ounce lime simple syrup (see below)

To make lime simple syrup, melt 3 ounces sugar with 3 ounces water, squeeze in an entire lime, then cut the lime into slices and add them to the mixture and stir. Let sit overnight.

Put ice into a cocktail shaker and add rum, lime juice, and simple syrup. Shake until cold. Pour into a chilled glass and serve.

ONE DRINK

Hawaiian Honeymoon

This drink is as sweet and old-fashioned as a Hawaiian honeymoon. The Blur is optional, but it adds a few antioxidants and makes the beverage a lovely pink.

Since this is a drink that requires no ice, chill your glass in the freezer—or by filling with crushed ice that you pour out—before serving.

2 ounces golden rum
½ ounce freshly squeezed lime juice
3 drops Blur, optional (this is a hibiscus
  extract that adds color, not flavor)
1 teaspoon honey
5 ounces brut sparkling wine

Fill a cocktail shaker with ice and add rum, lime juice, Blur, and honey. Shake thoroughly and pour into a chilled lowball glass.

Gently pour in sparkling wine, stir, and serve.

ONE DRINK

Honeymoon Stinging Nettle Tisane

Sometimes it happens to all of us—"honeymoon cystitis," or an uncomfortable UTI. Stinging nettle is traditionally used to settle that discomfort.

Rosemary helps relieve cramps. This tea is a woman's best friend sometimes.

When handling stinging nettles, wear plastic gloves. They do sting! It's not always easy being a witch!

1 cup chopped nettles, loosely packed
4 sprigs rosemary, plus more for garnish
4 cups boiling water

Place nettles and rosemary in a teapot, cup, or jar and carefully pour the water over them. Steep for fifteen minutes, then strain into a pitcher and serve warm or cold.

FOUR DRINKS

Champagne Punch

Most of my recipes are for single drinks, but this is for when you need all your girls to come over and cry with you. Or celebrate with you.

1 ounce brandy
2 ounces Cointreau
5 ounces strawberries, cored
1 orange, sliced thin
5 slices pineapple, cored
1 bunch mint, cleaned and leaves torn off
(discard stems)

1 bottle brut sparkling wine
1 liter club soda

Combine brandy, Cointreau, fruit, and mint carefully in a large punch bowl, stirring gently. Ladle into glasses (about half full) and top off each one with equal parts of the bubbly sparkling wine and club soda.

TEN DRINKS

Russian Tea

No Tang, no powdered iced tea mix, just a good old familiar flavor and some nourishing vitamin C for a cold.

1 cup orange juice
½ cup lemon juice
1 cinnamon stick
10 whole cloves
2 tablespoons honey
4 cups water
4 bags black tea

Combine everything but the tea bags in a saucepan and simmer for ten minutes. Remove from heat and add tea bags. Steep for three minutes, strain, and serve hot or iced.

FOUR DRINKS

Atomic Orgasm

Here's a favorite—lots of kick, lots of bloom in the cheeks afterward.

2 ounces vodka
1 ounce sweet brandy
2 teaspoons cream sherry
3 ounces brut sparkling wine

Put vodka, brandy, and sherry into a cocktail shaker with ice and shake until chilled. Pour into a glass or champagne flute and top with sparkling wine. Serve.

ONE DRINK

The Oracle

As you might predict, this name was too enticing to resist. Have enough and you'll see the future moving toward you in slow motion.

Since this is a drink that requires no ice, chill your glass in the freezer—or by filling with crushed ice that you pour out—before serving.

1 ounce rye whiskey
1 ounce jasmine liqueur
½ ounce freshly squeezed lime juice

½ ounce ginger brandy
2 dashes Angostura bitters

Fill a shaker with ice and add all the ingredients. Shake well to chill thoroughly, then strain into a chilled Old Fashioned glass. Serve.

ONE DRINK

Mint and Maple Tisane

This strange mix of summer and autumn transcends the seasons, letting you drift through space and time . . .

1 ounce mint leaves
1 tablespoon maple syrup
1 tablespoon fresh lemon juice
4 cups boiling water
1 ounce gin, optional (preferably one
    heavier on the juniper than the floral
    notes—try Bombay Sapphire East)

Place mint in a teapot, cup, or jar and carefully pour the water over it. Steep for ten minutes. Strain into a pitcher and add maple syrup and lemon juice. Add gin, if you like. Serve warm or cool.

FOUR DRINKS

French 69

Okay, this is basically a French 75 champagne cocktail, and granted I'm using a cheap-joke name. But there's nothing funny about this delicious confection.

Since this is a drink that requires no ice, chill your glass in the freezer—or by filling with crushed ice that you pour out—before serving.

2 ounces floral gin, such as Nolet's
1 teaspoon superfine sugar
2 dashes rose water
½ ounce freshly squeezed lemon juice
5 ounces brut sparkling wine
Garnish: strawberries

Fill a cocktail shaker with ice and add the gin, sugar, rose water, and lemon juice. Give it a few quick shakes to chill, then strain the liquid into a chilled champagne flute. Top with sparkling wine and add strawberry garnish. Serve.

ONE DRINK

Sidecar Sally

Oh, there's always that girl who feels like she's kept on the side, isn't there? Poor Sally. She needs to stand up for herself more.

This ought to help her self-esteem!

Rim your glass with superfine sugar by putting the sugar in a plate, running a slice of lemon along the rim of the glass, and dipping the rim in the sugar.

Since this is a drink that requires no ice, chill the sugar-rimmed glass in the freezer—or by filling with crushed ice that you pour out—before serving.

2 ounces cognac
1 ounce Combier Liqueur d'Orange
1 ounce fresh lemon juice (or to taste)
Superfine sugar for rim of glass

Fill a cocktail shaker with ice and add cognac, Combier, and lemon juice. Shake until chilled thoroughly, then strain into a chilled glass rimmed with sugar. Serve.

ONE DRINK

Rouge with Envy

There's no better cure for envy than to be the one everyone is envious of. With this adult smoothie in hand, you will be the envy of all.

  2 ounces vodka
  2 ounces frozen raspberries
  juice of ½ lemon
  ½ ounce simple syrup
  1 cup ice

Blend all ingredients together until smooth, then pour into a tall glass.

ONE DRINK

"He Makes Me Sick" Ginger Tisane

Ginger is excellent for whatever ails your stomach, be it anger, hurt, flu, hangover, or morning sickness. To make this tisane into a ginger ale, boil down to a cup of liquid, add sugar (to taste), and top with club soda.

  1 large (thumb-size) knob of ginger, peeled
     and chopped
  ¾ ounce Angostura bitters
  4 cups water

Combine ingredients in a saucepan and bring to a boil. Boil until reduced to 2 cups, then cool and strain the ginger out. Drink tepid for nausea.

TWO DRINKS

Rebound Tom Collins

Poor Tom. Always a groomsman, never a groom. But he's quite amusing and can be an excellent distraction while you nurse your broken heart.

2 ounces dry gin
juice of ½ lemon
1 ounce rose water
1 teaspoon superfine sugar
4 ounces club soda or seltzer water

Put gin, lemon juice, rose water, and sugar into a classic Collins glass. Stir to dissolve the sugar. Fill the glass with ice and add club soda or seltzer water. Serve.

ONE DRINK

Broke and Boozy

You can't buy happiness, but usually you can buy booze, no matter how ill-advised that might be. When things are low enough, it helps!

1 ounce white rum
½ ounce rye whiskey
½ ounce brandy
½ ounce grenadine
½ lemon, freshly squeezed
Garnish: lemon slice

Fill a cocktail shaker with ice and add all the ingredients. Shake until thoroughly chilled. Strain into a chilled glass, garnish with lemon slice, and serve.

ONE DRINK

Give That Diamondback

This is serious.

Chartreuse is known as a digestive, and, as such, it has miraculous effects on an upset stomach and jangled nerves. And if you've got to give that diamond back, there's no doubt your stomach is upset and your nerves are jangled.

Since this is a drink that requires no ice, chill your glass in the freezer—or by filling with crushed ice that you pour out—before serving.

1½ ounces rye whiskey
¾ ounce applejack
¾ ounce yellow Chartreuse

Combine the ingredients in a mixing glass and fill the glass with ice. Stir well and strain into a chilled cocktail glass. Garnish with a cherry.

ONE DRINK

Violet Femme

Strength is the word here. As in this elixir brings strength! Look at the protein in here! Why, it's a meal in and of itself!

Since this is a drink that requires no ice, chill your glass in the freezer—or by filling with crushed ice that you pour out—before serving.

 1 egg white
 2 ounces dry gin
 1 ounce freshly squeezed lemon juice
 1 ounce crème de violette

Shake the egg white briskly in a cocktail shaker for forty-five seconds, add ice, then remaining ingredients, and shake another ten seconds. Strain into a chilled Old Fashioned glass and serve.

ONE DRINK

What Ails You Cardamom Chai

This is a comforting warm chai to quell an upset tummy or cheer a chilling heart. You may use milk or any milk substitute you like. Cashew milk works particularly well.

Crush the cardamom pods with the bottom of a juice glass; they need to be cracked, not pulverized.

6 cracked cardamom pods
2 whole cloves
¼ teaspoon cracked pepper
½ teaspoon peeled and chopped ginger root
2 cups boiling water
1 tablespoon honey
Milk or milk substitute, to taste

Place cardamom, cloves, cracked pepper, and ginger in a teapot, cup, or jar and carefully pour the water over them. Steep for fifteen minutes. Strain; add honey, then add milk if desired—and enjoy.

TWO DRINKS

Absinthe Makes the Heart Grow Fonder

Absinthe today is not quite the same as the famous absinthe of old, yet people still do report a certain heady high from it. Also, like Chartreuse, it's a digestive that eases symptoms of tension.

  1 ounce absinthe
  ½ ounce lemon juice
  1 sugar cube, preferably raw sugar
  2 ounces water

Pour absinthe into a glass. Balance a spoon across the rim and put the sugar cube on it.

Mix 1 ounce water with lemon juice and pour it slowly over the sugar cube, so the liquid saturates the cube. Then pour another ounce of water, allowing the contents of the spoon to spill into the absinthe, creating a cloudy mix.

Serve.

ONE DRINK

Lemon Sage Tisane

Another nerve tonic; this one goes way back to ancient times. Smells delicious and is extremely refreshing when iced.

½ ounce fresh sage leaves
2 teaspoons grated lemon peel (avoid the
  bitter white rind)
4 cups boiling water
2 tablespoons sugar
Freshly squeezed juice of 1 lemon

Place sage and lemon peel in a teapot, cup, or jar and carefully pour the water over them. Steep for fifteen minutes, then add sugar, stir, and cool. Strain the mixture into a pitcher, add lemon juice, and serve.

FOUR DRINKS

Last Word

Sometimes everyone needs the last word.

Since this is a drink that requires no ice, chill your glass in the freezer—or by filling with crushed ice that you pour out—before serving.

1 ounce dry gin
1 ounce freshly squeezed lime juice
1 ounce maraschino liqueur
1 ounce yellow Chartreuse

Fill a cocktail shaker with ice and add all ingredients. Shake until thoroughly chilled. Strain into a chilled Old Fashioned glass and serve.

ONE DRINK

Center Point Large Print
600 Brooks Road / PO Box 1
Thorndike, ME 04986-0001 USA

(207) 568-3717

US & Canada:
1 800 929-9108
www.centerpointlargeprint.com